"I've Been So Happy."

"And Reeve, he's happy, too. Of course you've had to have seen it." Jaime laughed lightly, imagining the picture they must present to the world, mooning around, touching and smiling, forgetful of packages bought in stores, of time, of the entire world. "Every day of being together is like an ongoing miracle. Although—" and Jaime shook her head "—he worries that I'll leave him. Or that something will happen. Can you imagine he'd think that! As much as we love each other?"

"It's a great romance," Charlotte said. "Romeo and Juliet."

"Yes," Jaime returned, then with a laugh said, "No! That had a tragic ending. Juliet died."

"Ah," Charlotte said, "she did, didn't she?"

Dear Reader:

Romance offers us all so much. It makes us "walk on sunshine." It gives us hope. It takes us out of our own lives, encouraging us to reach out to others. Janet Dailey is fond of saying that romance is a state of mind, that it could happen anywhere. Yet nowhere does romance seem to be as good as when it happens *here*.

Starting in February 1986, Silhouette Special Edition will feature the AMERICAN TRIBUTE—a tribute to America, where romance has never been so wonderful. For six consecutive months, one out of every six Special Editions will be an episode in the AMERICAN TRIBUTE, a portrait of the lives of six women, all from Oklahoma. Look for the first book, *Love's Haunting Refrain* by Ada Steward, as well as stories by other favorites—Jeanne Stephens, Gena Dalton, Elaine Camp and Renee Roszel. You'll know the AMERICAN TRIBUTE by its patriotic stripe under the Silhouette Special Edition border.

AMERICAN TRIBUTE—six women, six stories, starting in February.

AMERICAN TRIBUTE—one of the reasons Silhouette Special Edition is just that—Special.

The Editors at Silhouette Books

JENNIFER WEST
Return to Paradise

Silhouette Special Edition

Published by Silhouette Books New York

America's Publisher of Contemporary Romance

SILHOUETTE BOOKS
300 E. 42nd St., New York, N.Y. 10017

ISBN: 0-373-09283-0

First Silhouette Books printing January 1986

10 9 8 7 6 5 4 3 2 1

America's Publisher of Contemporary Romance

Printed in the U.S.A.

Books by Jennifer West

Silhouette Intimate Moments

Star Spangled Days #31
Edge of Venus #71
Main Chance #99

Silhouette Special Edition

Earth and Fire #262
Return to Paradise #283

JENNIFER WEST's

current hobby is tracing her roots to see if she has claim to any European throne. In the meantime she writes novels, television scripts and short stories. Jennifer's husband, son, two Akita dogs and an indeterminate number of goldfish put up with her at their residence in Irvine, California.

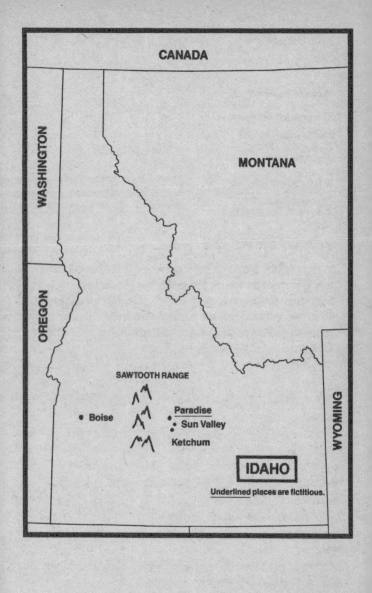

Chapter One

PARADISE   Population 62
EXIT 2 MILES

Reeve Ferris accelerated the red Porsche past the road sign. For the next two miles he drove at twice the posted speed limit. At the turnoff for Paradise, he kept his eyes straight on the road and his mind clear of the woman's face. It was a mistake. The decision to make the journey was a stupid, impulsive error of judgment.

He didn't slow down for another five miles, and then only because the Idaho State Police pulled him over.

"One-ten," the officer mumbled. He scratched the number on the pad to make it official.

The October cold poured in on Reeve from the open window. He zipped up the thin leather jacket that had been comfortable enough in the heated car. He hadn't thought to bring the right clothes. He hadn't thought. Like some teenager on a self-indulgent emotional binge, he'd let his feelings carry him nine hundred miles and ten years out of his way.

"One hundred ten miles per hour on a road with black ice." The officer clipped out each word in a flat monotone. "Twice the posted speed limit. Illegal, dangerous..." He ripped the ticket at its perforated line. "And expensive." The big man looked down at Reeve, really looked at him for the first time. "But I guess that's not a big problem for you now, is it?" His eyes skimmed over the lines of the expensive automobile, then went back to rest on Reeve with undisguised distaste.

Reeve's hand was already outstretched, complacently open. The officer slapped the ticket into the black-gloved palm.

"Now listen up," he said, steam following each word. "I don't care how rich you are, or how famous you are. Me personally, maybe I don't have much. But I got me this strip of blacktop." The officer raised his head for a second or two, surveying his domain with a proprietary air before his attention returned to Reeve. "Long as I wear this uniform, nobody—including you, Ferris, and any more of your kind comes up here—uses this road as a shortcut to hell."

"Appreciate the optimism," Reeve returned. He folded the ticket and slipped it inside his wallet.

"It's what I call being realistic. Knowing your reputation anyway. You'd need more oil than they've got in Arabia to squeeze that soul of yours through the Pearly Gates.''

The man leaned into the car, hunching down with his arm outstretched across the top of the Porsche. Inwardly, Reeve sighed. It wasn't the first time, nor would it be the last, that a stranger felt the need to prove himself against the image projected by his screen persona.

Reeve turned his head slowly. Variations on old tough-guy lines from his previous flicks played through his head. *Don't need no oil for them Pearly Gates, amigo. Only need this here Colt.* Or what was that bit . . . ? Oh, yeah, he had it now.

Squinting his eyes into the dusty sunlight of Baja, California, he had spoken his piece. *The Rio Grande didn't stop me. Poncho Villa didn't stop me. And no puny Pearly Gates' gonna keep me out neither.*

Any of them would fit the occasion; and any of them could get his head bashed in. He fought against the sense of absurdity he was experiencing. As he recalled, he had set out from L.A. to make love, not war.

He and the officer were at eye level. Their faces were close enough that Reeve could smell the remnants of a breakfast of coffee and doughnuts on the officer's breath.

''Does Jaime Quinn still live in Paradise?'' Reeve asked. He felt his stomach muscles tighten reflexively, apprehensive of what he might be told.

The man's face settled into a frozen mask.

Reeve couldn't make out the man's response, or rather lack of response. Had he not heard? It was certainly a valid question. Everyone in the area would know everyone else who was a permanent resident.

"None of your concern," the officer said finally, his voice low and colder than the air blowing in through the window.

"It's just a question. Not an assault," Reeve said amiably.

The mask altered then, showing feelings that hovered somewhere between fear and brute determination. The policeman's voice slid into a lower register. "This road runs two ways." He jerked his head to the left. "Sun Valley's that way. And L.A. lies that way." He made a jabbing motion with his thumb in the direction from which Reeve had come. "You pick either direction. Up to you which. But there's no exit to Paradise."

Reeve relaxed both wrists over the top of the steering wheel. Looking straight ahead, he flexed his fingers. "Funny. Could have sworn I passed a sign back there."

"You made a mistake, is all. Take care you don't make another."

Reeve turned his eyes on the officer. He itched to slam the door into the man's gut, but on second thought repressed the impulse. The man wore a uniform and this was no movie role he was playing; best not to push things too far. Nevertheless, he couldn't resist asking "Ever heard of a concept called personal freedom? It's got something to do with our government."

The man pointed at Reeve. The other hand had slid menacingly to the club at his side. Reeve thought it was a nice touch, perhaps overdone. "You stay out of touch with Jaime," the man in uniform advised. He waited a moment, then backed off.

"Yeah, sure...got ya. Thanks for the advice," Reeve said. "Nice chatting with you." He pushed the Porsche into gear and flipped the ignition. The car's engine revved.

"Hey!" the policeman called. "You don't want her." He said it derisively, accusingly, and it was only this statement that truly reached Reeve, because maybe, just possibly, it was true. If it was, then all was lost; or more precisely, he was lost.

Reeve had to narrow his eyes against the cold as he looked out at the man. Big boned, with his body stretched tall, he seemed a natural extension of the country's oversized surroundings, its vast open spaces and mountains that touched the sky. "How do you know what I want?" Reeve called back.

"Everyone knows what you want, Ferris."

"Yeah? How's that? I'd like to know how the hell everyone knows what I want."

For the first time, the man looked a little unsure, almost defensive. "We read about it."

"You read about it." Reeve shook his head. Then he looked away, his gaze searching down the road. He followed the blacktop to where it disappeared into the white, frozen jaws of the Sawtooth range. "Jaime...is she married?"

The policeman snorted. "What difference does it make? You're not getting within ten miles of her."

"Maybe I'd like to know she's happy."

"Maybe you and your fast car best get on."

Reeve smiled, tipped two fingers to his forehead in a kind of mock military salute. "Appreciate the hospitality."

"That's what us country folk are all about."

"Yeah," Reeve said. "That's what I read." He eased off the shoulder of the road, then floored the Porsche down the straightaway. In less than a quarter of a mile, he was burning rubber at ninety miles an hour. In his rearview mirror, he saw the patrol car start up after him. Reeve smiled and increased his speed. A mile down the road, he slowed and whipped the Porsche around in the opposite direction.

He was headed for Paradise at one hundred twenty miles an hour as he passed the patrol car.

Jaime Quinn had just finished serving her twenty-fifth cup of coffee that morning. The café catered to locals, mostly ranchers and farmers and the truckers who took the Paradise turnoff, driving out of their way for some of Jade Quinn's authentic Chinese food.

The café had no name. All that distinguished it from the other buildings in town was the weathered sign on top of the square clapboard building—Café, it announced in bold black letters. Other buildings were respectively identified as Hotel, Saloon, there were six of those, General Goods and Barber, Gas, and Feed.

For all of its apparent lack of glamour, during the summer, Paradise was a vibrant center of life. It was then, particularly on weekends, when the Basque sheepherders would come down from the hills and the cowboys would ride in from the range, that the town would take on its unique flavor, unparalleled by any other place in America.

Officially, there was only one street to Paradise. It was unpaved and ran straight as a Shoshone Indian arrow down the center of the commercial district, which of course was no more than the ratty collection of weathered wood-frame buildings fronted by sloping wooden boardwalks. Hitching posts and horse troughs shared the street with pickup trucks, jeeps and other four-wheel drive vehicles. By eleven at night during the summer, the streets and saloons were filled with men reeling from drinking beer and whiskey. Men danced on tabletops and smashed wooden chairs on one another's heads. Men lamented and celebrated life in Basque songs. Men sang along with Willie Nelson, who knew all the same things they knew about losing the woman you truly loved just because of a temporary lapse in fidelity. Now and then, through the music-saturated air, a gunshot would ring out as someone more lonely than all the others fired at the moon.

But in the winter, Paradise slept.

Jade Quinn refused to close the café, however, even though trade was sparce. The café was her hope. Every dime made was a dime bringing *The Dream* closer to reality. Someday, if all went well, Jaime could stop slinging hash and Jade could get out of the kitchen. They would find a buyer for the restaurant. They would turn the land back into a proper working ranch, the same as it had been before Grady Quinn, Jaime's father, had taken off for parts unknown.

It was *The Dream* Jaime was thinking of as she collected the tab for the trucker's breakfast.

She rang up the amount in the cash register, watching him as he went outside and climbed into his rig.

It was looking bad outside, she thought. It was a snow sky. If enough of the white stuff fell, even the main roads would likely be closed off. That meant fewer customers; possibly no customers at all.

Jaime gave her attention over to the cash box, tallying the morning's take in a ledger. She looked down at the figure—not bad, not good, just barely getting by. The story of their lives.

She looked up again, just as a bright red Porsche blazed to a stop in front of the café.

For a split instant she thought the car wasn't going to stop. She thought it would come hurtling straight into the restaurant at her. It had been going that fast.

Smiling ruefully, she shut the cash drawer. Nice red car. Expensive. There, at least, was one person who was doing more than getting by. And maybe, she thought, that's what it took, a bit of dash, some recklessness—stopping on a dime instead of scrounging for one. Chinese food and eggs-over-easy certainly weren't going to buy them their ticket out of the Paradise Café.

Another vehicle careered to a stop behind the Porsche, blocking it from behind.

Jaime stood transfixed as Pat Griffen tore out of his patrol car and raced toward the driver of the Porsche. She hardly recognized him. Pat's face was black with rage, his features contorted into an animal's snarl. Her mother's friend and self-appointed protector looked like a wild man.

With her attention absorbed by Pat, she hadn't taken any further notice of the Porsche's driver.

Now she did.

The tiny cluster of bells affixed to the door handle jangled daintily as the door swung open. A rush of cold air filled the room, but it wasn't the temperature that made her shiver and step back.

"Hello, Jaime."

For a moment, she could only stand there mute. It's not him, she thought. *I've dreamed it so many times, I've gone crazy. This isn't happening.*

But it was. It was real and she didn't know what to do about her heart, which was speeding faster than the engines of both cars put together.

"Hello, Reeve."

"Tell this friend of yours to get off my case." Reeve gave a slight backward hitch of his head just as Pat Griffen came barreling up behind him.

The officer's beefy hand was already on the soft leather of Reeve's Italian designer jacket when Jaime interrupted. "Pat . . . no. It's okay. Really," she said, feeling as though she were losing her physical balance along with her mind.

Pat threw her a wild glance. His eyes blazed like a demon's and his breath was ragged. "The sonofa—" He stopped, suddenly remembering his manners. He drew in a deep, rattling breath. "I told this guy to keep out of here."

Pat waited for her to say something, expecting her to back him up.

Maybe she should have, but she couldn't. Reeve was looking at her, talking to her silently with those electric blue eyes of his. "Piercing," a columnist had recently called them in a review of Reeve's latest film. Generally she tried to avoid any article having to do with him, only sometimes that proved impossible. He was in everything these days—television guides, even fashion magazines—and there she would be, innocently reading something about someone else entirely and up would pop his name.

"Not easy to get a cup of coffee these days," Reeve said. The barest smile played over his face, part happy, part sad. He was still staring at her. As far as she could make out, he had forgotten there was anyone in the room but the two of them.

Her eyes flicked over to Pat. "I'm all right, Pat. The man just came for a cup of coffee." She meant it sarcastically, not to hurt Reeve particularly, but to remind herself of what was the truth of the situation.

Reluctantly, Griffen removed his grip from Reeve's shoulder. "Look, it's none of my business, but—"

"You're right," Reeve said, without turning. "This isn't any of your business."

Jaime noticed an almost imperceptible change in Reeve's stance. Feet slightly apart, body relaxed, reflexes honed, he was prepared to defend himself. Along with that thought came the corresponding memory of his body as she had known it.

There had been a time when she had thought no one could know Reeve Ferris as she did. For a while, during the span of those innocent years when she had believed in herself and in the future, and most of all when she had trusted in Reeve, she had felt like a part of him. She had known the rhythm of his body as she knew her own pulse. But that had been a long time ago. She was smarter now. And Reeve? She looked at him standing there in the flat, hard-edged light of winter, saw him without the filter of the past obstructing present reality. Yes, he was still the most beautiful man she had ever laid eyes on. A lot had changed over the years, but that wasn't one of them.

"Ferris, I could haul your ass in for speeding," Griffen growled. "I could—"

"How've you been, Jaime?" Reeve asked, speaking over the threat as if it were no more than Muzak playing politely in the background.

"Okay," Jaime answered. "I guess I've gotten by."

"I've thought about you."

She didn't comment. Instead, out of self-preservation, she looked out the window. Nothing was going on; the sky was getting grayer. God help her—if she started to cry.

His eyes were on her. She could feel them as surely as she used to feel his hands on her body. Her fingers trembled as they gripped the handle of the coffeepot. Ashamed of her response, she took a quick look at Griffen still standing in the open door. Her secret was intact. Pat's face showed evidence of being lost in his own immediate melodrama. For the first time she realized how cold the room had become. "Coffee, Pat?"

"Hell," Pat sputtered abruptly, coming out of his thoughts. He fixed brown eyes on Jaime who waited expectantly for his answer as if weightier matters than a decision to drink coffee hung in the balance. Squaring his shoulders against the humiliation of defeat, Griffen raised a hand and pointed a stiff index finger at her. "Well, hell, you do what you want, girl. Just don't say I didn't try'n keep you from making a mistake." He stopped and shook his head. "No coffee. I've got a job to do," he said importantly and took hold of the door handle. The bells responded with inappropriate gaiety.

Griffen paused, seemingly reluctant to leave. "Tell Jade I'm sending Phil by with two cords of wood later on. He's to stack it, too. Make sure he does. It's all paid for." He stomped out, slamming the door behind him.

Reeve sat down at one of the small tables.

The room was silent. Then, a hard metallic sound echoed hollowly. Jade must have dropped a pot lid on the kitchen floor. Quiet again. On the wall a neon sign containing a clock in its center as part of its advertisement for a brand of beer, began to buzz and hum.

Jaime walked over to Reeve's table with the pot of coffee. She no longer felt attached to her body, but seemed to float above herself, viewing the scene as an observer might ponder the outcome of a chess game. A hasty or wrong move and you were in danger of losing your queen, the most powerful and versatile piece. It was always necessary to protect the queen.

Some kind of queen she was in her spotted apron over faded jeans. She brushed a lock of hair out of her eyes. She wished she had washed her hair that morning. Why hadn't she washed her hair?

Oh, why was she being so stupid? What difference did it make about her hair or the apron she wore or anything else? She was what she was, who she was. Nothing had changed since Reeve had left six years ago; at least, not for her.

She was still Jaime Quinn, daughter of a third generation Chinese-American woman whose great-great-grandfather had helped to lay the rails over which the country's first trains had traveled. She was also the daughter of Grady Quinn, Grady the incorrigible Irishman who meant well and did ill.

From Jade she had inherited wide, slightly almond-shaped eyes, their shade of dark green being as mysterious and impenetrable as a primal forest. Like her mother's, her features were delicately formed and she had the high, defined cheekbones of her Oriental forebears; yet, from her father—her departed, disappeared father, Grady Quinn—she had been given a complexion resembling fine white porcelain, flawless but for a light rainbow of freckles across the bridge of her nose. Her hair was raven-black. It was luxuriantly thick but not as heavy as Jade's tresses, which when loose fell in a single wave down the length of her back. Instead, the daughter's hair fell softly to her shoulders and curled in gentle wisps at her hairline where it was shorter. Grady Quinn had been proud of his riot of burnished copper curls, a fiery cap that caught the light—"hair dancin' in the wind with all the joy of life," was how he had put it.

Her father. Jade remembered little more about her father but that he was a spirited man, and a man of infinite vanities. She could still hear the lilt of his laughter and see the even rows of white teeth flashing in a smile that disarmed both women and men alike with its sincere charm. *Her father.*

Jade still loved him, would always love him, and continued to wait for him to return. Jade was a fool about that man, Jaime thought. But then, hadn't she been as big a fool? And after six years the object of that foolishness had just walked back into her life for a cup of coffee.

Reeve watched her pour. When she started to move away, he caught her wrist.

"I never stopped thinking of you, Jaime."

She stood very still, not looking at him. "No, of course not."

His hand rubbed gently up and down her wrist, as if he were soothing a terrified wild animal, captured for its own good. His voice was equally soft, lulling her into compliance. "Why does that guy—"

"Pat Griffen," she spoke out. "A friend of my mother."

"He really hates me."

"No—he loves me." She tried to get away from him.

Reeve's grasp tightened around her wrist. "Look at me." It was an order.

Hesitantly, Jaime moved her eyes to his face. Panic filled her, a fear that she was going to drown if she looked too long or hard into those blue eyes. He took the coffeepot out of her hand and set it down on the table.

He held her fingers in his. Her hand was warm, his still cold. "It's been a long time," Reeve said. His eyes suddenly filled with a fear of his own, and he looked down to where their fingers were twined together. "God," he sighed. "The way it used to be here. With the two of us. Jaime," he said, his eyes lighting again, "do you remember?"

Jaime swallowed. "I remember. Yeah, of course, I remember. I haven't gone senile yet." A weak, bitter joke, born of nervousness. Best to lay off the jokes, Jaime; bad jokes just give you away. Her throat felt dry, as if she had run a long way. She pulled her fingers out of his grasp and stepped out of reach. The queen was free again.

"So why'd you come back here, Reeve? Isn't this just a little off the beaten path you're used to traveling these days?"

He sank back into the chair. "I was passing through," Reeve answered, his response measured as if spoken to a reporter to whom he wanted to disclose only a certain portion of information and no more. "On my way to Sun Valley. I just took a chance that you might be here."

Jaime bit her lip, stemming the disappointment. So there it was. What had she expected, anyway? She wandered farther away from him into the room, an aimless journey that stopped when she heard Jade's voice calling to her from the kitchen.

"Just a moment," Jaime called back, too sharply. "Be right there."

She whirled around to Reeve who was watching her with what she recognized as apprehension. He looked like a man who had made a tactical error, like a man who had come expecting one thing and had been disappointed by encountering something else entirely. Well, let him be disappointed, she thought. God only knows she had been.

Unaccountably, as she faced him from across the room, the anger she had buried six years before beneath sorrow and humiliation and confusion surfaced. Unrealized feelings swept over her like a mountainous wave that had rolled placidly along during the years, its force undetected. With every mile traveled it had gathered momentum, storing fury.

From the kitchen: "Jaime! Jaime...?"

At her mother's voice, Jaime shut her eyes. Her fingers had clenched into tight balls at her side. "Coming..." she answered. "Just a minute..."

She was also suddenly, inexplicably angry, even at Jade, whom she loved more than life itself; and in one of those flashes of insight that comes like a streak of lightning out of nowhere, Jaime thought that perhaps that was it, the cause of the bitterness she now felt at the sound of her name being called by her mother. The fact was, she was sick of the café, and she was resentful for having no life of her own. She had somehow given up her own dreams, settling instead for Jade's crazy fantasy. Perhaps there was no one but herself to truly blame for her secondhand existence, if it could be called that—an existence consisting of endless days spent in a state of sleepwalking, months drifting into years, all lived in suspended animation.

She had waited like some dormant fairy-tale princess with a spell cast on her, but she had never known why. Certainly she had not waited for her prince to come, for it was he who had put the curse upon her. The prince—with his sparkling blue eyes, his dazzling white smile, the golden sun-streaked hair and hardened, sculpted body that was bronzed even in the winter's pale light—the prince was here again. Correction, he was passing through.

She was resolved not to let him touch her life again.

Jaime left her thoughts and brought the reality of the man watching her from across the room into sharp focus.

"It was nice seeing you again, Reeve. But there's better cups of coffee to be had other places. Better places than this. Just so you know," Jaime said. She backed off, heading in the direction of the kitchen.

"Don't go," Reeve said, standing. He took an urgent step forward, then stopped. "Please..."

"You did—you went," Jaime said. "Six years ago." She turned her face sideways, as if listening for her mother's voice. "I've got to see what she wants." She started away again.

Reeve rushed forward faster than she could escape to the safety of the kitchen. His arms swept around her, holding her back.

"Leave me alone," she said angrily. "Get in your car and get out of here." With a shrug of her shoulders, she tried to break away, but he only increased his hold on her, as desperate to keep her as she was to be free of him.

"Jaime..." The heat of his breath against her skin sent a responsive shiver through her body. Pressed against the length of him, she felt him harden, felt the quickening of his pulse. Reflexively, her eyes fell shut. The last time they had stood locked in an embrace like this she was only emerging from girlhood, just developing a woman's instincts. But this was different, she was grown now and she responded to him with a violent physical need that was as frightening in its intensity as it was unexpectedly pleasurable.

Reeve's finger traced a tentative pattern against the nape of her neck, then drawing her face to the side, brushed his lips lightly against an earlobe. A flash of white-hot light exploded inside her head. She shuddered, yielding all resistance.

"I came back for you. I want you," he said, turning her around to face him. He went to kiss her, but she drew slightly away, averting her face. She pulled back out of his reach again, and this time he let her go completely, the mood of eroticism splintering like shards of ice in the space separating them.

"Sorry," Jaime said. "It's just that I don't want you."

Reeve looked down. He looked away so that she was shut off from the light of those marvelous blue eyes and she was reminded all over again of the experience of being cut out of his life.

The room grew cold, and she grew even colder. "I can understand why you went away," she whispered, folding her arms around herself, "but how could you forget me for six years?"

He didn't answer for a moment. He walked to the window and looked out at the bleak sky. "I was seduced," he said.

"Oh! That was it . . . seduced. By Margaret Tanner?" A vision of a young woman with copper-colored hair and the smile of a cheerleader to go with sparkling brown eyes and apple-pie American features stung Jaime's memory.

Reeve turned his head toward her. Jaime read his surprise. "No," he answered. His eyes clouded for an instant as if he, too, were considering a long forgotten memory. His lips formed a weak, self-derisive smile. "Sadly, no . . . not Margaret Tanner. If only I could lay it on Maggie." He looked away again, out to the sky where beyond the roof of the saloon across the street, a mountain covered in snow jutted toward the heavens. "I was seduced by the world."

"Too bad," Jaime said without sympathy. "You shouldn't have left Paradise. Believe me, you'd have avoided the problem."

"I only wish I had stayed here," Reeve said. "Is it too late to come back?"

My God, Jaime thought. Reeve Ferris the movie idol, adored celebrity, golden boy—was standing across the room and pleading with her as if she held his fate in her hands. Hands that had washed pots and chopped wood and slipped dimes and nickles and quarters into her apron pocket, saving them for somebody else's dream.

"Yes," she said, the word a slice of cruelty she had not known she was capable of until that moment. "Yes, it's too late, Reeve." She gave him a short look and left him, going into the kitchen to see what Jade wanted. A moment later, she heard the jingle of bells and the sound of the door shutting.

Shutting her in. Shutting him out.

"Oh, God..." she whispered, closing her eyes against the passion, the fury, the hopelessness, the love.

Chapter Two

Jaime loaded a tray with dishes and took them to the kitchen. With only the two of them to run the café each action and every moment counted. Jade did not believe in wasting anything, be it food or time. This attitude, among others, was a part of Jade's Chinese heritage.

"Sorry," Jaime said, placing the tray on the sideboard by the sink. "Had a customer." An image of Reeve flashed before her. Just as quickly, Jaime banished it and looked toward Jade.

Her mother stood before the enormous stove. It must have been forty years old, at least. As far as Jaime knew, they didn't make stoves like that anymore. But then there weren't many women like Jade Quinn around either. It was destiny that the two had found each other, Jaime mused, the one made of hard iron and the other born with an unbending will of steel.

She knew Jade would have approved of her analogy. Jade was a firm believer in destiny, but without the romanticism people generally associated with predestination. Hers was a pragmatic acceptance of fate. What would be would be, like it or not. Jaime didn't particularly like this philosophy.

A large black iron pot simmered over a low gas flame, sending forth the aroma of that night's dinner special; Herder's Stew, four dollars and fifty cents. It came with rolls and a dinner salad. Coffee and dessert was extra. It was among Jaime's duties to scrawl the day's changing fare in chalk on the blackboard in the dining room.

"What cash amount did we take in this morning?" Jade asked in her usual soft voice.

"Sixty," Jaime replied in brief counterpoint to her mother's formal way of phrasing even the most mundane sentence. "But snow's coming," she qualified. The rest of the day's receipts would be paltry if the main highway closed, and it was a foregone conclusion that the herders would never be able to make it down through the mountain passes.

Her mother merely nodded, accepting the pronouncement without comment. She continued to stir the stew in a slow, clockwise movement.

As always, Jade's calm acceptance of whatever came her way baffled Jaime, and today, after seeing Reeve again, it downright annoyed her. She felt trapped in a time warp—Paradise, a town belonging in another era, she and Jade no more than remnants of other people's experiences.

"Who was it that you were speaking with?" Jade asked, still stirring.

Jaime watched her mother's hand as it continued its hypnotic rotation. Around and around the spoon went, like their lives, circular in scope, relentlessly unchanging from season to season.

Jade had turned her head and was waiting for Jaime to answer.

"Pat Griffen," Jaime answered. "He said to tell you he's having some firewood sent here later on."

She avoided mentioning Reeve. To do so was to summon pain, to heap salt on a reopened wound. Wasn't it misery enough that he had invaded her barren present? But she had sent him away, and away he must stay, even from her conversation.

"Wood's to be stacked," Jaime said. "And it's paid for, Pat said to tell you."

Jade nodded in response to this information. Just nodded. This, too, infuriated Jaime. Acceptance. Placidity. Patience stretched beyond any human reasonableness.

Pat Griffen was nuts over Jade. All Jade had to do was smile and the man melted. Her mother could do much worse than the policeman. He was kind and stable and had a good, steady income that could give her mother a rest for once in her life. But in another way, Jaime could understand Jade's disinterest in him romantically. For all his faults, Grady Quinn had been a modern-day cavalier. He was an exciting man, a virtual skyrocket of crackling energy. Anyway, he had been while he had been with them. To compare the two men, Grady was airborne in nature while Pat was firmly rooted to the ground. What it all came down to, Jaime supposed, was that her mother preferred the precariousness of free flight to a safe stroll through life.

Jaime moved to the sink, part of her listening for the jingle of the dining-room door, the other part of her lost in jumbled feelings of longing and resignation. She opened the hot-water tap, enlivening the suds that had gone flat, and then dropped a handful of flatware into the water.

"He's in love with you," Jaime said suddenly. "You've got to see that Pat's in love with you."

She looked to Jade, whose only response was to change the direction of the spoon.

"He would take care of you, Mother. You wouldn't have to stand on your feet all day. Look at your poor hands. You wouldn't have to chop onions and peel potatoes and slice carrots and—"

"I am not free," Jade said softly and finally, as if she had just made the concluding remark in an elaborate discourse.

"That's for sure." Jaime shook her head, knowing all too well what Jade meant, but seeing the situation quite differently. It would be a simple matter to obtain a divorce. Her mother had been deserted. But there were ties of the heart that bound her beyond any legal document. So, in another way, her mother was absolutely right; she was not free to accept another man.

Nor, Jaime had to admit, was she, herself, a totally free agent emotionally. Her meeting with Reeve had proven that.

She fished several utensils out of the sink and dropped them into a bucket of clear rinse water resting on the counter. Bubbles burst one after the other, like buoyant illusions. She closed her eyes tightly, thinking not so much of Jade anymore, but of her own foolish vulnerability. *Damn Reeve Ferris.*

Trembling, she removed her hands from the water and faced Jade.

"He's never coming back again," Jaime announced stridently, the sound of her voice seeming to ricochet back and forth against the walls of her mind. A rivulet of soap snaked down her arm to her wrists and dripped past her fingers onto the floor.

For a beat, Jade's stirring ceased, then took up again.

"Why can't you see the truth?" Jaime pleaded. "It's so plain. It's as clear and real as those mountains out there." As if Jade needed direction, Jaime hitched her head to the window, beyond which the glacial slopes of the Sawtooths loomed. "The man you're waiting for is never, never going to come back here. Your entire life is just this waiting. Waiting for nothing! And I'm waiting with you. I'm sick of it, don't you see?" Jaime's voice broke. She stood frozen, aghast at the torrent that had come spilling out of her.

Slowly, Jade removed the large wooden spoon from the pot and placed it neatly in a dish to catch the gravy drippings. There had been no discernible change in her facial expression, but her skin had paled and Jaime saw the hint of a flush forming.

"He will come back to me," Jade said adamantly, her head remaining lowered.

The fury that had spawned the barrage of words turned to compassion in Jaime. But if she were to agree with Jade as she had always done in the past, or continue to keep her own silent counsel, in the end it would not be a kindness. "No," she said. "No, Mother, it isn't so."

Jade stood a few feet from the stove, suddenly looking to Jaime, bereft and helpless. This vision of her mother's vulnerability came as a shock. Because of Jade's unshakable inner strength, Jaime had come to respond more to her mother's spiritual essence than to her physical form. But in reality her mother was a small woman with delicate Oriental features and green eyes to match her name. Thick hair, dark as onyx, was twisted into a roll at the nape of her neck. Standing there as she did now, an uninformed spectator would surely assume her to be fragile and mysterious, but Jaime knew from long experience there was little weakness in her mother. On that count, her appearance was deceiving. But that indomitable strength was also Jade's downfall for she had not learned when to surrender.

"I was eight years old when my father walked out the door," Jaime said. She spoke softly, without malice, but she continued with the grim determination that once and for all the situation would be acknowledged for what it was and life might go on, might begin, for both of them. "He didn't say goodbye, not to you, not to me. He just went. Either he's dead, Mother, or he doesn't care. But either way the result's the same for us."

"Not for us," Jade corrected. "You don't have to wait."

Jaime wanted to rush across the room and shake her.

"Don't I?" Jaime challenged. "What do you think? That I could walk out of here and leave you alone? You're so incredibly stubborn!" She cast her eyes to the heavens then back to Jade. "You can't afford to hire anyone to work here. And who'd even want to? So you'd keep the café open and you'd do everything yourself and...and you *couldn't*. Physically, you just couldn't. And one day you'd be forced to realize that,

Mother." Jaime moved into the center of the room, closer to where Jade stood looking paler with every word Jaime uttered. "Because one day, Mother, you'd just collapse in a heap on the floor and—"

Jade flinched. For an instant, Jaime thought her eyes were playing tricks on her.

Then Jade gave way to another, more pronounced physical spasm, and her arms clutched her stomach as she bent at the waist.

"Mother!" Wild with fright, Jaime crossed the distance, her arms sweeping around Jade who remained doubled over. "Tell me. What is it? Tell me what to do for you! Please..." Jaime cried.

Jade gasped, at the same time shutting her eyes.

Afraid to move or even breathe, Jaime waited. Her mind reeled with self-recrimination. She had brought on this horrifying spell by her insistence that Jade face reality. She had meant well, God forgive her, but now of course she could see that it was only her own frustration projected outward, it was anger at herself for not ever having gotten over Reeve, that had brought on the vitriolic outburst she directed at Jade.

The moment of Jade's physical anguish seemed to last forever, a time frozen in space.

Then finally, Jade exhaled and slowly righted herself, at the same time sliding out from Jaime's arms as if embarrassed over her lapse of dependence. With relief Jaime noted a modicum of color seeping back into Jade's face.

"A flu," Jade said. She turned her head quickly, and started back toward the stove.

Jaime came around just as quickly and blocked her mother's path. "It's stupid what I said," she confessed in a rush, seeking absolution for her behavior.

"Of course, he'll come back. I don't know what made me say those things."

"It wasn't your fault," Jade said, resting her hand briefly on Jaime's arm. A series of thoughts passed quickly behind the green eyes, none of which Jaime could detect. Yet she felt a chill brought on by a deep warning instinct that there was something dreadfully wrong.

"That wasn't from any flu, Mother," Jaime said with conviction, while inwardly she hoped that Jade would prove her suspicions false.

"It is a stomach pain," Jade insisted with equal vehemence. "For several days they have come and gone. This one was not even so bad. The flu is almost over. Did you refill the bucket with potatoes?"

"Yes," Jaime answered distractedly. She searched her mother's face for signs of deception. The private screen, lowered so briefly, was once more in place.

For a few moments there was silence between them as both women resumed their tasks. From the corner of her eye, Jaime kept watch. After a time she began to be convinced that her mother might have been telling the truth about the mysterious stomach pains. She had just begun to relax when Jade suddenly faltered again and with a sharp moan, clutched her middle.

"Go rest," Jaime said. "Go rest!" she shouted this time.

She was almost paralyzed with fright. Jade was even paler than before and for once, miserably, Jaime could read true emotion in her mother's expression. Etched in the green eyes was undiluted fear.

Jade disappeared quietly out the back door. From the window, Jaime watched her mother cross the frozen expanse to the small two-room wood cabin situated behind the café. Its construction was that of a modified log cabin with a high, peaked roof to carry the weight of the season's copious snowfall. There was one bedroom, belonging to Jade, a bathroom, and a sitting room of sorts with a pulldown bed on which Jaime slept.

It was only midday, but the low sky had become a hovering blanket over the terrain. Dirty gray clouds enveloped the upper half of the jagged Sawtooths, cutting the peaks off from view.

In spite of the day's crises, there were still the potatoes for Jaime to peel and hamburger meat to fashion into patties—a thousand small but significant duties to perform. Along with this, there was always the occasional customer to serve, who would appear when she would try to steal away to check on Jade.

But Jade appeared soon enough herself. She looked no better to Jaime, but she insisted she was fit enough to tend to the dinner if Jaime would go into town to fill a prescription for her. The druggist in Sun Valley would have it ready.

"So," Jaime said with scant pleasure at having her suspicions confirmed, "the flu that was nothing was bad enough for you to see a doctor?"

Jade shrugged, offering no comment. Jaime didn't have to ask when her mother had stolen off to be examined. Hindsight explained all. Generally Jade always had Jaime run errands in Ketchem or Sun Valley. But three weeks before, her mother had unaccountably insisted on tending to the routine matter of picking up supplies herself. Jade had asked Pat Griffen to drive her into town. It was then, of course, that Jade had visited the physician.

"Is this a refill?" Jaime asked as she slipped on her parka and coiled a narrow wool scarf twice around her neck.

"Yes," Jade replied. "It is a refill."

"It's not the flu then, is it?"

"No," Jade said. "It is not the flu."

Perhaps because she was afraid to know more, and perhaps because she knew Jade would not tell her more at the moment, Jaime only nodded and left to run her miserable errand.

From his room in the Sun Valley Lodge, Reeve had a view of the skating rink. Several children were practicing freestyle routines. A few adults shared the ice with them, one an obese man in an outlandish chartreuse ski parka, who was surprisingly agile on the thin silver blades, and a middle-aged couple who held on to each other, laughing, as they lurched around the rink's perimeter. A group of skiers, looking like aliens from outer space in their plastic moon boots and bug-eyed goggles, paused by the railing to cheer on the heavy man who was doing a fair set of camel spins. Once he might have been really good, Reeve thought; when young perhaps he had been thin and handsome.

Reeve watched the activity with stinging eyes. Fatigue weighed down his lids. Yet sleep remained no more than a wishful notion, unobtainable in his present state of turmoil.

He had rented the room at the lodge with the full intention of resting for a few hours, just long enough to give him the stamina to make the long haul back to Los Angeles. He had even gone through the motions of showering and slipping nude between the bed sheets, but to no avail. Whenever he shut his eyes Jaime's face would appear, and with her image the pain of loss would sweep through him with an almost paralyzing intensity. Three times he bolted out of bed in a sweaty panic.

He had lost her!

Always in the intervening years since they had been together, he had kept alive the firm conviction that one day, he would return to Paradise and get Jaime. It was only a matter of time. *The right time.* That had been his mother's phrase. He remembered it well. Always, whenever he had broached the subject of returning for Jaime Quinn, his mother had been supportive, but logical. Of course he would be with Jaime again, Charlotte had reassured him. Only first there was his quest for the Olympic Gold Medal that required all of his energies. Then there was the time he spent in the posh Eastern school. His life became as removed from Jaime's as if he had been living on the moon. Then came the movie deals and the ensuing complications of instant stardom. The right time to return to Paradise was an elusive dream, but one never forgotten by Reeve.

To think that he had lost his chance of realizing the only true happiness open to him was more than he could stand. To ward off the panic and despair, he turned his mind to other less important but more tangible aspects of his life.

No doubt there would be a certain amount of hell to pay for his irresponsibility when he returned to Los Angeles. But that sort of hell was nothing compared to his present condition.

He left the window and picked up the phone, dialing his mother's home in Beverly Hills. The maid answered and he waited while his mother was called.

Her voice was immediately anxious. "Are you all right? I've been frantic with worry, Reeve. I even called the police—had them search out the hospitals. Elliot's been absolutely crazy, too. He said he's promised DiLorenzo he'd have your answer about the Italian film deal by tomorrow. Where are you?''

"Idaho," Reeve answered.

There was a long pause.

"I see," his mother finally responded. Another long pause followed.

Reeve could sense his mother was gathering pieces of information and sifting through the possibilities of what the single word "Idaho" might augur in terms of his future—and hers.

"Are you coming home?" she asked, the voice well modulated, as always, in keeping with her social background, but with a hint of caution now.

"Yes. I need some sleep, then I'll drive back. I'd appreciate it if you'd call Elliot, extend my apologies for the walk-out—"

"It was dreadful of you, Reeve," his mother admonished. Her voice had taken on a more natural tone.

"I know." He also knew he'd be forgiven. Forgiven by all but Jaime.

The day before, on the morning of a television taping being held at his home by America's premier female interviewer, he had taken an aimless but precarious stroll through his Brentwood home.

Gingerly, he had stepped over the tangled mass of wires attached to light and sound equipment. He had dodged an interior decorator who was shrieking at a florist that the vase he had brought was vulgar, pretentious and tasteless. The florist might have had no taste, but he did possess a fine sense of invective. There proceeded an even more terrible row over this last insulting exchange.

It was amid this fray that his mother had appeared, her glorious smile intact as she introduced him to a young woman who looked amazingly like Charlotte Ferris herself. "Sandra from Boston," Charlotte had announced in dulcet tones.

She went on to explain that Sandra's parents were the so-and-so's of so-and-so, whom Reeve would of course remember founded such-and-such Industries, and as if all this were not enough, were cousins to Prince and Princess what's-their-crowns.

Reeve had listened with practiced politeness, all the while feeling himself suspended in a surrealistic world that in no way had any real substance.

Accordingly, he had walked past his mother without a glance and proceeded into his garage where he climbed into his red Porsche and calmly backed into the street.

He didn't even know where he was going exactly, except that sometime, an hour later, he caught onto the idea that a part of himself—a small surviving piece of himself that still lived and breathed autonomously without the aid of his mother or agent or business manager, not to mention an infinite number of other faceless beings on the Ferris payroll—was taking what was left of him back to Paradise, back to Jaime.

"What about the Italian deal?" Charlotte was asking him over the phone. "What shall I tell Elliot? He's on pins and needles, Reeve. This is the biggest deal he's ever put together for you."

"Tell him..." Reeve hesitated. He lifted the base of the phone and carried it to the window. At one end of the rink a small group of children had gathered. They surrounded a man, not in skates, who was gesturing with his arms and angling his body in such a way as to demonstrate what Reeve knew to be the setup for the rocker, a turn that joins two circles.

A silent wail shattered his soul.

He could still feel the air, sweet and crisp, as it had been that day when he had stood in a similar circle years before listening to an instructor demonstrate the proper slant of an elbow, the leveling of an arm when coming out of a turn. Along with the colors of the sky and the surrounding pines, the flashing eyes of a young girl with raven-black hair had captured his heart.

Oh, Jaime.

"Reeve? Hello? Are you there, Reeve?"

No, he thought, *I'm not. I'm back in another time when life was beautiful and real.* "I'm looking out my window," he answered. "Know what I can see from here?"

"No."

A single disinterested word.

It sounded as if she didn't want to know, or perhaps was afraid to know. He didn't care. She was going to hear it anyway, because he wanted to relive those times, however briefly. In a way, he supposed, it was his mother who had stolen Jaime from him. Unwittingly, of course. It was his mother's love for him and her ambition for both of them that had kept him from obtaining the only real treasure the world had to offer him.

"I'm looking out the lodge window at the rink." He laughed, happily as he watched the children skate. "There are a bunch of kids out there. Remember the way it used to be?"

"Reeve, that's over and done with. There's no sense in going back when there's so much in the present, in the future." Charlotte was speaking rapidly, almost breathlessly, as if she were bargaining for her life. "Elliot's going to ask two million dollars for you and—"

"God, Charlotte, you should see them out there!" He gave a sudden, free laugh. "They look so damned great!"

He fought down a wild longing to run out of the room and down to the rink, to gather them all into his arms and tell them, each and every one of them, never to lose their dreams—their own dreams; that was the important part, he suddenly realized. It was not enough to follow a dream, but it had to be your own and not your father's or mother's or teacher's. For if you did that, you lost yourself. If he knew anything in life, it was this one truth.

"We'll set up a new taping for your interview when you get back, so don't worry about that. Of course, we're going to have to look closely at your schedule to make certain you . . ."

Charlotte went on, her voice trailing off into the quiet of the room.

Reeve continued to watch out the window.

Two more children joined the others and more skiers were coming in from the slopes to take late lunches at the lodge. Suddenly he tensed. The phone dropped slightly away from his ear, reducing Charlotte's voice to a background buzz as he leaned his face against the window, trying to be certain, needing to be sure.

His heart raced wildly as the woman standing by the rink's railing raised her face into clear view. It was she. *Jaime.*

His grip on the phone loosened, and without thinking, as if he didn't know why he had been holding it, he dropped it into its cradle, cutting off the buzz.

Possessed, a man in a race against time, he searched the room for his clothes. Pants slung over the armchair, shirt on the bathroom doorknob, shoes, one sock, then the other, and his jacket. Item by item he collected each article of clothing and, dressing in a feverish haste, bolted out of the room without bothering to close the door.

Chapter Three

The druggist regretted that the order had not yet been filled. It wasn't something he usually stocked and he had sent to Haily to pick up a supply from a colleague in that town.

A veil of blackness drifted over Jaime. Not something he usually stocked. A powerful drug for a serious ailment.

If Jaime could wait just a bit longer, the drug should be arriving within the hour. The druggist's voice and expression bore genuine apology, and something more compassionate, a note of sympathy perhaps. The pall that had settled over her deepened.

Yes, of course she would wait, Jaime replied. Unless she wanted to see her mother clutch her stomach in agony again, had she any other choice but to wait?

"You don't have anything else on hand to substitute? Something, you know, generic?"

The druggist shook his head. "Nothing in a pain killer that strong. Nothing, anyway, that wouldn't have unpleasant side effects. Cancer's nasty enough without adding any more discomfort. She shouldn't wait so long to reorder," he added, as if to free himself from the guilt of not being able to provide the medicine sooner.

"Yes, of course," Jaime replied. Beneath the down ski parka, she was numb. "I'll make sure it doesn't happen again. I'll come back in half an hour," she said, and turned from the counter. As she passed along the aisles, the contents of the shelves and the other customers in the store swam before her.

The sounds of ordinary existence assaulted her as she stepped outside: the laughter of children, the hum of unseen adult voices, a shop door closing, cars starting up; the river of life flowing on. They were sounds that were suddenly loathsome to her, for they were alive and vibrant, and in the midst of so much vitality, her mother's life was ebbing away.

For a while she wandered aimlessly around the shopping area. She was vaguely aware that the ski shops and boutiques were decorated for the Thanksgiving season, but none of that was important as her mind fought to grasp the reality of what she had just learned from the druggist. It couldn't be possible. Try as she might, she was unable to form a connection between what the druggist had told her and the everyday world in which she and Jade existed. Emotions that should have arisen did not come. Instead they remained locked deep within her along with all her other unacknowledged fears, disappointments and desires.

She thought of her mother's desires, of how small they were, and of how reasonable and even wholesome they seemed when compared to the bloated demands some people made on life. Jade only wanted her man to love, and to live on a sheep and cattle ranch, which had been their first dream together.

A warning shout from a woman broke Jaime's melancholy introspection. There was no time to step aside before she took the full brunt of a young boy's body as he hurtled into her.

"Oh, sorry!" his mother apologized. She grabbed the boy by the hand, but the child wormed free and tore off in the same mad rush, a flash of bright light glinting after him like the gleaming tail of a comet.

Still in a partial daze, Jaime absently identified the sparkle as being the polished blade of a figure skate looped by laces over his shoulder.

"I'm terribly sorry," the woman said. "He gets so crazy when we're late for class. You're all right?"

Jaime nodded. "Yes, fine." She was watching the boy who had clattered into the skate office, a place that had once been like a second home to her.

"Well, I'd better go catch up with him before he leaves a trail of bodies."

Jaime laughed, and the woman hurried off in the direction the boy had gone.

In her mind's eye, Jaime imagined him rushing to the lockers and changing from street shoes to skates before making the final dash to join the others on the ice.

Absorbed as she had been in her worry over Jade, she hadn't paid any notice to the direction of her stroll. Finding herself at the site of happier times, moments out of her past leapt to mind.

A sense of peace enveloped her as she leaned over the railing of the outdoor ice rink. There behind the rink was the Sun Valley Lodge, venerable and stately as it had been when she was a girl. On the ice, a class was in progress. But for the change in clothing styles, it might have been one of the classes she had attended when she was a girl. Faces eager, eyes bright, the children listened raptly to their instructor. It must have been a school holiday of some sort, Jaime noted, for the time was too early for regular afternoon lessons.

With the outdoor sound system piping a changing medley of romantic and energetic musical arrangements, the young skaters were led through their paces by the instructor at one end of the rink. The other half of the ice was occupied by tourists, most of whom appeared to be more brave than athletic as they wobbled over the ice in varying states of precarious balance.

Forgetting herself for a time, she laughed good-naturedly, enjoying the spectacle of adults reclaiming youthful pastimes. But the brief flare of happiness was short-lived; an ache filled her as the notes of one song melded into a lyrical strain from the days when she and Reeve had skated together, and the world hardened once again into its present sober state of reality.

Motionless, she stood by the rail, jealous of the skaters' fluid buoyancy. In contrast, every part of her own being felt leaden, every cell, each muscle bound to a terrible present from which she could not imagine escape.

But once, in what now seemed like another lifetime, she, too, had flown over the ice as if she had wings on her heels. Absolutely no one could match her leaps! She had spun like the wind itself.

She stared past the skaters to the skate office. In her mind its form had suddenly taken on a sort of glowing light in the darkness that otherwise was her life.

Just one more time, she longed for an escape—a temporary one, but an escape nonetheless.

"Four dollars," the young woman behind the counter said.

Jaime handed her a five-dollar bill and waited for the change. Her heart beat so loudly she was certain others could hear it. It was as if she were cheating fate or at least thumbing her nose at destiny by reclaiming a portion of past joy.

The rental skates felt tight on her feet, but she didn't care. The tactile sensation of the icy steel blade against her fingers was thrilling, and just to tug on the laces brought a rush of pleasure.

In another moment she stood on the magical threshold of the ice rink. The tempo of the music now playing was fast and gay, and Jaime immediately caught its beat as her foot touched down on the smooth, frozen surface.

The last day she had skated was the day Reeve left town for good. She had gone to the rink as usual, determined that her life would go on despite Reeve's desertion. But it had been impossible for her to skate. Every turn, every twist of her body, even the sound of the ice grating under the serrated tip of her skate, had seemed alien without Reeve's presence. She had been only eighteen. The world was to have been hers. There was to have been a lifetime of loving and good times ahead. But on that day the seeds for the future shriveled and died within her, and like a widow who could not bear to be reminded of her lost love, the one true, great love of her life—Jaime retired from the scene and source of so much former happiness.

The rental skates were not good, but in spite of their mediocre quality and fit, Jaime sped over the ice, easily recapturing the flow of movement that many years before had enabled her to astound the top skating coach in the world.

God, she thought, spiraling down on one leg and coming out of the sit spin with a layback spin, and after a glide, daring to take a loop jump. *I'm doing it! I can still do it!*

Oblivious to everything but the sensations rippling through her body as she sped over the ice, her mind automatically sent signals to her limbs. Her limbs automatically accomplished the rotations and glides and leaps that only a handful of world-class skating champions could execute. In her own world, Jaime did not notice that the rink had cleared.

All other skaters had retired to the sidelines. Motionless and enthralled, the children stared, their eyes following Jaime like ball bearings attracted to a powerful magnet. A crowd of adults gaped at the edge of the rink, their numbers building steadily as the solo performance on the ice continued.

None of the onlookers noticed the man whose presence would otherwise have caused a flurry of excitement, if not a scene of total chaos.

As it was, Reeve Ferris moved unobserved from the flanks of the onlookers into the skate shop.

Outside on the ice, the music ended abruptly. Jaime faltered slightly, sculling while waiting for the new tape to begin. People yelled encouragement and compliments flew at her from the vast audience that now formed around the railing. It was ironic; here, now, years after her chance at fame and fortune had passed, she found herself a minor luminary without seeking the attention.

Her back was to the skate shop when the music began. She felt haunted as she recognized the song. It, too, was from the days she had skated with Reeve. A sadness swept over her, a longing that filled her soul and sent sexual impulses raging through her body as she relived the touch of his hands on her waist, felt again the warmth of his breath caressing the curve of her neck as he lifted her high into the air. All of it came rushing back to her, every nuance of their pairs' routine permanently imbedded in her memory.

She closed her eyes, closing out the present as she let the music flow through her, energizing her actions as she began to move in time to the notes.

An audible tremor pulsed through the crowd, drawing Jaime's attention.

Around her, the crowd's attention was still rapt, but their eyes were no longer on her alone. Again, an almost unanimous gasp filled the air, followed by an electrified hush. The current drew Jaime, forcing her to turn.

Stunned, all she could see were the radiant blue eyes dominating her senses as surely as they had on the first day they had met as children.

In an effortless, seamless glide, Reeve Ferris skated toward her over the ice, his gaze never leaving hers. Within the time it took to breathe again, she was swept into the fluid arc of his arms as he increased his command over her. His hands were quick and sure over her body. He repositioned her into the different stances necessary for each succeeding step as they moved rhythmically over the ice.

Locked in enchantment, there was only the two of them and the ice, the rest of the universe having faded into an inconsequential haze.

"I love you," Reeve said, spinning her into him. His breath was like fire on the curve of her neck.

She fought against the spell. "Keep out of my life, Reeve..." Gliding smoothly away, she escaped to safety.

"Never!" he shouted back across the ice.

Mechanically, without conscious deliberation, they had fallen into one of their old ice routines. Jaime was in position for her leap—*the* leap that had taken her two months of steady practice with Reeve to get it down so that it was smooth, not to mention safe. For an instant, as she looked at Reeve preparing for the catch, she wondered if she had lost her mind, but at the moment she was more disturbed over the possibility of a broken heart than of broken bones.

"You can't have everything you want in life, Reeve." She heard her voice sounding petulant, childish, and was instantly ashamed, yet at the same time she was unable, or unwilling, to hold her tongue. "Maybe most things, but not everything."

Reeve laughed, throwing back his head, rippling the shock of blond hair that was as much his trademark as the startling blue eyes.

"I don't want everything. All I want is you. You're everything."

"Yeah?" she called with her head over one shoulder as she did a preparatory loop.

"You got it."

"Then get ready. 'Cause here I come!"

Like a lightening bolt, she streaked across the ice, a determined ball of concentrated energy, her entire being focused on Reeve.

Airborne! She was flying! Caught in an invisible wind, hoisted weightless through space.

Into his arms.

A roar rose up from the crowd.

Reeve had caught her in midair, her legs in a split, and in one motion had lifted her over his head, at the same time twirling them both like a top.

In diminishing revolutions, he brought her down to earth again. Jaime's position changed automatically, her legs coming together in the form of a closed scissor, her body rigid as she made the descent. But instead of completing the routine as practiced, he held her there before him, not allowing her feet to touch ground.

"What are you doing?" she said, her breath short from the exertion and from exhilaration over their accomplishment. "Put me down."

His arms were straining. She could feel him shake slightly from maintaining his grasp around her waist. Still, he would not let her go.

"I love you," he said.

Jaime felt the blood wash from her face. She didn't want to hear it, none of it, and turned her head quickly for fear of losing herself in those compelling blue eyes that had taken her in so easily years before. "Put me down, Reeve."

"Listen . . . hear me, Jaime," he went on, ignoring her demand. "I should have come back for you years ago. I don't mind paying for that. I have paid for it," he said with some bitterness. "But don't punish me—don't punish the both of us—this way, Jaime. What we had between us was something rare."

"Did you get this out of one of your movie scripts?" Jaime returned.

"It doesn't ever die. It can't—" he was saying, and he was saying something else, only Jaime didn't hear what it was.

At the mention of death, the blackness of her present reality descended upon her again.

"Put me down, now," she said, her misery weighing each word with conviction.

The music was playing on, the dulcet romantic sound seeming cloying and almost obscene to Jaime as she wrenched herself free from Reeve's arms.

"It's too goddamned late," she said. "Everything good that might have been is over."

She started away, sweeping over the ice toward the skate shop.

Reeve followed her and caught her easily. He reached for her shoulder and spun her around to him again.

"Why?" he asked angrily, still holding her tightly. "Why does what we had have to be over?" he asked. "Where is that written? Show me the stone."

Jaime looked away, her eyes arctic green and slick with tears. "You've realized all your dreams, Reeve. But I only had one dream." She turned back to him, the tears gone now, and only an icy resolve left in their place. "I only wanted one thing. I breathed that dream every day, every night from the time I first saw you standing here on this ice, until the day you left with your fancy trainer and your fancy new skating partner. You knew it. And you never once, never once in all of those years, came back. You never even called. You never wrote. I wasn't even worth a lousy postcard!"

"Oh, God...Jaime..." He closed his eyes, bringing her tightly against him, squeezing her until she could not breathe. If he shut down the flow of words, he might also cut off the sting of truth.

In her anger she had grown strong, and being the target of that ire, he had grown weak. It was a simple matter to gain her freedom. With a push of one hand against his chest, she gained it.

She skated backward, close enough that he could hear her without having to raise her voice, and far enough to be out of his reach.

"So you don't know what it's like, Reeve, to have a dream like that and have it crushed. It kills something inside you. It gets you so you don't want to even try to wish for little things anymore. You learn just to put in your time, one day after the next. Nothing remarkable happens when you put in your time in Paradise, Reeve. But you get by without any more bruises."

She did a fast, spontaneous loop on her skates, then skidded to an abrupt, pointed stop closer to him. Chips of ice flew up in the air. One landed in his hair and for a crazy moment she wanted to reach out and brush it away, wanted to touch him. But instead, speaking to him but reprimanding herself, she said, "So, you see, this is one thing you just can't have, Reeve. Maybe the only thing. Now leave me alone, okay?"

Reeve looked away, as if in indecision. He tried to say something, but the words were inaudible. He cleared his voice, and looking back to Jaime said, "I'm sorry." Both hands reached out helplessly, palms up in supplication. "If it's what you want..."

Jaime nodded, then turned and walked up the stairs cushioned in outdoor carpeting to the skate shop. Just before she entered, Reeve called to her.

"Hey!"

Jaime looked down to where he stood. He wore a sad smile, like the ones that had made him so famous in his films, smiles that made women want to comfort him or ferret out the hidden sorrow. Jaime couldn't think of a single thing Reeve Ferris might have to feel disappointed about in life. He had always gotten everything. At least until now he had, but there wasn't any consolation in that thought, none at all.

"You still skate good," he called and hiked up his thumb.

Just the way he used to.

"You, too," Jaime said.

She hesitated, the green eyes lifting to his, and staying for a long moment, a giddy, excited, hopeful moment in which he felt the atmosphere changing. With certainty, he could feel her on the verge of reconsidering their relationship.

He dared not breathe.

Then, as if tuned to her mind, he felt her make her decision. There was an almost imperceptible withdrawal of warmth from her eyes. She looked away. Cold that had nothing to do with the temperature chilled him to the bone.

Jaime reached out to open the door and in a single movement disappeared inside the skate shop, leaving him alone on the ice surrounded by his adoring fans. Even then he knew it was a scene he would re-edit in his mind with variations of how it might have been had she turned back, had she called out to him to follow, had he committed some brutish act of masculine force and physically kept her from walking out of his life.

He experienced an odd series of emotions as he remained on the ice, staring at the place Jaime had so recently inhabited. He felt there was a hole in him. The space that she had filled in him over the years, even as a fantasy, was empty.

Around him, the crowd that had watched the skating performance in mute appreciation, now clamored like primitive natives for his autograph. Many of the onlookers rushed forward onto the ice without skates. Within seconds he was surrounded by jostling, avid autograph-seekers armed with pens and brandishing fluttering pieces of paper in front of his face. Trapped, and out of habit, he listlessly accepted his public responsibility with his outer smile intact.

Beneath the professional façade he was suffering. The woman he loved was lost to him completely and forever. Jaime was speaking the truth; this particular dream of his would not be realized. He had better face it.

"Are you working on any film now, Mr. Ferris?"

"Excuse me?" He had been operating on automatic. The question from the outer world came as an intrusion.

The woman repeated the question.

"Soon," he said, looking up as he passed out another autograph. "But not another western."

"Are you ever going to get married?" a teenage girl asked.

The question was typical, one he had answered at least a thousand times before, but now it cut into him like a knife. Stunned, he heard the words as if for the first time. He felt as if the future would evolve from this single response.

Everyone was waiting for his answer; so was he.

"The next script calls for a bachelor."

A mixture of titters and groans was heard from the circle.

"In real life," the girl persisted.

"Do you like happy endings?" he asked.

"Yeah, hey...well, sure," the girl responded, thrilled to have involved herself in an actual dialogue.

"So do I," he said and winked.

The girl and several other women appeared as if they were about to swoon. If only they would, he'd be off the hook.

"You didn't answer," an older woman chimed in.

"I don't see it in the cards," he responded sharply.

As soon as he finished the abrupt sentence, a sadness engulfed him. Perhaps the crowd sensed it for an unfamiliar silence followed his answer. It was a self-conscious, overly respectful lapse of animation, the type of mood people reserved for funerals. Appropriate, he felt, under the conditions.

"Maybe I ought to get a new deck," he joked. It was a mistake. It was a bald effort that rang out false. A couple of nervous laughs sounded from the crowd.

It was not part of his basic nature to give himself over to depression. For one thing, defeat of any real consequence had never been part of his life. The fact was that Jaime was right, whether from luck or from personal effort, Reeve had pretty much gotten everything he had ever wanted in life. He had, however, learned with some surprise that this condition was viewed by others as aberrant to the point of being suspect. They would poke around, they would delve into his past, even into his family's past, in search of dirty linen and dangling skeletons. None were ever found, because nothing was there to discover; he was as he appeared—a fortunate being.

Well, he thought as he handed back his signature scrawled over a fan's bank deposit slip, it looked as if he had finally made the grade. *Welcome to the human race, Ferris. You're no longer an emotional freak: you feel like hell.* If my friends could only see me now, he mused, stepping back slightly as he prepared to make good his escape.

"What kind of a woman do you like?" another woman yelled, her friends laughing and nudging her, all eyes alight with renewed excitement.

Women who don't ask silly questions. "They're all good," he said. He was drifting to the edge of the circle, and finally he was free of playing movie star.

From the skate shop, he made his way back into the lodge. Weighed down by a blanket of dejection, he hardly noticed the interested and admiring stares he drew from those he passed. It wouldn't have mattered to him one way or the other, anyway. He was not caught up in stardom. It was only something that he did, something that had happened to him the way the rest of his life had happened, the same way that some men became plumbers or accountants. Life just happened.

His thoughts were fixed on Jaime. He was obsessed. There had to be something he could do to counteract the prophesy of their doomed relationship.

Then, while passing the lodge's Duchin room, he believed he'd found it.

Chapter Four

Reeve watched as the woman wrapped his purchase. Her fingers moved quickly and expertly, fashioning the ribbon into a perfect red bow over the glossy blue paper.

With a smile, the woman handed him the package. "They're beautiful, Mr. Ferris, the best made. But then you'd know that, of course. I hope she enjoys them." The woman's eyes were alight with curiosity. No doubt firsthand knowledge of his love life would have been worth a considerable amount of gossip over lunch with her friends.

"So do I," he said cordially and left it at that. "So do I."

He felt almost jaunty as he placed the package in the passenger seat of the Porsche. The present was more than just a gift: it was his link to Jaime.

At the lodge he gave the front desk orders to wake him by six the following morning, but even though exhausted, he awoke several times during the night. Each time he sat up and turned on the light, unable to resist the impulse of making certain Jaime's gift was still where he had placed it on the dresser. In his mind, the package had taken on magical properties. Indeed, if it had suddenly begun to glow it would not have surprised him. Beneath the blue paper bound in red ribbon was his future with Jaime.

Or so he had to believe, as once again he switched off the light by his bed.

A good foot of snow had fallen during the night. The wind had piled up drifts that were much higher in places, but in terms of the kind of snow Sun Valley saw during a season, this was nothing. The snow blowers were out early, making the roads passable and safe for vehicles with tire chains or studs if one excluded the ever-present threat of avalanches along the passes.

Jaime served her first cup of coffee to a trucker at six that morning. He ordered one of Jade's homemade cinnamon rolls and a plate of potatoes with eggs and sausage, along with orange juice. Several other customers walked in shortly after the first man, and Jaime found herself having to write down orders rather than trusting her memory as she rushed between dining room and kitchen. She was glad for the activity; she had lain awake the entire night. Her thoughts had been fuzzy, her mind clouded with worry over Jade. Then there had been the recriminations over having skated with Reeve. She shouldn't have. Better she should have played with fire than to have allowed him to touch her again and leave her with empty torment. The look in his eyes, the stance of his body across the ice from her, a thousand subtle reflections of a past she had wished to bury and feelings she had struggled to forget.

In the kitchen, Jade moved swiftly, performing her tasks with an exaggerated and faultless precision that Jaime recognized at once as being unnatural.

"How much does it hurt?" Jaime asked, taking up a plate with biscuits and gravy.

"The pain has gone. There is no pain anymore." Jade's voice was as bland and noncommittal as her facial expression.

"I don't believe you," Jaime countered defiantly. "The food is getting cold." Jade turned back to the stove.

Jaime dogged after her. "What are you going to do about it?" It was somehow necessary to avoid the actual word, the disease itself, as if to mention it aloud would make it real.

"It will be all right," Jade said evenly.

"What! What on earth are you saying?" She put the plate on the counter and turned to face Jade, forcing her mother to look at her.

"There's nothing to be done," Jade said.

"What did the doctor say?"

"He said it was in my stomach. He said it was this, it was that, how it grows... very interesting, like a history lesson."

"Sure, sure. But this isn't some far-off country. It's you, your life and your body. And it's now. What about an operation?" Jaime pressed.

Jade shook her head. "No operation."

For an instant, Jaime felt unbalanced, as if she'd been hit in the stomach. Then she remembered she was dealing with Jade, and in that case she could not necessarily take anything at face value. "Wait," she said, "let me get this straight. No operation because the doctor says so? Or no operation because you've made up your mind not to have one?"

In the dining room, the front door jingled.

"Ah, another customer," Jade said happily, the tiny crows'-feet at her eyes crinkling in pleasure.

Jaime shook her head. Another customer, another dollar. One more dollar closer to making the ranch a reality. But it was still a pipe dream as far as Jaime was concerned. Besides, didn't her mother realize that in the present circumstances, customers and ranches didn't matter anymore?

Jaime retrieved the plate with the biscuits and gravy and backed away. She pointed her index finger at Jade. "Don't think that this is the end of it. I want real answers."

Jaime entered the dining room with her mind still absorbed by Jade's trouble. She was halfway across the room before she saw him.

Reeve stood in the doorway just as he had the previous day. For an instant Jaime thought that perhaps she was imagining him, that he was just an image left over from the previous night's dream. But no, he was as real as he had been the day before, and looking beautiful to her, the same golden man who had claimed her heart at age fourteen—and who had since gone on to claim the hearts and minds of half the world's female population, Jaime reminded herself. Just standing there, he had the amazing ability to appear at the same time tender and hard, vulnerable and arrogant, a man who radiated maleness in every fiber of his being. The critics said he exuded charisma. All she knew was that his presence in her life was dangerous.

"Get your coffee somewhere else," she said in a low voice, and passed swiftly by on her way to deliver the biscuits.

She left the plate of biscuits and the check for the breakfast on the table. When she turned back, she saw Reeve hadn't moved. This didn't strike her as a particular surprise; he was accustomed to having things his way.

She couldn't avoid him. In order to reach the kitchen, she had to pass him again. In the same low voice, she said, "Didn't you hear me? I said—"

"Yes," he returned mildly. "I heard you say it the first time. A bit rude, perhaps, but you said it very well."

She glared at him. "Then why are you still here?"

"I didn't come here for coffee."

Jaime paused, her body tense, then turned away from him. "Then, what?"

He remained slightly behind her. "You know that as well as I do."

She spoke to him in profile, not willing to offer any more of herself than was necessary or safe. "Well that's not on the menu anymore," she returned.

She had on faded jeans and a yellow turtleneck. Her black hair was drawn back off her face and was fastened in a fake tortoiseshell clasp, and she hadn't bothered with any makeup. As if from above, she saw them both standing there, inches away but a world apart. How clear it all was now, and what a fool she had been all those years to believe the differences between them did not count.

Standing there, looking every inch the movie star, Reeve reminded her of the other people who came into the area. It was really a joke. The tourists would come, uptight in their expensive leisure outfits, faces gray and pinched from city living, and in a few days, swept up in the natural beauty of the surroundings, they would become frantic to collect a piece of a world that was so different from their own. They would purchase Indian arrowheads and sheepskin jackets such as the Basque sheepherders wore, carrying these things and other similar items back home with them like talismans to ward off the plasticity of their existences.

And that, Jaime thought, was what Reeve was doing. He had merely returned to collect a piece of her to take back with him, something that would remind him of the fresh air and tall mountains. She was a wholesome souvenir.

"Look," she said, shrugging, "I love shooting the breeze and all, but I've got work to do." She stepped ahead.

"Jaime...!" He came forward, stopping her. In his hands he held a large package that she only just then noticed. "For you," he said.

She stepped back, as if threatened by the offering. "No," she said, shaking her head, "keep it."

"Please, I want you to have it. You'll see...it's—" He broke off. "Look, not that it should matter to you, but it would mean a great deal to me...everything, it would mean everything...if you'd just accept this."

She looked down at the blue paper and red ribbon, stared at it as if studying it intently. It wasn't the gift she was afraid of accepting, but the giver. She did not want to be one of those people who collected scraps of a life they would never lead in full. That seemed so phony. Better to live her own life as it was and to live it honestly, than to be left with nothing more than a piece of someone else's.

"Jaime, please, what can it hurt?"

She looked up. His nearness made her tremble and the blue of his eyes almost blinded her with its radiant intensity. He was holding the gift out to her as if it were a living thing, something priceless and fragile.

"No," she said. "I don't want your package." She measured out each word so that he would know she was serious. "And I don't want you."

He nodded. His expression held something more than disappointment and she had to look away, unable to stand the look of sorrow, feeling it somehow as her own.

"Look, I've got customers," she said listlessly. "It was nice seeing you again." She sighed and ran her fingers through her hair. She wanted to touch him, to smooth his face with her hands. "Time passes, and you know, you just can't go back. Anyway, it didn't work before. I've gotta get back and see about hotcakes and sausage, that kind of thing."

"Sure, that kind of thing," he echoed.

Reeve scanned the room, taking in the several occupied tables before his attention rested on her again. Smiling slowly, but without much humor, he said, "I didn't know you could be such a hard woman."

"It happens sometimes." She stepped forward, but got only two steps away before he caught her wrist and drew her back.

A couple of the men seated nearby looked up from their conversations. They were men who liked a good fight. Jaime knew that nothing would please them more than to have an excuse to bash heads.

"If you don't want to have your teeth knocked out, I suggest you let go of my arm," she said calmly in a voice low enough so that only he might hear.

"You still have freckles," he said, smiling.

"The man in the plaid jacket can single-handedly lay a five-hundred-pound steer flat. I've seen him do it. You'd be a piece of cake."

"Okay, I'll say it. You're forcing it out of me. I love you."

Her face burned. Her body was on fire and her ears rang. "You aren't listening to me."

"No, you aren't hearing me. I always loved you, Jaime, back then and I still do. Nothing's changed." He squeezed her wrist tighter as if to emphasize each word. "Do you think I'd mind losing a few teeth if that's what it took to convince you?"

"I don't know about your teeth, but I care about my cups and table and chairs, okay?"

Slowly, he released his hold on her.

Their eyes locked one final time before Jaime fled to the safety of the kitchen. Seconds later she heard the sound of the door close and when she returned, Reeve was gone. The package was left on the counter by the cash box.

It was late afternoon before Jaime had any time to herself. In an unprecedented act, Jade herself had put the Closed notice on the window. Jaime wasn't certain if that was a good or a bad sign. It could mean her mother was becoming more realistic; it was a waste of human energy to remain open during winter afternoons when hardly anyone ever stopped in for more than a cup of tea and pie. But on the other hand, Jaime considered, closing the café could also be taken as an outward sign of despair, evidence of Jade's deteriorating physical condition.

Jaime remained in the café, telling Jade she would join her in the cottage soon.

She stood in the dining room, staring across the room at *It*. The presence of the box had tormented her all day. It seemed animate, as if Reeve had left behind a piece of himself.

Several times she approached it, then backed off. Finally, feeling like Pandora, assailed by curiosity and foreboding, she hoisted the box and carried it to a table in the center of the café.

She tore at the paper and ribbon, and with her heart racing wildly, she lifted the lid of the box. More white tissue paper, and then . . .

Skates.

Jaime stared at them.

For a moment she was reluctant to touch them. Then she gave into the urge to run her fingers along the shiny silver blades, letting her fingers lightly trace the white leather. She could hear her heart in the stillness of the room, the rhythm of the past taking hold of her pulse.

Slowly, she lifted the skates from the box.

"Oh, damn you, Reeve. Damn you. I loved you so."

Slumping into a chair, she held the skates, cradling them in her arms as if they were living entities, as if they breathed all the memories of her life. Her life back then . . .

The café was very quiet, everything was still. Jaime raised her eyes, staring out the window to the mountains. That day, the day when everything had begun, had also been quiet. She remembered perfectly.

It had been an unusual time. There were not many people around Sun Valley. It was one of those slow periods between seasons, no longer winter and not yet spring, a period when patches of snow stubbornly refused to melt, creating a mottled blight on scenery that only weeks before had presented an image of a glistening white fairyland to the international jet-setters who came in droves to play during ski season.

But on that day, all the beautiful people had drifted away. They had flown off to Rio or Maui or Tahiti to get a head start on their tans, or had flown to Paris to shop furiously for their summer wardrobes. So it was not really the kind of day from which anything much could be expected by the ordinary citizens of Sun Valley.

Certainly, not even Jaime—who, as Jade's daughter, had then believed in miracles—could have anticipated the moment of magic that was to occur. As it was, the day had dawned in a personal sense; it was Jaime's eleventh birthday. She had been given a gift of money, the proceeds of a collection taken up by some of the merchants and miscellaneous townspeople of Paradise.

Jade had not wanted to accept the money, considering it charity, which of course it was. But when a fuss was made by the good-deed doers, she was forced to relent and Jaime found herself fifty dollars richer.

There were still potatoes to peel and carrots to chop before she could leave the small café her mother ran singlehandedly, if one did not count Jaime's assistance. But after the chores were done, Jaime peddled her bicycle to Sun Valley. With her money snugly wrapped in a tissue tucked deep within her jacket pocket, she passed by the boutiques with their splendid clothes and the gift shops with their exotic treasures, thinking only of her intended destination.

When she arrived at the outdoor ice rink, there were just a few children skating, those who could afford the semi-private coaching sessions.

Jaime stood on the sidelines where the rail divided spectators from participants. She watched for a time with her fingers buried deep in her pockets. One hand was clutched around the thick wad of bills as if she half expected them to disappear. Vicariously, as she had so many times before, she experienced the glide of silver metal over ice and thrilled to the harsh scraping sounds of the serrated points of figure skates. Ice crystals flew into the air and fell about the skaters like tiny shooting stars. No matter how many times it happened, Jaime would catch her breath, silently gasping at the spectacle.

No one in the skate shop paid her any attention as she wandered through the displays, examining the merchandise with the eye of a jeweller purchasing a perfect stone at great cost. Her face was long familiar to the sales staff: Jaime Quinn, the little dreamer from Paradise, the noncustomer.

It took her forever to make a decision.

Laying the tissue paper on the glass counter, she unwrapped the birthday gift and let the bills fan out before the clerk.

"Those," she said with authority, pointing to her choice. "I want to buy those skates, please."

The world seemed particularly still. Perhaps, she thought as she laced the skates, the earth had stopped its spinning. Such was the momentousness of the occasion as she gingerly made her way onto the ice. Her heart had gone silent and her body seemed weightless as gleaming metal met frozen water. A false start, a glide of sorts, a dangerous wobble, and then as if she had been caught suddenly in the flow of an invisible stream, she was being carried over the ice. She was skating!

Several of the children paused in their routines, marking the occasion with curious glances. The instructor noted her as well. Jaime felt his eyes on her and encouraged by the attention dared to execute a wide circle, arms extended gracefully, head thrown back, just the way she had watched the other children do it. She felt a rush of energy. She was a star, a shooting star caught in the light, dazzling, bright, alive and invincible. Later, one of the kids told her that the instructor had said her turn was almost perfect, in fact he couldn't believe it when he learned that she had never studied.

Jaime peddled back to Paradise with the skates slung around her neck. It was a trip she repeated a thousand times over the following years. With the money she made doing odd jobs for some of the local merchants, she paid for Saturday group lessons. By the time she was fourteen, there were whispers of "Olympic material" coming from the tables where all the mothers sat on the patio outside the lodge, their attention divided between their knitting and what was happening on the rink.

For as long as Jaime or anyone else could remember, there were only a few kinds of people in Sun Valley; the local townsfolk, the part-time residents, and the rich, reclusive artists, writers, and other creative types, who were rarely seen except when buying booze or bread. Naturally, there was also the steady stream of tourists, and of course the "players," beautiful young transients of both sexes, who worked in the discos and restaurants and on the ski lifts in order to be part of the Sun Valley scene.

It was on a Tuesday afternoon that Jaime saw Reeve Ferris for the first time.

She was practicing on her own after school. Her time on the ice was precious to her, as Jade depended more and more upon her services at the café now that she was fourteen and could wait tables and handle the cash register. Although she could not afford the private lessons that her closest competitor, Margaret Tanner, took three afternoons a week, she managed stealthy glances from the corner of her eye. With her natural skill and determination, this technique was almost as good as the coveted individualized attention that Margaret received.

Someone else watched the activity on the ice that afternoon. A boy stood off to the side, leaning against the rail. He was new; of that Jaime was certain. She pretended not to notice him, but she could see him following everything intently, as if he might be technically aware of the steps being executed.

He was the handsomest boy she had ever seen. He was, she thought, worthy even of the term "beautiful." Slender and tall, he wore what she knew to be expensive clothes. His hair was a golden blond color and was worn brushed off to one side where it dipped in careless elegance across his forehead. There was nothing disproportionate about him; every facial feature was even, yet oddly distinctive in its perfection. He had a strong, clearly defined jaw, and lips, which although not curved into a smile, hinted strongly of a sunny disposition. It was a mouth, Jaime thought idly as she kicked off on one skate to prepare for a leap, that had never *had* to turn down. Probably, she thought, nothing had ever come into his life that warranted sadness. The thought came to her without jealousy. It was merely an observation, a fact that she accepted as she did everything else in her existence. The flagrant inequalities of her life compared to those of other children in Sun Valley were never brought up for conscious review. Things were just the way they were.

A few minutes later, the boy whose name she learned was Reeve Ferris, was on the ice. He was sixteen, two years older than Jaime, but he had come to Sun Valley with a lifetime of experience that would be impossible to realize if she lived a thousand years in Paradise, Idaho.

His father was an airline pilot, therefore "rich" by Jaime's standards. Reeve's mother was also fair-haired and beautiful, once having been a model and, according to the local gossip, a former debutante in some town in Virginia noted for its horses and famous families. She wore her hair sleeked back off her face and knotted at the nape of her neck. She had a face that was a match for her son's in perfection, except for being totally feminine in every way, while Reeve's was totally masculine. Reeve had lived in Hong Kong and South Africa and Australia. He had traveled throughout Europe and had been educated in a wonderful school in Switzerland where he learned to speak several languages. It was in Switzerland that he had learned to skate.

And Reeve Ferris skated beautifully.

That day, Jaime watched him take over the ice, just as in the future she saw him command the student body, and later, her body.

Each movement, the slightest gesture he made, was like a moving symphony. She could not take her eyes off his face. The radiance of his smile broke over her like warm sunlight, and the eyes—such eyes as she had never seen in her life—sparkled with blue light.

That first day, he swept the entire perimeter of the rink, taking it in a graceful arc, his arms floating in counterpoint to his body, like the wings of a magnificent bird in free flight. He moved solo over the ice, for the rink had been abandoned to him by others.

Jaime was taken with him instantly.

She was the best skater in Sun Valley, even better than Reeve. That was the indisputable, incontestable fact that was no doubt responsible for drawing her into the orbit of Reeve's sun. He selected her to be his skating partner.

While Reeve took his private lessons after school, Jaime peeled potatoes and chopped celery and sliced tomatoes like a demon, after which she peddled her bike like a maniac from Paradise to Sun Valley and worked on routines with Reeve for as long as Jade could spare her services from the café.

Jaime's substitute on the days when she could not attend their pairs' skating practices was Margaret Tanner. This drove Jaime wild. Not only was Margaret Tanner an excellent skater, but she was quite beautiful and rich. The two of them, Reeve and Margaret, looked like a prince and princess, beings cut out of the same heavenly pattern labeled "Aristocrats."

The most terrible moment of Jaime's life occurred in November, during her sixteenth year.

After school, she had swiftly completed what had seemed like a limitless set of demands from Jade and she had arrived twenty minutes late for her practice with Reeve. She was flushed and breathing hard when she skated onto the ice. At first she thought Margaret Tanner was with Reeve because he must have thought she wasn't coming. But a sense of wrongness hit Jaime as Reeve shifted his glance away from her. Except for the fact that Margaret was observing her with an air of amused triumph, Jaime would have thought herself suddenly rendered invisible.

Then she saw *him*. He had been standing off in the sidelines, talking to Reeve's mother, but now he was skating over the ice. His face blew up in Jaime's mind like an explosion. Peter Egri—the most successful coach of Olympic skating stars in the history of the sport—had just laid his hand on Reeve's shoulder. Egri spoke to Reeve, then to Margaret, issuing some sort of instruction, which they began to follow.

Jaime backed away, almost stumbled on her skates and hit the railing hard with her backbone. She didn't feel the pain. She was overwhelmed by another kind of pain, the unbearable agony of facing the truth of life as it was and not as she believed it would be. Her face burned from shame—the shame of recognition of being who she was—the daughter of a third generation Chinese-American woman with no resources but her two hands and a will to survive, and a fun-loving man who made promises and dreamed dreams, but who in the end was a coward, leaving his wife and daughter without explanation.

She peddled home and locked herself in the bathroom, for Jade's sake stifling her sobs in a terry cloth towel. Sinking into a ball on the cold linoleum floor, she swallowed down dry screams of rage and sorrow for being, like her mother, left behind, a cast-off convenience in the life of a man who was moving on.

The news was all over school. Reeve was being trained for the Olympics and Margaret was to be his skating partner. It was strange how no one really thought to offer condolences to her, but that was just as well as Jaime did not think she could stand any kindness at that time. Her strength came from anger, and it was building every day. It was funny how everyone but she had been aware of "the way things really were." She was Jaime from Paradise, Jaime from the café, Jaime who was the best natural skater in Sun Valley, but whose boundaries went no farther. The rest of the world belonged to Reeve and Margaret.

She stayed away from the rink for a week, nurturing her fury until she was strong enough to do what she had to do.

Reeve and Margaret were on the ice, just as she knew they would be when she reappeared. Egri was there with them, hovering and scolding, the benevolent guru to whom they had surrendered their futures. With a show of nonchalance, Jaime moved onto the ice. Reeve turned his head; Margaret did too. Jaime waved. A look of relief relaxed Reeve's features. Then Jaime began.

She had never before skated so forcefully. With full concentration, with energy of anger to propel her, she moved over the ice like a goddess. When she leaped, she flew; turning, she became a focused blur of light.

Reeve and Margaret had stopped their practice. Egri stood on the ice, face like stone, his gaze fastened on Jaime's movements. Reeve's mother had put down her magazine and watched intently from the bleachers. A gathering of onlookers stood motionless by the rail. Never, Jaime knew, had anyone seen anyone skate as she was skating. When she finished there was applause. At first, she noted with elation, it was only Egri who clapped; after a moment, as if initially stunned, Reeve joined in, and finally, lazily, Margaret. The others watching also applauded, but that didn't matter particularly; they were merely background. All that mattered to Jaime was Egri's and Reeve's reaction.

Jaime's only acknowledgement of their appreciation was the slightest of nods. Regal, her head high, she left the rink like a princess disdainful of unworthy subjects.

For the next three hours she walked by herself through the countryside, not wanting to speak to anyone or to dilute the energy that had taken a week to build. It was dark as midnight when she approached the rented condominium where Egri lived. Discomfort described his expression as he let her in.

She knew he was expensive, she said, and she didn't have the money to pay his fees. But he had seen her skate and she believed in herself enough to promise him she would take the Gold Medal for the United States if she could train under him. She would work harder than anyone he had ever known or would ever know. She waited for Egri's response, which was a long time in coming. In all the old movies she had watched it wasn't like that; a talented young person would make her plea and a smile would break out on the benefactor's face as he said, "Yes, by George!" and the violins and trumpets would swell around them. This wasn't like that.

Egri's face became clouded. He went to a sidebar and pulled out a pack of cigarettes, opening it and taking one in his fingers. He stuffed the cigarette into his mouth and lit it, never once looking at her. "No," he said, exhaling. "I can't help you. You're an excellent skater. That's for the record, for whatever good it will do. And for all I know you might even take the Gold, although it's not quite that easy. Nothing is," he said, but not really to her. "I'm not a charitable organization, young lady. I busted out of Hungary with Russian bullets flying at my heels. I took that chance because I liked the idea of living well enough to die for it. I'm sorry I'm not a true hero, like some of my compatriots."

She pleaded with him with all the intensity of a film heroine, but in the end there were no violins and horns. There was simply the door shutting at her back and the first fall of snow, the frothy crystals dissolving into her hot tears.

Reeve graduated that spring. He attended college out of state, an Ivy League school in the east. Margaret was a year behind him and remained in Sun Valley to finish high school. Reeve returned during school breaks and for summers to train with Egri.

Jaime never skated when the two Olympic hopefuls were in Sun Valley together. Anyway, she rarely had the time, even when they weren't there to practice. Jade needed her more and more to help at the café. With every passing year, Jade's spirit seemed to drop a notch. Sometimes when Jade did not have her splendid guard up, it seemed to Jaime that her mother was shrinking before her eyes, not so much physically as in essence.

It was during one of those increasingly rare occasions when Jaime had the opportunity to skate, that she looked up to find Reeve watching her from the sidelines. Since the time Egri had entered their lives, they had rarely spoken, Reeve curtailing their relationship from what she assumed was a sense of embarrassed guilt, and she from a sense of anger and betrayal. She saw him, and he waved. She waved back, continuing to skate.

Her heart was thumping wildly and she felt her legs go numb beneath her as he entered the rink. They skated together for three hours.

Before, when locked in close physical proximity, they had been no more than children incapable of realizing their own physical destinies, just as they were unable to command other aspects of their lives. The attraction was there, but so were the warnings of society not to give reign to the frequent floods of warmth through limb and loin, nor to take seriously the aching itch of desire that affected body and mind long after they had left each other's presence.

Now, as they skated, emotions belonging to developing adults overrode the bounds of their childhood relationship. For those three hours it was the same as when there had been no Margaret or Egri, but only she and Reeve and the ice. There was not that same intimacy that came when their bodies moved in simultaneous flow, catching hold of their minds, their very souls, bonding them together. But now there was a difference, a subtle change in the rhythm of their bodies as they joined and swept away from each other.

Reeve was no longer a boy. He was a man. It was not just the obvious response of his body hardening against hers, but the look in his eyes. Evident as they moved in and out of each other's arms over the ice, was the entire biological history of mankind: the male's instinctive need to possess the female; the woman's response of giving herself to the man.

They were shy toward each other as they removed their skates. Reeve walked with her to the bicycle rack. It was a painful moment, that exhange of goodbyes. As she rode home, Jaime cursed herself for having been such a fool as to give her heart to him once again. She was only a convenience, in Margaret's absence.

The motor was a purr behind her, then close beside her. The car slowed, stopping just ahead of her at the curb. Reeve put her bike in his trunk, lashing it closed with a piece of rope. Jaime got in. Saying nothing, he pulled her close against him. They drove like that, heading in the direction of Paradise but he passed the exit and continued to another turnoff.

The barn was abandoned, but it was dry inside and surprisingly warm, with straw still lying in smooth heaps like the rolling swells of ocean waves. Reeve undressed her and himself simultaneously. His mouth was on hers, and their tongues twined together in an undulating rhythm that matched itself in their bodies as they came together on a bedding of shed clothes thrown atop the straw.

She had never been touched before by a man. All the imaginings of her life as to what sex might be like could never equal the ecstatic pleasure she experienced as his hands roamed like silk over her breasts and down her belly, tracing the line of her hips, the smoothness of her thighs. She was drowning in pleasure. His body was covering hers and she felt him hard as iron against her. For a moment she was frightened. But his mouth was on her breast and she arched up instinctively, her legs parting as she cried out and dropped her head back in reflexive abandonment. Reeve moved into her, separating her thighs with his leg. Still drawing her nipple into his mouth, he took her hand in his and guided it to his body. A deep sigh was accompanied by a series of shudders, his muscles rolling in a kind of electric trembling the length of his body.

Jaime felt his effort to be still, and for a moment he was above her, all motion suspended. He continued to hold himself quiet until finally she felt him relax and his body again began its slow, spiraling rhythm.

She had never known such a sense of power before, that she had the capacity to give such pleasure, and in that giving, that she could receive such delight. She felt him against her, the powerful male need pushing into her with a single thrust. There was a moment of pain and she cried out. His hands clamped to her tightly, as if afraid for her but unable to stop what he had begun, and her fear vanished into the fluid heat that made all else in life insignificant and superfluous. He cried out then, and along with him she was unexpectedly caught. Lost to time, lost to her body, she was sensation itself.

They dressed themselves in quiet embarrassment. The act hung between them like a third party awaiting further order. If it had only been the act of sex, that could have been understood more easily than the experience they had just shared together. There was genuine feeling as well as passion exchanged. As they had been born to skate together, so their bodies had naturally come together in the act of love. And they both knew it.

But there was nothing to be done.

"I'll only be here another week," Reeve said, the apology also a warning. She was on notice. Did she understand that in telling her, he was being fair? "Egri's coming to work on something with Maggie and me."

"Are you coming back at spring break?" Jaime asked as they started to walk in the direction of his car.

"No, I don't think so. Margaret's coming east. There'll be some initial tryouts."

"And not in the summer, either," Jaime predicted dully.

He was quiet. "I can't help things!" he exploded as if she had accused him. "Look Jaime..." His voice was leaden in frustration. "You know what all this means to my mom and dad. They've spent a fortune on Egri, not to mention all the years of training. I'm their only son. I can't just walk away from this now."

He was quiet and so was she. Their footsteps crunching over the frozen earth sounded like the ominous marching of guards. The third party, that unseen specter, still followed along, awaiting its own final dispensation. At the car, Reeve took hold of her shoulder as she was about to get into the passenger's side. "I'll come back for you, Jaime. After it's all over, I'll come back for you."

Jaime closed her eyes and fell against him, her face turned sideways against his chest and her arms entwined around his neck. "Reeve," she said, and had to begin again because her voice came out in a choke of torn emotion, "Reeve, I'll wait for you. I'll wait, Reeve."

His arms clamped around her, and although she couldn't be certain, she thought he, too, was crying softly. There was moisture on the top of her hair as she touched her fingers to her head on the silent drive home. It made her feel good that she could have such an effect on him. The knowledge that he had also cried at their parting was one of the main things that gave her heart during those endless nights when she waited for him to return to her.

But Reeve Ferris didn't come back as he had promised.

Mr. and Mrs. Ferris moved out of Sun Valley shortly after Reeve and Margaret took the Olympic Gold Medal in the pairs' skating competition. Some people claimed that the couple who skated for West Germany were better and more deserving of the award—Jaime included—but Reeve Ferris had conquered that arena with his golden looks and invincible charm, just as he was soon to expand his reign into new territories.

Jaime had sent a telegram to the site of the Olympics, congratulating Reeve. It was possible, she thought, that he had never received it. It was possible he might have waited to hear from her and when he didn't he might have thought she had forgotten him. Of course she did not believe any of that. It was ridiculous. But it was something she had to think then or she would have died of grief or madness or a combination of both.

Immediately following his Olympic triumph there were guest shots on all the big television shows for Reeve, then the two commercials, and the movie—a western—that made him the newest, biggest box office star since Steve McQueen had hit the screen. After that, there were other movies, and Reeve's fame grew beyond McQueen's and Redford's combined, perhaps because he was single, perhaps because he held out the hope to so many millions of women that he might someday be captured and tamed. Jaime saw two of Reeve's movies and never went again, but it took her longer than was sensible to stop waiting for him to return. God only knew Jade was even more dense than she was. Grady Quinn had left Jade high and dry, without even so much as a promise to return, and yet Jade remained convinced he'd come back someday. It was not going to happen. Never in a million years would Grady Quinn step over their threshold again. Never in two million years would Jaime ever expect Reeve Ferris to come riding into Paradise on his white charger to carry her away with him

But she was wrong. It took six years, but he came hurtling out of the past in a fast red sports car, dropping a pair of skates into her lap and telling her the same lies she had believed when she didn't know any better.

That was then, she thought, and this...this was now.

The sun had dropped low in the sky and it was cold in the café dining room without the heat from the kitchen stove drifting in for extra warmth. More snow coming, Jaime thought, as she lifted the skates from her lap and placed them back in the box. They were beautiful skates. What she wouldn't have done for skates like this once! Once upon a time, she thought sadly.

As she put the lid on the box, a small white card fluttered to the table top.

Gingerly, she fingered the envelope, then pulled out the slip of paper with the message: *If you ever want to skate again—I need a partner. Just call me. Seriously.*

Below, Reeve had scrawled his now famous signature.

Only she wasn't a fan of his anymore.

Carrying the box with her into the kitchen, she placed it on the counter while she started a flame going under Jade's large caldrons. Then she went outside and brought in three armloads of wood for the fireplace in the dining room. When she was finished, she stood at the window looking out at the Sawtooths.

Beyond them, somewhere, traveling away from her in his expensive red sports car was a man she had once loved with every particle of her being.

Chapter Five

Pat Griffen stomped over to the window and then back across the dining room to where Jaime stood by the cash register. He repeated his journey several times before he finally came to a halt by the counter. Draping his arms over the cash register, he dropped his head, remaining that way for some time, as if in silent prayer. When he looked up, his eyes were red-rimmed and his brow creased with deep horizontal slats.

He let out a great, heaving breath. "She's not going to die. I'm not gonna let her."

Just having Pat with her made Jaime feel less desperate, although she didn't know what he could do actually to make things better. Yet he was big and solid and caring, and that in itself was of immense comfort.

When the doctor told her it was possible for Jade to have an operation, and that it was possible, although not certain, that she might be cured, Jaime was ecstatic.

But her relief was short-lived.

In the next breath, the doctor told her the cost of Jade's reprieve. The operation, plus hospital expenses, could total fifty thousand dollars.

"Don't worry about the money," Pat said, sweeping his hand in the air, the matter dispensed.

"Don't worry? I don't have fifty thousand dollars," Jaime said. "All I've got is what Jade's managed to save for the ranch and that wouldn't buy much more than a few bandages."

"I said not to worry about it. I'll take care of it," Pat insisted with a blustery authority that Jaime guessed consisted of equal amounts of hyperbole and good intention.

"You've got that kind of money?" Jaime questioned, skeptical but more than willing to be proven wrong.

"Nope," Pat said, rocking back on his heels, "but my insurance company does. Working for the government has certain advantages, and this is one of them."

"For you it is. Pat, you know Jade's not covered on your policy."

"She will be when I marry her," he objected forcefully.

"No," Jaime said, shaking her head. "She can't get covered after the fact. It's not insurance then; there's no gamble. It's just a big bill."

They were both silent, the weight of the situation crushing them.

"I'd sell my soul to save Jade," Pat murmured, his eyes casting around as if to seek out a buyer.

"Yeah," Jaime concurred. "Me, too. Not that mine would bring much on the open market."

She began to clear up the day's accumulated debris, odd pieces of paper lying on the counter with reminders to herself or Jade to buy something or do something or tell someone something.

Pat, who had been lost in a reverie of his own while she went about her mundane duties, suddenly slammed his fist down. "Hell, girl! If I had a body worth selling, I'd sell parts of it piece by piece."

Jaime stared at him, as if suddenly struck by something.

"What?" Pat asked.

"Nothing." Jaime clutched the side of the counter. Her knuckles were white, her body as tense as a drawn bow.

"What's going on?" Pat demanded, rushing around to her.

"Nothing, I said."

"Bull! Something." He caught her by the shoulders and gave her a gentle shake. "I know you just the same's I know your mom. So don't try to pull one on me." His eyes probed beyond her guarded expression.

Jaime twisted away, trying to keep her secrets safe from his piercing inquiry.

But Pat was not to be put off. He caught her chin, and guiding her around to face him again, ordered, "Tell me, girl."

"Reeve came back today," she said, her eyes wavering as she caught the immediate affront in Pat's expression.

"Sonofa— What the hell did he want?" Pat's coloring flared, his face a bright scarlet. "He did something! I'm gonna kill him," he raged. "L.A.'s not so far that I can't take myself for a ride and—"

Jaime interrupted. "He brought me a gift." She bent down and retrieved the box with the skates from under the counter. "This."

Slowly, as she had done the first time, she lifted the lid.

Pat looked down, then back to her. "Skates?"

"And this," Jaime said. She handed him the white card.

Pat read the message slowly. He shook his head, letting Jaime take back the card. "He wants you to skate with him again? The guy's a genuine fruitcake. Thinks he can come marching back in here and take whatever he wants."

"Whomever he wants," Jaime corrected.

"Well he got a lesson this time," Pat said darkly, then with less certainty, "Didn't he?"

Jaime only nodded. With her head bent, she replaced the lid on the box.

"Sure you kicked him right out the door, outa your life," Pat said with relish. "And a good thing, too. Guys like that..." He shook his head disparagingly again. "Oh, they think their money can buy the world, but in some places it's counterfeit. And this just happens to be the—" Pat stopped abruptly. He stood stock-still, seemingly to have turned to stone. Only his eyes moved. Various emotions, ranging all the way from cunning to fury to resolution, played like shadows across his face. "You gotta do it," Pat said, emerging from his trance.

His eyes were bright, his voice clear. There was no chance that she could have misunderstood him.

The worry lines had miraculously vanished from his forehead. Issuing a mighty whoop, he grabbed her up and spun her in a circle. He was breathing hard when her feet touched down on solid earth again.

She was furious. "Let me get this straight. You want me to skate with Reeve Ferris?"

"The money, Jaime." He clenched his beefy fist and raised it above him with a triumphant shake. "The money!"

Suddenly feeling unsteady, she felt for the security of a straight-backed chair and eased herself down into it. She raised incredulous green eyes to Pat. "You hate him and you expect me to—"

"Girl," Pat said with a sigh, "girl, love's stronger than any kinda hate. I love Jade. I love that woman. If you love her like I know you do, you'll get that money."

"But—"

"Anyway, you have to," Pat finished.

Jaime composed the letter. It took some effort to strike the right tone. The final result was an official and businesslike communication. She could just as well have sent it to her banker, if she had one. Which of course was the whole point of her groveling, wasn't it? To get money. She was merely involving herself in a commercial enterprise, she reassured herself as she signed her name.

Oddly, as it turned out, the composition of the letter was not to be the greater of her difficulties; the real problem became the task of contacting Reeve. In spite of all his impassioned urging for her to contact him, he had left her without an address.

"There!" she said to Pat who had joined her in the café. It was during the afternoon slack period, between two and four. "You see, he really wasn't serious. If he had been, he'd have left his address with me.

Where do you think I'm going to send this? The North Pole?''

"He's a movie star. They're used to having other people take care of details for them."

"Oh, yeah?" Jaime asked sarcastically.

"That's what I hear."

"Well, great, la-di-da. Hurray for Hollywood." She glared down at the page on the table. "It just so happens that I'm not one of his minions! I don't have to take care of his blasted details."

"Yes, you do," Pat argued. "At least this one you do."

He lifted the paper off the table, as if sensing she might rip it to shreds. The possibility of such an action had, in fact, crossed her mind.

"You know what this makes me, don't you?"

"I know what it makes me," Pat grumbled. "Which is sick."

"Fine, you be sick. For me, sick is nothing. Nothing, Pat!" She sprang out of her chair, paused indecisively, and having no target for her energy, collapsed back into the chair. "This makes me feel like a prostitute. For money, Pat...I'm doing this for dollars and cents."

"Girl, you're doing it for Jade. And I don't want to hear that kind of talk from you, neither," he finished sternly.

Jaime turned her head, properly rebuked.

"Anyway, you aren't sleeping with him. You'll be skating with him, s'all. You'll get the money and bring it back here so your mama can get herself fixed up. It's going to be okay, Jaime. It's going to be good for all of us. Jade's gonna get well and I'm going to see to it that she gets that ranch of hers. I've been telling her. Oh, you should see the light in her eyes..." But Pat's eyes had clouded over, and now Jaime could see the mist in them turning to liquid.

She touched his hand, covering it with her palm. "I'm going to get the money. I will," she promised.

Between them, they decided to send the letter to the studio that had released Reeve's last film. Then came perhaps the worst part of the entire ordeal—the wait. The long, interminable wait. After three weeks of hearing nothing, she was beside herself.

Pat wasn't much better off. He stopped in at least twice a day, to check if she had gotten word from Reeve.

Sometimes he would charge in, his spirits revved. "It came!" he would shout, or something similar to that. "I know it came because I had this feeling come over me right up on Galena Pass." He would wait expectantly, his eyes shining, for the confirmation.

"That feeling? Most likely something you ate," Jaime would say.

"Hell," Pat would mutter. "Well, no matter, it'll come tomorrow. I know it will."

"Sure," Jaime would mutter back. "You and Jade. The two of you should get paid for waiting. You'd be millionaires."

"Faith," Pat would argue, "can conquer anything."

"I thought that was love."

"Same thing, girl. Exact same thing."

"He was just playing around, Pat," Jaime would lament, knowing that Pat would argue, needing to hear him argue. "He had some nostalgia bug. Now he's over it. The last thing Reeve wants is a hick girlfriend from the sticks trotting down there with her skates thrown over her shoulder. How cute," she scoffed. "I can see it now. Me arriving in my faded jeans, Reeve lying among satin pillows, surrounded by partly clad starlets peeling the skin off grapes and popping them one by one into his mouth. Yuck.'' She shivered, the scene of humiliation real in her mind.

"He didn't get the letter," Pat said. "Send another one."

"Where to?"

"What do you call those guys? Managers... agents. Agents, that's it! He's got to have an agent. I'll ask around in Sun Valley. There's always one of those hotshot celebrities hanging out at Whiskey Jacks. Someone'll know how to get hold of our guy."

Jaime had to laugh. Pat had everything but the sirens going as he raced away in his patrol car. A modern-day Lancelot on his mechanized steed. True to his word, in less than an hour, he telephoned the café with the information.

Jaime scribbled the name down and called the Los Angeles information operator. "Elliot Cohen," she said and waited.

"There's an Elliot Cohen in Beverly Hills," the operator returned. "Elliot Cohen, Incorporated. Artists' agent."

Jaime took down the information, and redialed the area code.

The secretary for Elliot Cohen sounded busy, professionally polite, and said that she would relay the message to Mr. Cohen, who would then decide to act on the information.

"What does that mean?" Jaime asked. "Act on the information?"

The secretary sounded less polite. Jaime could hear the buzz of phones in the background. "I can only deliver messages to Mr. Cohen. I cannot be responsible for what Mr. Cohen decides to do."

"But this is a matter of life and death!" Jaime rolled her eyes. God, did she actually say that?

The secretary ignored the dramatics. "I'll tell Mr. Cohen." She hung up. Jaime said thank you to a dial tone.

The wait that ensued after the call was almost unbearable, even when compared to the preceding vigil.

Jade's discomfort had increased with each succeeding day. Jaime had already gone to the druggist twice, each time picking up a prescription strengthened to higher doses in order to relieve the pain.

Jaime called Elliot Cohen again two days later. The same secretary told her that Mr. Cohen had received the message. She would tell him that Jaime had called again. The secretary sounded peeved.

"You've got to go down there," Pat said.

"What?"

"Get yourself down there to that office. If you've got to grab Cohen by the ankles, that's what you've got to do."

Jaime went white. "I've never been out of the Valley, Pat."

"Well, it's time for you to see some different scenery. Start packing."

Jaime sat in the back of the cab, staring out the window and trying to make sense of it all. She felt disconnected, even disembodied. Instead of the towering peaks of the Sawtooths, billboards surrounded her. Cardboard blonds in black velvet gowns reclined beside giant bottles of liquor. An enormous blown-up face of a Latin American singing sensation actually had eyes and lips that moved. Jaime blinked and looked again. A trio consisting of two teenage girls and one boy was dancing down the sidewalk. They all had short, spiked, rainbow-colored hair. Their clothes were shredded strips of material, also rainbow-colored, beneath which they wore tights in fluorescent colors, ending at their feet in army boots.

Sunset Strip. It was all too much. What was real? What was fantasy? All of it, she told herself grimly; the whole thing was real and the whole thing was fantasy. Here they were one and the same, the area less a geographical place than a state of mind.

This was Los Angeles, and Hollywood. She'd read about it, just like the rest of the world and now she was seeing it live and in the flesh. This was the land where souls were gobbled up by magicians posing as accountants and writers and producers. The exotic-looking creatures she saw around her had probably looked like her at one time, she mused as a fat man in a Mercedes-Benz convertible winked leeringly at her through the cab window as they stopped at a light.

Elliot Cohen, Incorporated was located in a rather ordinary-looking modern office building. Jaime signed her name at the security desk and lied that she had an appointment. Nothing was going to keep her from getting to Elliot Cohen and eventually to Reeve.

She had dressed presentably, abandoning her usual outfit of jeans and a sweatshirt in favor of a long, straight, charcoal-gray skirt with a side kick pleat, over which she wore a long white sweater. She had on flat-heeled black boots and carried a white wool jacket she found to be unnecessary in Southern California's moderate winter climate. Her hair was drawn neatly back into a clip, her dark bangs feathering to just above the slightly upswept green eyes. No one would suspect her of being the desperado she was, the crasher-of-agents-offices and stalker-of-movie-stars.

She slipped into the elevator and pressed the button for floor five. In less than a minute, she was giving her name at Elliot Cohen, Incorporated's sliding glass reception window and stating her request to see Elliot Cohen.

"A personal matter," she said and smugly enjoyed the curiosity in the receptionist's eyes.

After that, she found little else to please her.

In fifteen minutes, Elliot Cohen's secretary appeared at an electronically controlled door. There was a general look of great weariness about her. She had red hair and hazel eyes surrounded by large, elegant glasses. The brown leather pants she wore squeaked as she moved farther into the room.

While Jaime was waiting, two other people had been cheerily invited through that same door. Only in their cases, they had hosts who invited them into the inner sanctum.

Well, she decided as she rose from the couch, she would lay odds that she wasn't about to get the red-carpet treatment from the readhead.

"Mr. Cohen received your messages," the secretary said crisply.

"But he didn't call me."

"He doesn't call everyone who calls him. He can't. There'd be a million calls a day for Reeve Ferris. Every lunatic under the sun would be—"

"I'm not a lunatic," Jaime said, feeling the opposite.

"I'm sure you aren't," the secretary said. She shifted her weight from one foot to the other, anxious to be back to the realm of sanity behind the electronic door.

"I don't need your condescension. I need to talk to Mr. Cohen."

"Mr. Cohen can't see you."

"Look, Reeve Ferris and I grew up together. Really."

The woman tossed her flame-colored hair and shifted her weight back to the other foot.

Dismissal was imminent. Jaime wondered if they bounced people out of offices in Hollywood as they did in the bars of Sun Valley. Because, she vowed inwardly, that was the only way they were going to get rid of her.

"Reeve visited me in Paradise," she said.

"Give me a break." The secretary made a move to turn.

Jaime stepped quickly in front of her. "Paradise— it's a town, not, you know, the other place. It's near Sun Valley."

"That's nice," the redhead said. She stepped away again.

Jaime flew after her. "Wait! Wait a minute, I can prove it." She dug frantically in her purse. "He gave me this."

Jaime waited, her heart beating rapidly, as with reluctance the secretary took the white card from her.

She glanced at it, then handed it back to Jaime.

Jaime was confused. "But that proves it."

"Look, I don't know who you really are, and I don't care. I'm too busy to care. You look like a nice girl, but maybe you've got a little problem with reality, and believe me, in this town you've got plenty of company in that department." She looked down to the note still held in Jaime's hand. "I can read. But frankly I'm not a handwriting analyst, and my educated guess is that someone other than Reeve Ferris wrote that. Reeve's gone a little beyond his ice rink days.''

"He wrote it," Jaime said emphatically.

The secretary ignored her. She backed away. "I'll tell Mr. Cohen you stopped by."

It was an efficient kiss-off.

"You didn't ask for my telephone number where I'm staying. Just in case," Jaime said sarcastically.

Jaime wrote down the name and number of the hotel, along with her name, which was hardly necessary. She might not have been among the agency's famous, but she was fast becoming infamous.

The secretary squeaked off in her tight leather pants, closing the door emphatically behind her.

Jaime could imagine the secretary tossing her telephone number into the trash. Finished business.

She had her hand on the doorknob to leave the office when the electronic door opened again. A young man stepped out carrying a box of files. Dismissing Jaime with a glance, he placed the box before the door, using it as a wedge while he went back inside to get another box.

Branded a lunatic, she may as well live up to her reputation. Without hesitation, Jaime slipped through the open door and headed quickly into the inner sanctum.

She followed a long corridor, with no idea of where she was going. The walls were covered with smiling photographs of famous stars. She passed closed and open doors, and a couple of people who, rushing by, gave her no notice.

Then, at last, she was there. She knew she had reached her destination because of the large desk guarding double doors. One door was closed and bore a plaque with the inscription Elliot Cohen; the other door was open. Through it, Jaime recognized the voice of the secretary and heard the squeak of her leather outfit as she moved about.

Jaime wasn't interested in the woman any longer. Her attention was fully fixed on the man.

In clear view was a man with a clipped gray and black beard. He was leaning back in his swivel chair, sometimes rocking forward, as he listened to several disembodied voices filling his room.

Jaime waited, her heart beating a frantic tattoo, until he had finished with the conference call and put down the phone receiver.

The secretary was just leaving, holding a ream of papers cradled in her arm, when Jaime skipped past her into the room. "Hey you!" the redhead cried.

But it was too late.

"Mr. Cohen?"

He looked up from his paperwork. "Yes?" His brow was wrinkled, and he seemed unsure, like a man who had awakened from a sound sleep and couldn't make out his whereabouts. Jaime could see his mind working, trying to place her.

"I'm Jaime Quinn."

"I'm sorry Mr. Cohen," the secretary said, rushing up beside Jaime.

Jaime made up her mind then and there that if the woman laid one finger on her, she was going to get decked.

"I called several times and left messages. I need to speak to Reeve Ferris. He's a friend of mine—"

"Then why didn't you call him at home?" Elliot Cohen asked wearily. "Please, young lady, I have a lot of things to do." He immediately backed up his statement by giving his attention to some papers on his desk.

"All you have to do is tell him to call me."

The secretary took a timid step forward. "Mr. Cohen, I'm terribly sorry—"

"No you aren't," Jaime snapped, cutting her off. "Mr. Cohen, if Reeve gets my message, he'll call. I know this whole thing seems very strange—"

"It does," Cohen said, looking at her again.

"I'm only acting crazy because this system you've got here is making me crazy. Reeve will call me. I know it."

"You know it." Cohen sighed.

"Please," she said. "Just mention my name. Tell him that I want to skate. That's all."

"Find another partner, he's out of the country."

"I don't care if he's on the moon. Look, I come from a long line of very determined people."

"I never would have suspected," Cohen said.

"I'm not giving up."

"That I would have suspected." He let out a burst of air, signaling defeat. "You'll get out of my hair?"

"I'll even get out of your office." Jaime grinned.

Cohen looked to his secretary. "Carolyn, send a cable."

The arches cast deep shadows over the stone floor. Only one moving shadow upset the calm atmosphere.

Reeve Ferris stepped from midnight shadows into full moonlight. His expression was wary, brooding. A jagged scar ran lengthwise along his cheek. Danger pervaded the hush, broken now by the soft fall of his steps.

Suddenly, out of a shadow, another figure pounced. There was a bright flash of steel. Then out of nowhere a knife lunged downward accompanied by an eerie cry like a crazed banshee.

Reeve's arm shot up. Too late. There was a sudden flash of red as the knife met its mark.

Close together, their labored breath mingling, the faces of the two men were illuminated in silver light as they struggled for control over the blade.

"Why?" Reeve asked the man, who had missed his mark and driven his sword into a stone arch. "You had everything. Why me?"

"You defiled her!" the other man rasped. He struggled to free his blade.

"I loved her!" Reeve shot back, the words strong and true like a bullet hitting its mark.

"Tanya was—"

"Cut!" bellowed a voice from beyond the shadows. "Cut the moon, cut the shadows, cut, cut, cut. Damn it! Her name is Vanya. Vanya. What kind of a love-crazed man dies for a woman whose name he can't remember?"

"I ate something bad at lunch," the actor said.

"I didn't even eat lunch and you're giving me heartburn."

"I don't like the way you're talking to me," the actor said. He turned to Reeve. "I don't like the way he's talking to me."

"And I don't like the way you're saying my lines," said the director, who had also written the script.

The actor continued to complain. "He's in my moonlight," he said, hitching his head toward Reeve.

"He can afford to be in your moonlight. He's a star. And if you want to know the truth, Reeve Ferris could be in a black hole and he'd still shine brighter than you even if you swallowed a thousand-watt bulb." The director sighed. "Oh," he said, casting his attention back to Reeve, "got something for you. Cable from your agent." He reached into his breast pocket and handed Reeve a folded piece of paper.

Reeve opened the note, distracted for the moment by two workmen who were carrying off part of the Styrofoam abbey. "Are they supposed to be taking that? I thought we were going to shoot that—" His eyes fell upon the message, then he stiffened.

"What's the matter?" the director asked.

Even the other actor seemed to have forgotten about the moonlight.

"You all right, Ferris?"

Reeve looked up slowly, his attention clearly unfocused on his surroundings. "What?"

"What's the problem?" The director bobbed his head toward the paper.

"I've got to take off," Reeve said.

"Take off? What do you mean, take off?"

"I've got to go back to L.A."

"A death? If someone croaked, forget it. There's nothing you can do."

"No," Reeve said. "A rebirth."

"What? We're talking religion here?"

"We're talking my life." Reeve started to turn away.

The director grabbed his shoulder. "Uuhh-uh. We're talking my picture, buddy."

"Look," Reeve said, turning. He towered over the small director whose eyes were bloodshot from late nights in the editing room, "I've got to go. Someone I once let down is counting on me."

"A broad?"

"A woman I loved. Love," he corrected, putting it into the present tense. He felt better even as he said it. Joy spread through him at the public admission.

"Okay, okay," the director said, clearly panicked. "No problem. You can send for the lady. All women love Rome."

"No," Reeve said.

"No? Why no?" The director was practically nose to nose with him. Reeve stepped back. He laid his hand on the director's shoulder.

"Because it's important that I go back to the States for her." He peeled off his scar and taking the director's hand, patted the rubber into his palm.

"Oh, no," the director said. "No, no, no. Put that scar back on."

Reeve started to walk away, the director hurrying to keep pace with Reeve's longer strides.

"If you walk out on this film, Ferris, I don't care how big your name is, I'm going to drag you through the most expensive lawsuit you've ever seen. Let's put it this way, baby. Putting this movie out is a calculated risk, but a lawsuit like this I'm gonna win. Between my insurance and a lawsuit against you, I can make more money than I can at the box office. And you end up with minus zip," the man screamed.

Reeve continued moving forward. "You do what you've got to do. I'll do what I've got to do."

"Put that scar back on, Ferris!" the man hollered.

Reeve smiled. He kept going, his footsteps no longer sounding hollow as he passed over the eight-hundred-year-old stones. At least some things were real.

Chapter Six

Some trait of her mother must have taken hold of her. Whether dogged determination had been instilled through genetics or environment, was anybody's guess. The only fact that Jaime could rely upon for certain as she lay on the hotel bed, staring at the ceiling and waiting for the phone to ring, was that she was not going home without the money for Jade's operation. If she didn't hear back from Reeve soon, she'd simply try some other tactic. The resourcefulness was not a dramatic gesture, but a necessity.

The small travel alarm clock that Pat Griffen had given her for the trip ticked loudly on the nightstand. It was a cheap but clean room in an old hotel in what Jaime assumed to be one of the seedier parts of town. Even so, the twenty-nine dollars a night bargain rate was twenty-nine dollars a night that was eating into the money that could be used for Jade.

However much she resented it, all she could do now was wait. She could listen to the clock's ticking. She could examine the swirls in the ceiling plaster for patterns of faces and animals. But mostly she could wait.

When she thought about it, she had no real reason to trust Elliot Cohen even to send the telegram to Reeve. Her vigil might be in vain.

No, she cautioned, she couldn't allow herself to wallow in negative thoughts. Wasn't Hollywood the place where people put their faith in the power of bad vibes and good vibes? Cohen would send the cable. He had to.

Jaime sighed, and closed her eyes, which had grown heavy from the strain of staring at the same spot on the ceiling.

"In Rome," Cohen had said. Reeve was thousands of miles away in Rome, Italy, separated from her by an ocean and a continent. Italy, from her perspective, was as mythical as a garden where unicorns might be found.

It was hard for her even to imagine the kind of life he led as a matter of course. While she sliced carrots, he flew first class to exotic places where he was greeted by people whose names appeared on the covers of national magazines. A knot tightened in Jaime's stomach as the image of Reeve with beautiful people—with beautiful women—came into focus.

It was not another woman; it was herself cast in the fantasy that grew more real every moment.

Warm, pleasurable feelings traveled through her. Her limbs relaxed as Reeve stroked her prone, unclothed body. His lips were on her mouth, then lower. The heat of his mouth caressed her breasts, while his arms twined beneath her, arching her into him.

"No!"

She shot up from the hotel's bed, her eyes wide as if awakened at a crucial time from a nightmare.

Disoriented, she stared into the vacant hotel room. A light film of sweat covered her body. She brushed wet tendrils of hair from her forehead and the side of her face. Within her loins, tiny spasms, pinprick reminders of her aroused state, ebbed.

How real it had all seemed, the dream so authentically physical.

Ashamed of her body's betrayal, she left the bed. She stripped off her jeans and sweater, dropping them on the floor as she hastily made her way to the pink-tiled bathroom. Reaching into the tiny, dank shower stall, she turned on the cold water tap full force. The spray exploded against the squares of pastel tile, and then upon her as she entered the cubicle to take the cure for her impossible desires.

Five minutes later she was dry again, her body sober and stable, possibly trustworthy. Even so, she rejected the jeans and sweater as reminders of her weakness, and instead selected a beige skirt and white pullover sweater, after which she took time to put on makeup and fix her hair. It wasn't as if she had somewhere to go, yet the familiar rituals were reassuring.

She was applying lipstick when the clang of the telephone sliced the silence. For a moment she stared at the apparatus while feelings of dread and wild elation seesawed through her. Across the room the telephone rang again, like an impatient creature demanding her attention.

Standing beside the bed, she leaned down toward the nightstand, and clutched the receiver with icy fingers. "Yes, hello—"

"Jaime Quinn?"

"Yes, speaking." Although she recognized the voice, the man's tone told her nothing.

"Elliot Cohen, here. Reeve called."

Jaime sank slowly to the edge of the bed, awaiting the punch line.

"Reeve's returning on a flight out of Rome. It arrives at L.A. International tomorrow afternoon at two."

A wave of tension dissolved in Jaime. "Oh," she said, "oh, that's great."

"No," Cohen snapped, the sharp retort overlapping her last word. "It's not great at all. It stinks, as a matter of fact." He paused briefly. Jaime could feel him gathering control. Cohen took up again, his voice a tight knot of aggravation, all of it directed her way. "Young lady, I don't know what the hell you have going, but you've just cost a great many people a large amount of money."

"Excuse me?" Jaime asked, feeling that odd sense of unreality taking over again. She was Alice, after slipping into the rabbit hole. No one and nothing made sense; it was a world turned upside down and inside out. "I don't know what you're talking about."

"No? Then let me fill you in, honey." The *honey* was clearly laced with strychnine. "Reeve Ferris just walked out of the biggest deal I've ever put together for him. He walked out of the film because of you, baby. I've already talked to two lawyers who are going to sue the pants off my client. Because of you."

"I'm sorry," Jaime said, mostly because she couldn't think of what else to say. She still wasn't sure what he was talking about. However, whatever it was, it certainly sounded serious enough to warrant an apology, if for no other reason than form's sake.

"Yeah, sure you are," Cohen slurred nastily. "Reeve's got your address. I just hope he's got your number."

"I told you I'm a friend."

"No, what you are is bad news. Just be there tomorrow afternoon." Cohen dropped the receiver onto the hook, releasing the connection.

A slow smile crossed Jaime's face as she lowered the phone into its cradle. *Well, how about that, Quinn? You've made your mark on Hollywood.*

It wasn't as though she enjoyed causing trouble, but there was a certain satisfaction in not being ignored. She hadn't experienced that feeling in a long time, not since she and Reeve had skated together as teenagers; deluded times, they were, too. Metaphorically speaking, it was nothing to get into Paradise, while it was everything to be able to take the road out.

Anyway, she thought, rising from the bed, for a brief period of time, on this, the saddest and most desperate of occasions, she had finally managed to squeak through the gates of Paradise.

And how do you find the real world, Miss Quinn?

She looked about her. With surprise she noted the room suddenly seemed brighter. Even the clock sounded jauntier in the silence. The mission was no longer futile, the wait no longer infinite.

He was coming! Reeve was coming, and he'd walked out of a film deal for her. For her—Jaime Quinn of Paradise, Idaho.

At the mirror, she brushed her hair into a chignon and examined the effect. Just as her surroundings appeared altered, so did she seem subtly changed. Yet the amazing metamorphosis had little to do with the hairstyle. There was a light behind her eyes, a green brilliance to the cast that had veritably changed her face.

Maybe, Jaime thought, just maybe Jade was right to believe in miracles.

Elliot Cohen greeted Reeve outside customs.

"You didn't have to meet me," Reeve said, not bothering to cover up his annoyance at his agent's presence.

"Have you gone crazy?" Cohen said, ignoring Reeve's displeasure.

"No, sane is more like it," Reeve replied, taking off at a rapid clip with Cohen trying to keep stride with him and talk at the same time.

A sea of bodies parted as Reeve made his way through the milling crowd, scores of faces turning speculatively to gape at the famous figure passing among them. In contrast, Elliot Cohen had to dodge and bump shoulders as he made his way down the same path.

"Jeeze," the agent grumbled. "Who are you—Moses?"

"It comes with the territory, Elliot. Like a lot of other stuff, not all of it pleasant."

Elliot gave him a sharp look. "Right, you're a movie star. In case you've forgotten, that bears some responsibility. You don't get something for nothing in this town."

"Yeah? Tell me about it," Reeve returned, the quick, slanted glance at his agent heavy with sarcasm.

"That's precisely why I'm here—to tell you about it. Because it seems you've lost your marbles."

Reeve stopped dead. Turning, he appraised the pinched countenance of his agent. "Elliot, for the first time in my life I know what I want and I'm doing it, both at the same time."

Elliot stared as if accosted by a foreigner whose language he didn't speak. "What are you saying?"

"I want my life back."

"What is this, some sort of dry run on mid-life crisis? It's too early in the game for you to go weirding out on me."

Reeve started off again. A woman called out his name in a high-pitched scream of elation. Her husband looked excited and embarrassed. Reeve kept going, stepping up his pace just in case.

"Call it anything you want," he said. "I know walking out of the film was a suicide move as far as my career goes. I am fully cognizant of that fact. So, no, if it makes you feel any less insecure, I haven't lost my mind."

"You're going to lose your financial ass," Elliot spat, one-upping him.

"It's my heart I'm concerned about."

"Who the hell is that woman?" the agent grumbled.

"Jaime Quinn and I go back a long way. We used to skate together." Reeve's eyes softened, focusing on the past. Instantly, a warm, liquid sensation filled him. Transported back to the clean air of his youth, to the sound of birds trilling in nearby trees, he and Jaime circling again and again, meeting and parting on the ice, the rhythmic flow of their bodies sensual and innocent.

He was in the barn again. She was giving herself to him. He could feel it, smell it, taste their love. It was all happening again, the melding together, not only physically but in a higher sense.

It was a way he had never experienced with any other woman, nor would he. In that fiery, molten act, he had realized a part of himself that had lain dormant. For just that one time, he had entered the magical, enchanted realm of love.

Reeve pushed through the glass doors leading to the street. The blast from an automobile jarred him back into the ordinary present.

Cohen ran frantically after him. "Where's your luggage? You're forgetting your bags."

"Didn't bring any."

"You're bonkers," the smaller man reiterated. "We've got to talk," he whined in desperation. "I'll drive you over to her. We'll hash this out on the way."

Minutes later, Elliot Cohen maneuvered the black Cadillac out of the airport's circular double-decker drive and onto Century Boulevard, heading toward the San Diego Freeway with a murderous expression in his eyes.

Reeve switched on the car radio.

Elliot snapped it off. "There's no good news, no new music. Let's talk," he ordered.

"Okay," Reeve replied agreeably, and shifted himself around, his left arm stretched over the seat's back as he spoke. "Set up a skating deal. Something big and lucrative with the networks. They've pitched you on it before. Make it seem like we're doing them a favor."

"Television?" Elliot asked, shooting Reeve a horrified expression of disbelief.

"Right—the tube."

Elliot Cohen gripped the steering wheel and stared straight ahead with eyes fixed on the road. "You don't do television."

"I do what I want, Elliot. Not what you want."

"Your mother won't—"

"Not what my mother wants, what I want, Elliot. And this is what I want—a deal to ice skate. Major network. The contract's got to provide for national publicity, a total all-out advertising campaign. You know—the whole works."

"Do you mind my asking a cheeky question?" Elliot asked pseudo-sweetly. He turned to face Reeve. His eyebrows were triangular peaks over round eyes filled with the sorrow of Pagliachi. "Why?"

"Because Jaime Quinn is going to skate with me. A long time ago, she was cheated out of something she deserved. In a way, I suppose we were both cheated."

"Cheated?"

Reeve smiled. He could see the wheels turning in his agent's eyes as he contemplated the possibility of a nice, juicy lawsuit.

"Shortchanged by circumstances," Reeve elucidated and couldn't resist another smile as the avarice faded from Elliot's eyes.

The exchange, thought Reeve, was typical of conversations in Hollywood, just the usual banter between people who lived the proverbial life in the fast lane, as the journalists were so fond of putting it. Well, he had been traveling far too long. It was time to put on his brakes before they failed.

Jaime stood back from the open door and blinked. A tall, dark form stood before her. In contrast to the hotel room's cell-like atmosphere, the afternoon sunlight was violently bright. Her vision quickly accommodated itself to the comparative brilliance and the shadow became a man.

Reeve was smiling down at her. There was tenderness and affection in his eyes, as if for some beloved creature he had happened upon by chance.

Jaime shrank from the intimacy of the blue eyes.

"No staring," she said with forced lightness. "It's not polite."

"It's just that you remind me of a girl I once knew."

Jaime chewed on her lip. "You're mistaken."

"I don't think so," Reeve said softly.

Jaime's heart constricted. The way she had worked it out in her mind the deal was to be cut-and-dry, and already he was making things difficult. For one thing, even his physical presence invited tenderness from her. It was the first time she'd seen him looking peaked.

Although he had shaved, there were faint blue circles beneath his eyes, and, amazingly thin character lines had appeared by his mouth and eyes. He wore a leather jacket of a muted moss color. It had wide shoulders, but the leather was so supple it draped elegantly to the top of his slacks.

His pants were of a heavy cotton blend, their design European, she decided, from what she remembered of some of the jet-set tourists who frequented Sun Valley.

Reeve looked tired and masculine and, interestingly, unlike the man whom she had last seen in Sun Valley, a man whose face was devoid of even the slightest shadow of disappointment.

"That girl's been gone for a long time, Reeve."

"Maybe she'll come back?"

"No, never," Jaime replied.

"I can't believe that, Jaime." Reeve reached forward and before she could escape, he stroked the side of her face with his palm.

Jaime flinched, jerking her head to the side. "Don't—" she said, and obediently, he dropped his hand. "Don't think things that can't be, Reeve."

"The cable—"

"You offered me a deal," she cut in.

"I offered you myself," Reeve said quickly. "I thought that was understood."

"I need a job, Reeve. I need a lot of money, and I need it fast. If you came here thinking anything else, I'm sorry, but there it is—the truth."

There was hurt in his eyes and it pained her to see it there, but she reminded herself of the years she had suffered her own lingering pain and was able to move back several steps, distancing herself emotionally as well as physically from the inherent danger of their proximity.

"Come on in," she said. "It's not much, but it's home," she joked lamely as he followed her into the room.

When she turned around, he was staring at her.

"Don't look at me like that."

"Like what?" he said and stepped closer.

Jaime backed away, and instinctively, her hand went out to ward off any physical contact he might be contemplating.

"Your fingers are trembling, Jaime," he accused. "Why, if it's just business between us, are you shaking like a leaf?" He wasn't making fun of her; he was merely pointing out a fact.

Jaime hid the arm behind her back. "I had to come here. It has nothing to do with us, Reeve. Truly."

She shook her head, then dropped it, letting it hang limp as she went on to explain. "My mother's sick. She has to be operated on or she's going to die, Reeve." Jaime looked up.

There was alarm and compassion in his eyes. This time, she allowed the connection between them to remain.

"That's the only reason you took me up on my deal."

"Sorry, but that's it."

"Ah," he said. Now it was his turn to look away. He moved slowly, taking a few aimless steps. Without turning back to her, he said, "You were desperate."

"Yes."

"I'll do what I can to help," he said without meeting her eyes. "Of course, I understand the situation, and I apologize for putting you in such an awkward position. I just thought—" He shrugged. "Well, it doesn't really matter what I thought. Like you said, you can't reclaim the past."

"No," she said, "you can't."

He started to move toward the door, paused with both hands in his pockets, and then looking back to her, said, "I've already spoken to my agent about setting up the skating deal. It could take a couple of weeks, more, depending on who's out of town and what kind of musical chairs are being played in the studios at the present time. I'm out of touch."

"Too much Italian wine and beautiful women," Jaime joked lightly.

"No women," he said pointedly. His stance was tense, his face drawn. "But you're right about the wine. How much money must you have?"

Jaime swallowed hard. "Fifty thousand dollars. Possibly more."

Without a beat he said, "I'll cut you a check now. You can forget the deal we have between us and go home tomorrow. Tonight, if you want."

"No," she said, genuinely affronted. "I'm not going to take a handout from you."

"I don't think of it as a handout," he said. "I can see how you might, but it wasn't meant that way. You gave me something of yourself that was incomparable, irreplaceable—"

Jaime felt herself flushing. "My virginity? I'm sure I'm not the only virgin you've had in your career, Reeve. You'll get writer's cramp from filling out check stubs."

Her words might just as well have been bricks hitting him.

"I loved you."

"You loved me," she mimicked. "You loved me so much you left me and you never came back for years."

"You don't understand—"

"Oh, I do, Reeve. I most certainly do. I'm like a favorite toy from your childhood that you misplaced. One day you started wondering whatever happened to that toy, so you took a ride back to a place that no longer exists. Except in your mind. The toy you left behind is no longer on the shelf, Reeve. It broke a long time ago."

"You really hate me, don't you?" he said, wonderingly.

Neither of them moved.

"Yes," she said. "I expect I do. In a way."

He nodded. "You're right, I really didn't understand that. I thought—" He broke off. "Look, I'm not going to push you into anything. The money's yours if you want to take if from me—*gratis*. If you want to go through with the deal instead—we'll keep it that, a straight transaction."

"That's what I want," Jaime said. "I want to skate."

"Okay. Then you'll skate. Couple of things," he said, making plans. "Whoever picks up this show, is going to want to see you. That means you'll have to hang around. Is that a problem?"

Jaime's stomach churned. "Uh..." Her eyes circled the room.

"I could recommend a better hotel—"

"No, it's not that. Not exactly."

"Oh," he said, suddenly understanding. "How much is this place?"

"It's cheap and it's a dump," Jaime admitted, "and I don't even have the money for it."

"Stay with me," he said, and when he saw the objection in her eyes, he said, "Without any strings attached. I swear it, Jaime."

"Only until I get some money of my own. Then I'm out of there."

"Agreed," he said. "So, uh, welcome to fame and fortune."

"It's a one-shot deal, Reeve. When it's over, when I've got the money, I'm going back to Paradise."

"You can't," he said. "Don't you know? You can't go back to Paradise from here. Someone told me that. A woman with green eyes, I recall."

Chapter Seven

It's not much, but it's home. The phrase Jaime had uttered at the motel mocked her as she stood in the entrance of Reeve's home.

This, she thought, *was a great deal, and, amazingly, it actually was home.*

As a girl, she had occasion to visit some of the more elegant homes of friends in Sun Valley, but never had she experienced luxury of this magnitude. The floor on which she stood consisted of varying shades of pink marble, scored by swirls of deep green. The foyer was large and octagonal in shape. It had a high-domed ceiling, latticed and glassed in, through which streams of pale light illuminated walls covered in material. The cloth was not merely decorative, but also served the utilitarian purpose of smothering sound even as soft colors reflected the soft hues of the marble.

Beyond the foyer, Jaime could make out a vast room, the colors of its modern furnishings blending in a shimmering haze of pale peaches, soft greens, and silvery whites. A white grand piano, with its top up at an angle, occupied a corner of the room. Sheet music was spread open, and she realized that, of course, like so many other talents Reeve possessed, he would also have an expert command of the keyboard.

She sensed she was no longer alone, and turned. Reeve stood watching her. He had sent her in ahead while he took care of the cab fare. Her suitcase was still in his hand.

"So, what do you think?" he asked. His weary gaze reached out to her from behind the shadowy fringes of his dark lashes. But there was still humor lurking in the blue eyes, which in the muted surroundings, appeared all the more electric in intensity.

"It doesn't look like you," she said bluntly. Then, her candor forced her to admit, "But it's beautiful."

Reeve acknowledged her observation with an easy smile. What wasn't easy for him?

"My mother's the culprit," he said, without taking offense.

An image of Charlotte Ferris flashed into Jaime's mind. Of course, that was it. The room, the house, was a reflection of the pale, cool beauty of Reeve's mother.

"How are your parents?" Jaime asked. She found herself genuinely curious, the way one becomes curious about the fates of daytime soap opera characters.

"My parents, yes..." Reeve paused reflectively. "That's right, you wouldn't have known. It all happened after Sun Valley. As a couple, they're history," he said with only the mildest sense of regret evident in the disclosure.

He left the suitcase on the floor and walked to the wall where he opened a small panel disguised by a cloth overlay. He pressed a button and a moment later a distant voice sounded on the intercom. "Lupe, I've brought home a house guest. Please make up the big bedroom for her. And her suitcase is in the entry hall." Turning back to Jaime, he said, "Suppose we see what Lupe's hidden in the refrigerator?"

Jaime followed Reeve, listening as he continued talking about his parents.

"Of course they were never happy," he said. "Never for as long as I can remember, anyway. Perhaps briefly, in the beginning it might have been all right. But it was a union more or less doomed from the start. There was no way my father could ever hope to measure up to my mother's expectations." The statement was a fact rather than a condemnation of Charlotte Ferris.

"But he did very well, your father."

Reeve's response was a light laugh, ironic. "Very well? Very well was never good enough for Charlotte."

"What did she want?" Jaime asked.

They had entered another spacious room. The kitchen. There was an enormous black cast-iron stove, its character in keeping with the room's European flavor. Jaime couldn't help but compare it to Jade's hopelessly outmoded model. The tiles were all hand-painted and the floor was of highly polished, and highly impractical parquet wood inlay. In the center of the room was a vast wooden counter over which gleaming copper pots were hung on a round metal structure, its center filled with plants, the trailing vines receiving their light artificially from above.

"A castle," Reeve replied. "She would have liked to have lived in a castle and looked down from some lofty parapet at her surrounding kingdom. But of course, then she would have wanted other kingdoms." He was speaking with amused tolerance rather than malice. "Think of Marie Antoinette, and you have my mother."

He opened the doors to an enormous refrigerator and for a few seconds peered intently into its interior. "My mother's heritage was one step removed from European royalty. The myths of what might have been...ah, ham, cheese, salami...good woman, Lupe." Reeve gathered the items into a crooked arm. "The myths," he continued, as he scanned the shelves of Lupe's sacred domain, "influenced my mother greatly. From the time she was fed with her first silver spoon, she was brought up on a never-ending supply of what-might-have-been stories. If only this or that had transpired way back when...things would be this way today." He looked back at Jaime and grimaced as he said, "God only knows I got a similar fallout from my mother. In a way, Charlotte never had much of a chance. She was raised to see herself as a kind of Grace Kelly, I suppose."

"Then why did she marry an airline pilot? Why not hold out for the prince on the white charger?" Jaime asked.

Reeve nudged the doors of the refrigerator closed and returned with his booty of luncheon cold cuts and some rolls. With a nod, he gestured for Jaime to take one of the wooden stools, and she waited at the island while he returned to the refrigerator to gather condiments for the prospective feast.

"Passion, I suppose," he said. He set jars of may-onnaise and mustard and pickles before Jaime, then went off for utensils.

Jaime couldn't imagine Charlotte Ferris being pas-sionate about anything. Passion required spontane-ity. The picture that formed in her mind of Charlotte was of a woman whose every plan was premeditated and exacting.

"And the flame burned out," Reeve said. He was back at the island with napkins and silverware.

"Passion never lasts," Jaime said. "It's a state of the crazies. Then you get cured."

"Really?" said Reeve. He twisted the top off a jar of pickles. "And then what happens? What do you have then?" He leaned toward her with both palms flat on the counter. "What do you have when the flame has gone out?"

"Real life," Jaime said.

"No life," Reeve retorted.

"And how would you know?" Jaime asked. "As far as I can tell, your entire existence has consisted of following a road with clearly marked signs. No de-tours along the way, just keeping your head pointed in the right direction. And you reached your destina-tion. So save the pretty speech about flames and such. Remember, I live where the wind blows. Fire doesn't last long in Paradise." Jaime looked away. She had said too much, and what she had said was bitter enough to belie her claim of disinterest. Speaking more evenly, she said. "You made some choices, and they were good choices, Reeve. You've got it all. What everyone wants, the fame and the fortune."

"What do you want, Jaime?" he asked.

The question caught her by surprise, and she couldn't answer. Then she said, "The money for Jade."

"For Jade. What do *you* want?" he repeated.

"I don't know," she said haltingly. "That is, I've never thought about it." But she had. Once when she was young, as she skated with a boy who was golden and beautiful, when all of life was bathed in golden light, she had wanted him. And glory, she had desired that, too; with all of her heart she had wanted the Olympic Gold Medal around her neck. The sound of trumpets blaring, the explosion of hands beating together as she spun on the ice, as she leaped higher and farther than anyone—all of that and more she had once dreamed of having. She had wanted the entire world, and had settled for Paradise, Idaho.

"Then save yourself the search," Reeve said quietly. "There's only one thing that matters. Only one thing, Jaime... The flame. It doesn't have to go out," he said. "Not if you take care of it. Jaime, people can have it all. If they really want it, if they—"

Jade's face flashed before Jaime's mind. How did she attract these incurable optimists, these professional dreamers?

"You've been in too many movies," Jaime said sharply.

"You haven't been to enough. Art imitates life, or didn't you know?"

There followed an uncomfortable silence, the kind that follows conversations begun innocently enough on the subject of politics or religion then suddenly turn incendiary with no way out but termination of the topic or the relationship. With elaborate care they concentrated on the serious task of making sandwiches.

"So, anyway," Reeve resumed his topic, placing a piece of rye bread over ham, lettuce and tomato, "my father finally had enough and walked out on her."

"It must have been dreadful for her." Jaime's sympathy was a natural reflex. She remembered Jade finally putting away the dinner she had saved for Grady to eat the night he had disappeared. She saw her mother's eyes searching out the window, day after day for a man who never came back.

"She couldn't believe it. But surprisingly enough," Reeve said cheerfully, "it had little effect on Charlotte. In a way, I think she was almost relieved. My father's proletarian roots cramped her social image. With him gone, she was free to do as she pleased, with no restraints."

"And it pleased her to decorate this," Jaime commented, glancing around slowly. She looked back at him, her gaze direct and meaningful.

Reeve nodded. "You've got it. My life is her life."

"It always was." Jaime thought back to the days of Sun Valley, when the shadow of Charlotte Ferris hovered over Reeve's every activity.

"She was my mother and she took her position seriously. Maybe too seriously. Not an excuse, just a fact of life."

"And now? What are the facts now?"

"Different time, different facts. There've been changes. Or," he qualified "there will be soon." He raised a can of imported beer to his lips and downed a hard swallow.

There was no doubt in Jaime's mind that the room assigned to her as a guest had been designed by Charlotte for Charlotte herself. It was fitting in every detail for a princess or in the case of Charlotte Ferris, a queen. Like all the other rooms in Reeve's house, it was large. The same cool, pale colors from the living room and foyer had been used here.

Jaime showered, then found her clothes, which had been neatly put away by the efficient Lupe.

She laid her clothes out on the bed, its covering a silvery comforter, silken and tufted with a design of an immense lotus in its center. The gray slacks and matching gray sweater looked ridiculously drab and out of their element.

Jaime did not belong there, that was for certain; but as she dressed she was also sure that to find herself in such luxurious surroundings was not entirely bad. To deny the pleasure she experienced in bathing in the sunken pink marble tub would have been more than hypocritical; it would have been crazy. She liked it. Across the room, small glass perfume bottles glittered on the dressing table. Yes, Jaime thought, she had nothing against this kind of a life.

Charlotte Ferris might easily have been mistaken for a piece of the living-room furniture, so perfectly did she blend into the surroundings. Her hair was awash with silver light, her dress of white silk, her purse and shoes a luminous frosty peach.

Jaime had not expected to see her there. She had entered the room, looking for Reeve. But, clearly, Charlotte was not surprised to see her.

The two women stared at each other, Charlotte arranged neatly on the striped silk sofa, and Jaime, in her gray outfit, standing in the doorway, feeling like an unsightly dark blot on the pristine surroundings.

Charlotte's eyes glittered like blue ice cubes. "Jaime, isn't it?"

Jaime nodded. She felt stupidly young again, the presence of Charlotte resurrecting feelings of insecurities, long forgotten. "Jaime Quinn."

"It has been a while, hasn't it, Jaime Quinn?" Charlotte spoke with a slight drawl, more the result of affectation than her southern origin. Jaime was reminded of the silken comforter on her bed, so cool, so limp.

"It's been a while," Jaime concurred. "People from Paradise don't get around much. We just watch the cars come and go, same as always. I'm sure you remember."

"Yes, very well." Charlotte crossed one slim leg over the other and draped her arm languorously along the sofa's back. Her hand dangled, flashing a large diamond ring. She appeared thoughtful when she spoke. "A long way from Paradise...aren't you, Jaime?"

Jaime smiled. "It's down the road a piece." She knew Charlotte wasn't speaking of geography.

"And how do you find our world?" Charlotte asked. "How do you find Hollywood?"

The question was not meant to be conversational. "It's different," Jaime replied, prolonging the cat and mouse game until she had a better grasp of the pitfalls and rewards.

"And only temporary, of course," Charlotte prompted.

"Of course," Jaime said. "I'm just passing through. The way people pass through Paradise," she finished, having her own point to make.

Charlotte caught the sarcasm. She appraised Jaime, then nodded, seeming satisfied enough with the answer. She had been assured that they understood each other.

"Reeve will be right back. He's changing," Charlotte said. She removed her arm from the sofa.

A cat pulling in its claws, Jaime thought.

Then, in a manner of a woman ringing her hands, Charlotte twisted the huge ring on her finger. "Poor darling. He's exhausted from the flight, and of course there's this terrible thing in Rome..." Charlotte's voice drifted off. It was left to Jaime to complete the disaster with her own imagination.

"Because he walked out of the movie in Rome?"

"To do this skating thing," Charlotte said at once. "I've been on the phone with his agent for hours— you've met Elliot, I understand." She shook her head and sank more fully against the sofa's back, sapped of strength by the very thought of the ordeal.

"And I'm to blame," Jaime said bluntly. There was no point in continuing the charade any longer. She was not a child anymore, bewildered and trusting as she had once been. She refused to play Charlotte's games of social pretense.

The veil of feigned politeness lifted. Charlotte's face became instantly more mobile. She sat forward on the sofa, upright and alert, all traces of the limpid belle erased from her manner.

"Why are you doing this?" she asked. "I want to know what the hell reason you have to march into Reeve's life? Out of nowhere—"

"Out of nowhere?" Jaime flared back. She had nothing to defend, but she would not be discounted as a person. Charlotte would not do that to her again. "I was a part of Reeve's life. A big part once."

"Granted," Charlotte conceded. "But childhood romances belong where they ended, in the past." Her eyes darted back and forth from Jaime to the door. "So what do you want?"

"Money," Jaime said flatly.

Jaime watched Charlotte's reaction. Her blue eyes were like prisms, catching light as thoughts twisted in her mind.

"I'm honestly surprised," she said with a short laugh. The smile faded quickly. "I thought myself a better judge of character. Money. From someone else it would have been expected, but from you . . ." Charlotte abandoned the editorial. "Name your amount." A cautionary hand went up. "Within reason, of course. It's never wise to be too greedy. Anyway," she said shrugging, "whatever it is, it's going to be a lot cheaper than if Reeve has to settle the Rome production deal in court. He can still go back. He can clear up the whole thing." Charlotte reached for her purse and pulled out a checkbook. Her pen was poised in the air. "So tell me," she said, "what do you want?"

Jaime was about to reply that Charlotte could take her check and do several things with it when Reeve suddenly appeared beside her. Even before he spoke, Jaime sensed his anger.

"Put your pen away, Charlotte." A nerve in his left cheek twitched.

Charlotte paled. "Reeve, don't be foolish. You'll ruin your career."

"Perhaps," he said.

"I can't stand by and let this happen, Reeve. I'm not speaking as a mother, but as a manager now. Be sensible," she pleaded.

"I don't want to be sensible, Charlotte. I want to feel alive."

"Yes, yes, of course you're right," Charlotte said, her face softening along with her voice, but her eyes remaining like mica. "You have every right to kick up your heels and let loose once in a while, darling."

Charlotte rose with agile grace, and walked to where Reeve stood beside Jaime. Kissing her son lightly on the cheek, she said, "You've always been so good, Reeve. I've never had a complaint. I just want you to know I'm always behind you, darling."

Then, switching her attention to Jaime, she extended her hand. "And, truly, it's wonderful to see you again, Jaime. You were a beautiful child, and you've grown into an even more beautiful woman. If I've appeared cranky and over-protective, it's only because I'm a mother. I'm sure you understand."

Jaime took the proferred hand, which was cold to the touch. A surprising sympathy arose in her for the frightened woman. "I understand," she replied.

"Thank you," Charlotte replied. A smile lit the cool blue eyes. "And welcome to our world," she said.

It was still early when Jaime retired to bed. Her flannel nightgown of yellow and white squares, so right for Paradise, took its wrongful place between the silk sheets.

When the knock on her door sounded, she was still awake. She rose up in bed, and switched on the lamp on her table. "Yes?" she called, supposing it to be Lupe who had appeared before to stock the bathroom with additional soaps, towels, shower caps and sachets for the drawers.

"It's me," Reeve said, his voice muffled by the thick wood.

"I'm already in bed."

"This can't wait," he pressed. "It'll only take a moment."

"Only a moment," she parroted back, and immediately the door swung open.

Reeve was also dressed for bed. He wore a dark blue robe, its color emphasizing the hollows beneath his eyes. A thick forelock of fair hair had fallen lower over his face, increasing the shadowy effect.

If she had been afraid of a sexual encounter, she could relax. He remained just inside the door with his back against the wood, as if perhaps he didn't trust himself any more than she did.

"After I left Paradise—when I went to school back east—I missed you terribly."

"You don't have to go into that. It's over—"

"I want you to know that it wasn't the way you thought. I didn't just walk out of Paradise, out of sight, out of mind. It's important to me that you know, Jaime."

She sighed, turning her face away. "But it's not important to me."

He moved to place himself in the immediate range of her vision. "Charlotte had advised me to concentrate on the Olympics. It made complete sense then, just as what she's saying about the Rome deal makes sense now. She told me it would be worse for you to feel like a small, insignificant part of my life than to be nothing at all. She convinced me the relationship would be cruel, that it would be torture for you. After the Olympics, it was agreed that I'd go back to Paradise and then we'd be together. That was the deal I struck with her."

Reeve took a few steps closer, narrowing the distance between them. Jaime drew the bed covers up higher, shielding herself from the current of physical attraction always present when they were in close proximity. Already the atmosphere was heavy with possibilities and they both knew it. He stood quite still, his hands at his sides while he spoke softly and earnestly, as if to the wild creature who would surely bolt if threatened.

"But it wasn't working for me," Reeve said, "the promise I made to my mother. Sure it was logical, but it didn't feel good. And one day I sat down and wrote you a letter. Everything in me exploded. I had never felt so free before, so wildly ecstatic."

Reeve's face had taken on a glow. Jaime could see him as the boy he had been, a young man at a desk, his pen flying over paper, fervent at his task of expressing himself to the girl he loved. The girl he loved!

That girl had loved him so, had loved him with every fiber of her being, and had waited to no avail. The pain of remembrance ripped through Jaime, the recollection of the days spent waiting for letters that never came, as her spirit succumbed to the slow poison of an impossible love. Those tormenting might-have-beens and if-onlys; God save her from the delusions of Charlotte Ferris.

Reeve was still speaking. "I told you all kinds of things." He smiled sadly. "It was the kind of letter only young men in love can write, I suppose. Filled with misspelled words and overdone phrases. Along with the truth."

As if drawn to her by an invisible string, he moved yet another few feet closer to where she lay in the bed. The coverlet was drawn modestly up to the top of her chest, with only the top portion of the yellow and white checked nightgown visible. Only a small pool of light was cast from the lamp, making the scene seem more dreamlike than real.

"I never got the letter," Jaime said in a flat voice. There, that was reality.

"I never sent the letter," he said, and shook his head as he remembered the scene. "My mother had chosen that weekend morning to surprise me at school. The letter was already stamped and addressed. It was on my desk, waiting to be taken downstairs to be mailed. And Charlotte saw it." He paused, his face contorting slightly as if he were reliving the event. "She was understanding and sensible as always. The letter would hurt you, she said. We'd start up a correspondence, and I would write to you of the parties at estates you'd never see. I'd talk of my training for the Olympics. I'd talk of the future. And Charlotte pointed out how all you had was your life in Paradise. She told me to finish with what I had to do, and then go back for you. When she said it, even the way she said it, it sounded so romantic. I was to return, the conquering hero, and sweep you off your feet."

"I sent you a telegram," Jaime said. "When you won the Gold for the United States."

Reeve stared at her from across the room, and she could see the impact of her words on his face. "I never got it. I got a thousand telegrams, but I didn't see yours. I even asked my mother—" He stopped.

"Maybe it got lost," Jaime said, feeling inexplicably protective of the foolish Charlotte, the very person who had done so much to damage her life.

"Perhaps," he said, but Jaime doubted he believed that. "Anyway," he continued, "there was a letter. I only wanted you to know."

He finished. There he stood, equidistant from the bed and the door, a purgatory suitable to their situation, Jaime noted.

He allowed her time to comment, and when she didn't, he didn't press her. He said only, "Thanks for listening," and rather than step toward her, he turned and strode out the door, taking time to close it softly after him.

For a time, Jaime remained sitting upright. She could still hear his words ringing in her head. But what good was such honesty now? It was a ship arriving too late to save a drowned person.

In a swift motion, she turned off the lamp and slipped fully into the silken cocoon.

But if he had stayed at that moment, if he had stepped toward rather than away from her, she wasn't sure she would have turned him from her bed.

No, that wasn't true; she was sure. It would not have been a sensible thing to do, but like Reeve, she wanted to be alive again, even if it were only a brief rebirth.

Sleep came slowly, bringing shifting images of a queen in black velvet. Filmy, handwritten letters spiraled upward in a whirlwind. A white horse bore a handsome man dressed in silks to the bottom of a turret clouded in mist. He extended his hand to a woman in the tower window, but she turned away, unable to see his hand through the vapor.

"Where is Reeve—uh, Mr. Ferris?" Jaime revised, watching as Lupe poured coffee into a fragile china cup.

"Mr. Ferris left early. He will be back soon, he said to tell you. Would you like anything else for breakfast?"

Jaime, accustomed to pouring others' coffee, smiled at her new situation. "Thanks, no. I'm not very hungry."

Lupe left after giving assurances that anything Jaime might want would be provided. Jaime had only to step on the buzzer beneath her foot.

The breakfast room was charming, done as a green and white gazebo, and again in its design, Jaime detected the deft hand of Charlotte Ferris.

If it hadn't been for Charlotte... A look of rage had crossed Reeve's face last night.

"Good morning!"

Reeve pulled out a chair and sat down.

"Good morning. I didn't hear you come in." If he had slept, the rest had done nothing to alleviate the distressed appearance he still presented.

"It comes from sneaking around in films. You never know when an Indian might pop out at you." He glanced swiftly at her, then concentrated on pouring a cup of coffee for himself. Lupe had left the silver urn. "Did you sleep well?"

"Yes," she lied. "No," she then admitted. "Not very."

"Neither did I."

"Probably overtiredness."

"Unlikely," he said over the rim of his cup.

"No," she said, "I guess not."

He paused, then said, "If I had come to you last night—"

"I'm glad you didn't," she replied.

"But if I had?"

"Then it would have been a night's pleasure. And a lifetime's regret."

"Ever optimistic, aren't you?"

"I have every reason for my skepticism," she said. But added in a lighter tone, "Besides with Jade around, someone's got to keep her feet on the ground. A little pessimism goes a long way in our house."

"Speaking of mothers, I saw Charlotte this morning. Make that—I dealt with Charlotte this morning," he amended, and as if reliving an exhausting scene, he fell back against his chair. "Something that should have been done years ago." He looked across to Jaime. "She didn't admit to taking the telegram."

"Did you think she would?"

"No. But of course I'm certain that she did."

Jaime shook her head. "She really hated me."

"It wasn't anything personal. She wanted me to bring her the kind of life she wasn't able to have from my father. The last thing she wanted was for me to marry a girl from Paradise, Idaho."

"She wanted a princess for you," Jaime said, "not a waitress."

"She wanted someone who would reflect her values. A woman who was compliant."

"Did you just discover this?" Jaime asked, incredulous that an intelligent man could be so blind to a woman's wiles. "After all these years?"

Reeve looked into his coffee. "I suppose I always knew it on some level. I just didn't deal with it."

"Why now?"

"Because the future we were always striving for has somehow caught up with itself. The future, with all of its proposed goodies—the cars, the house, the fame— is here. It wasn't ever really my future, anyway, although I suppose I thought it was. Charlotte can have a compelling effect on a person. So here I am, the dream achieved and it isn't such a good deal, after all. Certainly not worth a man's whole life."

Jaime glanced around. "It doesn't look like a half-bad trade to me," she said and laughed.

Reeve was not amused. "You don't mean that. I know you couldn't."

But that was the strange thing; in a way, she did mean what she had said. In the few days she had been in Los Angeles, she had found herself intrigued by the deal-making prospects of Elliot Cohen, had found enjoyment in the lovely surroundings of Reeve's home. She had even gotten a mild charge out of the power she wielded over the fates of people as far off as Rome, Italy.

If it had been she rather than Margaret Tanner who had won the Olympics with Reeve, how different life would have been. This, or a home like it, could have been hers. That was something she had thought a lot about lately.

Reeve's gaze drifted beyond Jaime to the garden. "I've never seen Charlotte particularly contrite before. She's given her promise never to meddle in my personal life again."

"I assume it was her solemn promise?" Jaime asked dramatically.

Reeve laughed. "Yes, pretty hard to swallow, isn't it? Unless you believe in miracles."

"Frankly, no. I'm in charge of negative thoughts, remember? The miracle department belongs to my mother."

"Any miracles in particular?"

"Sure, the fantastic variety. The more preposterous, the more she believes."

"For example?"

Jaime leaned back, staring through the window where a gardener toiled, clipping hedges. Her thoughts were focused elsewhere, though, and instead of Reeve's estate, Jaime saw a different scene, one which Jade viewed from the café window. There was the expansive prairie, brown in the summer, white in the winter, with that brief respite of spring greenery, and through it all, there was the long road dissecting the flat monotony, seeking the Sawtooths at its end. Jade would glance up during the day, her eyes following the stretch of road for sight of the man who would never come.

Jaime looked back to Reeve. "In particular? Oh, that love conquers all. That kind of rubbish."

Lifting his cup to her, Reeve said somberly, "My money's on your mother."

Jaime noted the gesture as gallant, one which might have fit nicely with one of the film characters he portrayed, but in reality lacking conviction. And that, thought Jaime, was the difference between Jade and most other people. Jade truly believed in miracles, while others only hoped for their wishes to come true.

The days that followed would have been remarkable enough for Jaime, for Reeve made it his mission to show her the city in detail. But the time was particularly memorable for its lightning passage. Hours were minutes, a minute flying by as the mere beat of a second.

She called Pat Griffen often, checking on Jade, from whom she would never get the truth. Jaime didn't know if Pat was deluding himself out of his own need to believe, but he reported that Jade seemed to be in a state of remission. There was less pain and she was managing the café, along with help from Pat's sister in Jaime's absence.

Jaime was both glad and disturbed to hear this. Jade had proclaimed the disease a temporary phenomenon, one which could be dismissed by maintaining proper thoughts. Optimism run rampant! But given the remote possibility that this could be true, that Jade was somehow healing herself, then in Jaime's mind it created the equally remote and disquieting possibility that Jade's other incredible theories about life might have some basis. Jaime had grown comfortable with her ironic view of life; this late in the game, she was not willing to cope with the notion of hope. From past experience, it was too dangerous a belief.

In her direct conversations with Jade, Jaime could tell she was missed. The tone in her mother's voice told her as much; but of course Jade could never bring herself to say so outright, for fear, Jaime knew, of sounding dependent. It was bad enough to Jade that Jaime had gone off to earn money for an operation which she still insisted was unnecessary.

"Everything happens in its own way, in its own time," Jade had said before Jaime had left. This was at a time when the pain was at its zenith, and even Jade could not deny its reality. Yet even then her mother had the nerve to say, "And everything happens perfectly."

Jaime had merely stared at her with the look one reserves for the insane.

Now Jade was saying, "I am completely well. The money is no longer an issue."

Of course it was still an issue. But aside from that, the idea of packing up and returning home was suddenly inconceivable to Jaime.

If it were possible to be gradually poisoned by small doses of happiness, so slight as to go undetected until the effect had taken irreversible hold, then a part of her old self was being murdered bit by bit; it was a curious notion, but one that occurred to her as the days flew by. Still, in all fairness, she could not fault Reeve for any outward attempt at physical or psychological seduction. He was the perfect host, nothing more. Their days together were spent in friendly camaraderie.

Yet at odd moments during those rare quiet times she spent alone, she felt as if pieces of herself were slipping away. She, who had prided herself on her sense of reality, could no longer lay claim to any hard-and-fast rules. The fixed principles of life that had guided her for so long seemed as insubstantial as the white clouds that formed and dissolved against the deep blue of the Los Angeles sky. At particularly joyful times, she would catch herself, and shuddering with insecurity, she would step up her vigilance, seeking to discover the deceit underlying her present happiness. Each time she was confounded by the lack of such negative evidence.

Two weeks had passed swiftly since she had moved into Reeve's Brentwood home. Every other day Reeve rented time on an ice rink for them to practice. They were moments Jaime cherished, for they brought not only the past back but gave her a present that was even more precious. Besides the moments they spent together, Reeve's time was occupied by closed-door telephone conversations with his agent, mostly discussing tentative offers on the skating deal. He read new scripts sent to him for possible acceptance, and more recently, Reeve attended meetings with an attorney regarding his walkout in Rome.

She found herself concerned about the legal threats that seemed serious, despite Reeve's pretence otherwise. Still, she couldn't bring herself to disclose openly her fears over his welfare; to do so would undoubtedly invite a discussion of their relationship again. It was, after all, his feelings for her that had precipitated the drastic measure of leaving the film in the first place.

Along with the other activities, visits from Charlotte Ferris would punctuate their days. Even under Jaime's harsh scrutiny, it appeared that Reeve's mother was a changed woman, particularly regarding her attitude toward Jaime.

It was late on a Friday afternoon, and Jaime and Reeve were just getting in the Porsche to take a run to the Farmer's Market for a special cheese, when Charlotte's white Lincoln Continental sped into the circular driveway.

Charlotte threw open the car door, and with no trace of her characteristic reserve, strode energetically to where they waited.

"The skating deal's been put together," she announced.

To Jaime, Charlotte's blue gaze, ever tinged with crystalline flecks of silver, brought to mind frost on a pond.

Charlotte's attention roamed back and forth from Reeve to Jaime. "I was at Elliot's going over some of your video royalty statements when the call came," she continued. There was a note of caution in her explanation. "So I told Elliot I'd give the two of you the news in person. It's a terribly good agreement," she stated. "Everything you wanted. But you'll see for yourself," she emphasized, and her full attention fell on Jaime. "How marvelous for you," Charlotte said. "You'll have the money in no time, and can take it back with you to Paradise. Of course, since it will be a few weeks until the show will be ready to film, you don't need to hang around here anymore. The waiting must have made you terribly anxious, poor darling, always worrying about your mother. Well, now it's all over. You can pack with the assurance that everything's taken care of."

Jaime suddenly felt herself to be in an airless vacuum. The sky, which had seconds before been a comforting blue, seemed to have been drained of its color, and the surrounding shrubs no longer seemed three-dimensional, but paper cutouts. None of it had been real. For two weeks she had lived a fantasy.

Reeve was similarly quiet, both of them unresponsive to Charlotte's news.

The light in Charlotte's eyes dulled slightly as she said, "Well, I had expected some show of excitement. Perhaps not fireworks, but at least some mild display of…"

As Charlotte spoke, Jaime experienced a feeling of water being poured on top of her. The impression came not as a shock so much as a sensation that she was simply being washed away.

"You'll want to call Jade immediately," Charlotte said. "Or perhaps it might be better to book your return flight and then call your mother. My travel agent is—"

At a half run, Jaime bolted from Reeve's side and made for the front door.

She was vaguely aware of Charlotte calling out behind her for Reeve to let her go, that she was just excited and would probably want to be alone. The words were crisp, clean and spare and cut in the manner of fine, steel blades hurled through the air by an expert knife-thrower.

Jaime pushed through the double front door. The luxury of the house seemed to absorb her sorrow, the cloth walls muffling her breathing, the thick carpeting swallowing her rushing footsteps as she took the now familiar path to her room. *Her room!*

In the safety of the bedroom, she threw herself face down on the bed and heaved dry sobs into the beautiful silken bedspread. The fine fabric was bunched into balls beneath her fists and she found herself clutching the material as desperately as a rock climber on a crumbling ledge.

She was in danger of losing her grip when she heard her name called through the closed door. "Jaime! Are you all right?"

She caught her breath, panicking that her state of despair would be discovered. It would be the final humiliation. In another second she could have collected herself. She would have told him that she was fine, and he would have gone away; but Reeve didn't wait for that second before he stepped through the door into her room.

Twisting around, she dabbed at her eyes, liquid with unfallen tears.

Reeve closed the door behind him. Several feet into the room, he stopped to observe her. "Jaime..." he said, at a loss for further words.

No longer did he appear untouched by life. The facial lines she had taken to be the result of fatigue on his return from Rome were still in place. Even the remarkable eyes had altered, becoming deeper ovals in this new face, where varying emotions had taken residence. Gone was the careless gaze that had contributed to his success as a movie idol; the radiant twin suns had become blazing blue stars.

And she, sitting in miserable disarray on the bed, was exposed by their light.

He knows. He understands my feelings, she realized with crushing dismay. This made her ashamed. It rendered her vulnerable and weak, and again she identified with her mother and her need to show her strength.

"So," she said, forcing herself into an upright position at the edge of the mattress. "That *was* good news! Sudden, but good." She made an energetic attempt to neaten the folds of her skirt.

"So good that you took off?" Reeve asked quietly.

"Oh, yes, that. You refer no doubt, to my untimely, unorthodox departure?" She quirked her mouth into what was supposed to be a smile, but came out as a lopsided grimace.

"The very same," Reeve replied, going along with her attempted lightness but losing none of his seriousness.

"Obviously, Charlotte's number one son is not acquainted with ancient Chinese principles. Strange behavior is part and parcel of my heritage. 'Always run from good news, for the reverse is not far behind.' So says Jade, who sure as hell ought to know," Jaime finished with more truth than humor.

"Jaime," Reeve said, coming toward her, "it doesn't have to end."

"That's an aphorism I don't know," Jaime said.

"It's not an aphorism. It's the simple truth, plainly stated." Almost imperceptibly, he had advanced even closer to her, and just as he had known the fear and disappointment in her mind, she knew his thoughts by the tension of his stance, and understood the tight clenching of his jawline to be restrained male need.

"No. No, Reeve." Her breath quickened as he moved forward. She held herself together long enough to say, "It wouldn't do any good to—"

But he was already gathering her in his arms, and she was twining her arms around his neck even as he said, "I left you alone. I waited, Jaime. I thought that eventually it would happen the way it should happen, with both of us wanting each other."

Her lashes fluttered open, yet the dream continued, with him still in control. His fingers lightly brushed her jawline, sought the curve of her lips, sought to possess her more completely.

Her fingers caught his as she made the eternal gesture of female resistance; he, in his turn overcame the resistance. With little more than a shudder, she accepted defeat as they both had known she would, as he leaned over her to claim dominion over her body. With a cupped hand and his mouth, he grazed the taut nipples evident beneath her cotton blouse. With his lower body he strained against her pelvis.

"I'm leaving here, this will only—"

His mouth was upon hers, silencing the storm of regret with another kind of tumult.

Jaime gave into her need, meeting his with a force that had built over long years of lonely nights. But her body was a woman's now and she was no longer the uncertain girl who had given herself to the boy on a bed of straw. Instinctively, her form molded itself to his, and she felt the certain throb of his desire pulse against her.

"Jaime . . . Jaime . . ." he said, and with the greatest gentleness, shifting her slowly but with unmistakable intention to a recumbent position on the silk coverlet.

He placed himself over her, but only partially touching her, as if to assure them both that the act was not merely to be a wild frenzy of desire, a turbulent physical encounter that might easily be dismissed later as a momentary impulse, and therefore, a mistake.

His fingers moved deftly to the top buttons of her blouse, releasing her breasts.

There was a moment when he did not move, and she watched his eyes travel languorously over the swelling of flesh visible through the white, lacy bra. Still, he made no overt move to dominate her, as if by each sacrifice of his base masculine drives, he was gaining her irrevocable compliance.

She could stop him easily, by a word, by a silent gesture. He wanted her to know that.

His lips lingered on her shoulder, delicately grazing her skin like the wings of a butterfly warmed by an afternoon sun. She sighed, trembling slightly as her body relaxed into a deeper reverie of sensual abandon.

He was softly stroking the curve of her hip now. She lifted herself, not to stop him, but to hold his face between her hand and let him look into her eyes.

"You're positive?" he asked, seeking the truth in her eyes as well as her words.

"Absolutely," she answered.

"For so many nights I've wanted this," he said just before exploring her mouth with his tongue. "If you only could imagine."

There was no imagination necessary after that.

They came together in the waning afternoon light, liquid fire, melding into each other.

The muscles of his chest glistened smooth and hard as he rolled beneath her, bringing her astride him. Then he arched into her, bringing her by slow rhythmic movements to the point where everything was forgotten but the mounting pleasure. With every thrust he stoked a fire deep within her loins. His hands roamed over every inch of her body bringing her to ever higher levels of ecstasy.

"With me," he breathed raggedly, tensing beneath her, "with me, Jaime..."

Together they were riders of a rapturous force, components of an energy, exploding and coming together, over and again...

"With me, Jaime," he cried out.

And she was, entirely.

Chapter Eight

Absurdity of adsurdities; to think she could ever have denied it. Of course she was in love.

In love. The term was a caress. It was music vibrating in every cell of her body. Ah, *in love.*

And yet, after all, what a paltry phrase it was for such a monumental state of being. Could any word, any chain of letters, phrases, sentences strung together, come close to approaching the actual experience? Never.

She had realized her love, succumbed to its absoluteness, not during the heat of that afternoon's passion, but in a moment much like a void, when all was still.

They lay on their sides, he against her back, one hand still on her breast, the other resting lightly over her hip. In the air lingered that lovely scent of his cologne, her perfume, and the blending of the natural musks of their bodies. If she moved slightly his leg was sure to seek hers. If he shuddered in his half sleep, she would quickly clasp him against her, prepared if necessary to protect him from the universe.

His breath had become even and deep. Slowly, she extricated herself from his hold. Covering him with the discarded white silk sheet, she remained propped on an elbow, experiencing fierce delight in watching him sleep.

It was late afternoon now. The drapes were open to reveal a panorama of towering eucalyptus, lacy green jacarandas, and lofty Italian cypresses outside. Now and again Jaime's gaze was drawn to the view. The property off her bedroom dropped sharply into a ravine, which unlike other parts of Reeve's well-tended estate, had been left to follow nature's design. Beneath the stateliness of the large trees there existed another kingdom of vegetation. A variety of rambling vines and spindly shrubs were interspersed with clumps of prickly pear cacti and other kinds of cacti, whose spindly tentacles splayed out in all directions like a deep-sea creature. Beyond the fringe of green the winter sky had paled, and in contrast, the rest of the world was thrown into sharp, crisp relief.

Her gaze dropped again to where Reeve lay. His face in repose revealed the inner man. It was then, when she suddenly became aware of the strength, the gentleness and purity of his construction that she understood why he was so beloved by so many, and begrudged by those who didn't have it themselves. He had always been what she had first recognized, only to lose that sense of him later through bitterness. It was Charlotte and Elliot Cohen and others who had exploited the natural man to their own purposes. They had pruned and clipped and shaped what was already perfection.

In a sense, Reeve had tried to tell her this when he came to her bedroom that night. Instead, she had taken his explanations for his desertion as excuses, a bid to reclaim what he had lost. He had not suspected Charlotte's treachery for so many years because there was no corresponding emotion in him. He had not been selfish nor stupid. He was only what he was and as he lay sleeping before her, she saw him as generous and good, a man blessed within and without.

His arm was bent at the elbow, with the palm flat and open. Reaching down, she touched her own palm to his, and in his sleep he automatically interlocked his fingers with hers.

It was like the first time they ever met. She, a girl on skates, had glided over to him, the boy on skates. Their hands had met, his fingers closing over hers, joining them to each other.

She loved him then. On that long ago day, she had innocently given her heart to him, and now it was the same. She loved him, then, now, and always. There had never been a moment when she had not. Her fervent protestations to the contrary had been pretense; the love was real.

She called Pat the following day to tell him of the ice contract. The money—the full fifty thousand dollars—would be forthcoming within two weeks of completing the legal formalities; papers had to be stamped, sealed, signed and filed to everyone's satisfaction. Jaime explained it all to him, as it had been told to her by Elliot Cohen.

Also, she wouldn't be required to begin rehearsals for another month, so naturally she would come home. This was, of course, the upsetting plan initially brought forward by Charlotte. But, just as Reeve had proclaimed, when Charlotte had steered the course of his actions as a young man, his mother's promptings were always as "logical" as they were disruptive. Now even Jaime herself could not deny the sense behind Charlotte's proposal.

"You sound bad, Jaime," Pat said over the wire, picking up the vibration of her gloom. "What's wrong, girl?"

She wanted to tell him about Reeve, about how wrong she had been about him, and that she loved him more than life itself; but she didn't. She knew it would be a selfish confession under the circumstances: Pat's own great love was in such jeopardy.

"Nothing. How's Jade?"

"Still good. Still real good." There was relief, even pride in his tone. The dark horse having made the finish line in good time.

"Do you think she might be over the..."

"It's almost like before she got sick, Jaime." There was that lilt to his voice again, and the denial.

Sick? The term seemed trivial, misplaced. The word was cancer. Cancer was an eviction notice to vacate life's premises. There was little hope of appealing the judgment.

"She's bustling around here," he went on. "Hell," Pat exploded with a laugh, "Sis can't hardly keep up with her."

"She won't have too much longer. I'm flying back tomorrow afternoon. I'll land in Boise and then take the bus back to Sun Valley."

"I'll check the schedule and pick you up in town," Pat said and Jaime could feel his smile over the distance. "It's going to be good to have the whole family back together again. Jaime," he said. "It's going to be okay. It's all going to work out. I can feel it in my bones, girl."

Jaime identified with his desperate conviction. "It will, Pat. It's all going to work out."

"Jaime?" She had been ready to say goodbye. "I'm hearing it in your voice again. What's going on?"

"Then your bones are smarter than your ears," she said lightly. "I'm fine, and I'll see you all tomorrow. Hug Jade for me."

She was anything but fine, and that night as she dined with Reeve and Charlotte at The Palm, she barely touched the three-pound lobster set before her.

Reeve had bought her a suit for their last night in L.A. together. She learned from Charlotte that it came from a boutique on Rodeo Drive. It was white knit with a black collar and black piping, and fit her as if the designer had had her in mind when he created it.

Had she not been so depressed she might have enjoyed the attention she was receiving from waiters and customers alike. Her dark hair fell in a soft sheen to her shoulders, curving under at the ends. In her sadness, her green eyes seemed deeper, holding as they did the compelling mystery of a beautiful woman's private sorrow. To cover the blotches formed from a crying spell she'd indulged in that afternoon, she had resorted to camouflage, and the effect of facial makeup was extraordinary. She looked like a porcelain doll, fragile, feminine and exotic, and there was the unexpected glow of summer ripeness to her skin and form, brought about by the satisfaction of loving fully.

It was Charlotte who made the comment. "I believe, Reeve, you are being eclipsed by a brighter star this evening."

He had been engrossed in Jaime, and at first didn't catch his mother's meaning.

"Look around you, darling," Charlotte explained, her own eyes sweeping the restaurant. In slanted looks and unabashed gawking, the admiration of other patrons was being leveled at Jaime. "She's clearly the most stunning woman here tonight," Charlotte commented magnanimously. She herself was dressed impeccably in a black sheath, looking as thin as any twenty year old, and ten years younger than her fifty years.

"They have excellent taste," Reeve said, and reaching for his glass, lifted it in Jaime's honor. "To the most beautiful woman in the world," he said extravagantly, topping his mother's assessment.

"Reeve..." Jaime protested with pleasure, but Charlotte seconded the toast.

"There are many beautiful women in this city," she said, "but there's something about you, Jaime. You have a quality, my dear, which no amount of artifice or money can presume to duplicate."

Although she made an effort to be cheerful, for Jaime the meal proceeded with all the atmospheric undertones of a funeral procession. There was a soundless ticking in her heart, measuring out the moments of happiness left to share with Reeve.

Her sad mood was quite foundless, since her parting from Reeve was merely temporary. But she couldn't shake the sense of history repeating itself. The play was different but the theme was the same. She, the heroine, was being called back to her proper place. She was becoming a secondary character again, relegated to a drab corner of the stage where her role would consist of lackluster lines and the performance of mundane actions. It was an ongoing melodrama in which she had been haphazardly cast, and there was no relief in sight unless the horrible denouement of Jade's possible death were to be considered. And this Jaime could not, would not, consider as an alternative to her own situation.

As if infected by her despair, Reeve's conversation drifted subtly into the negative with phrases such as, "If you come back to me" and "Maybe we'll be able to travel someday if..."

Misery fed at their table, a boorish bully dominating the scene.

Charlotte had been in the middle of a story about her ancestors when Reeve suddenly interrupted. "I won't be alive until you return here, Jaime," Reeve said, his eyes burning into hers.

There was a brief silence, during which time Charlotte must have decided to ignore the obvious: her presence was insignificant and her information immaterial to her dinner companions. She went on with her tale with increased animation when Reeve again broke in.

"I'm going to go with you," he suddenly announced. "That's the only way, Jaime." He had reached across the table and held Jaime's hand in his own, as if fearful she might, even then, slip away from him.

"No," Jaime replied firmly. "It wouldn't work for us in Paradise. It would be depressing. Oh, Reeve, after all of this..." She looked around, the gesture accentuating the luxury. "I don't want to spoil things," she said.

"I don't care about any of this," he said.

"But I do."

"All I want is us," he insisted.

"Let it be right, though, Reeve."

"When we're together, it's right. Paradise or here— or on the moon, for that matter."

Charlotte had been quiet during the interchange, forgotten, in fact. Now she made her presence felt, saying, "Reeve's absolutely right. Now that you two have found each other again, why thumb your nose at fate?"

Both Jaime and Reeve exchanged glances, neither having expected Charlotte to be an ally.

"I've made a mess out of things in the past," Charlotte went on, as if reading their thoughts, "and I agreed never to meddle again. But in this case I feel it would be a disservice to keep quiet. If you have the chance for love, grab it. Take it now. It may not come again." To Jaime, she said, "You said this friend of yours—this man Pat—insisted your mother is doing well enough on her own. And she has other help, besides. So for the time being, stay. Stay, Jaime."

With both Reeve and Charlotte aligned on one side, it became impossible to reject the logic of the proposal. Charlotte herself put the telephone into Jaime's hand and stood by her while she explained her change of plans to Pat.

That night, as she lay in Reeve's arms, she felt secure and happy. "I feel almost guilty," she said, "not trusting Charlotte. She really does love you. All she wants is the best for you, even if it includes a ragamuffin like me, I guess."

"It would seem that way," Reeve said. "But don't count your chickens."

"My, aren't we suspicious?" Jaime, who had been lying on her back, shifted to her side and propped herself up on an elbow. "And I thought you were too generous to let a disparaging thought cross your mind. I'll have to cancel the shrine."

He didn't laugh. "There's a difference between discrimination and meting out judgment." His eyes were dark hollows. Now and then the wind would cause the eucalyptus trees to bend, and the moon would shine through, striking them with a cool shaft of light. "I've learned you should be careful."

"So ominous," Jaime said, watching him.

The look he wore changed. His glance moved fleetingly from her face to her form, then back. His expression was the reflection of his love, mixed with his appreciation of her physical beauty, and, disturbingly, fear. Jaime reached forward with her free hand and stroked the side of his face, as if to rouse him from a bad dream.

He clasped her hand in his, brought it to his lips and kissed her open palm. Dark lashes covered the blue eyes.

"What is it?" she asked.

His breath was warm on her skin. Lightly, he brushed his lips over the tips of her fingers. "I took it all for granted," he said. "Life, you know. There was always this flow of good things, one after the other. And now..." Jaime felt a tremor pass through him. He looked up. "Now I care so much about something, for the first time. Consciously care about it, see all the angles, appreciate even the smallest amount of time. I'm afraid." Jaime winced slightly, not wanting to disturb him, but he had tightened his hold on her fingers. "I don't want it to end. I want it to stay exactly the way it is. I love you, I love you," he said, then shook his head, at a loss to express himself more completely. Frustrated, he dropped his head onto the pillow, his eyes turned upwards, a man seeing nothing and everything. "I want to hold on to you."

Jaime pressed her body over his, protecting him from his fears. "There is no need to worry," she said. "I'll always be with you."

He wrapped his arms around her. She knew he did not believe her.

Charlotte invited her for lunch.

"There's no sense in hanging around the house," Charlotte had said. "Reeve's going to be tied up with his attorneys for heaven knows how long. It could be weeks before anything's settled about the Rome thing. If it is ever is settled," she inserted darkly, but went on brightly enough in the next breath, "You and I shall share some delicious times together."

Jaime was constantly revising her opinion about Charlotte. No sooner would Jaime's suspicions take form when some deed or word from Charlotte would counteract her assessment.

The "delicious times" to which Charlotte referred turned out to have as much to do with shopping as with their dining-out extravaganzas. Charlotte was correct in her projection. With apologies, Reeve reluctantly trudged off to the lair of his Century City attorneys, meeting with Elliot Cohen and the "opposing interests" in the hope of an out-of-court settlement.

"It's just rotten..." Charlotte said, sliding the Lincoln into position before a Rodeo Drive boutique. Two valets bounded forward to swing open the car's doors. Charlotte took the parking claim slip. Still talking, she said, "Reeve's going mad, wanting to be with you and instead..." She sighed. "That damned Rome thing."

It was not a mere tour of the greener side of life Jaime received from Charlotte, but an indoctrination

into a world Jaime had previously viewed only
through the pages of fashion magazines. At a certain
level, Charlotte explained, style and social position
were one and the same, defining the person.

It was, of course, totally superficial, this wafting
from shop to shop where dresses cost as much as
Jaime had earned in a single year. Accessories to
complement a single outfit might cost ten times the
amount of the basic garment.

But it was fun.

Wearing the suit Reeve had bought her gave her a
sense of confidence. More than one saleswoman
commented upon the outfit. They also admired Jaime
in it. For a time Jaime thought their praise and seeming interest in her were no more than sales tactics. But
after a while, even she could not deny the evident sincerity behind the comments.

"This would look incredible on you," a saleswoman said, bringing out a dress. It was black, strap-
less, cut low in the back with an intricate design of
sequins.

"It is incredible," Jaime said, laughing. "But not
for me."

"But of course it is!" The saleswoman was baffled, almost insulted.

"I have no use for it."

"She most certainly does," Charlotte said. "I'll
hold your purse while you slip into it." In what appeared to be a single movement, Charlotte took her
clutch purse while the saleswoman shepherded Jaime
into a spacious mirror-lined enclosure.

A moment later, Jaime stepped from the dressing
room, the dress a black sheath clinging to her body.

There were whispers and wide stares from the store's
several employees and considering looks from other

shoppers. Charlotte's head was tipped, her eyes unblinking. For a moment, Jaime thought that perhaps she had put the dress on backward.

"She'll take it." Charlotte's voice broke the silence.

The room became an instant buzz. Unfamiliar faces clearly registered feminine jealousy and admiration for the stunning creature in the black gown.

"Charlotte, I don't have the money for this," she whispered frantically. The price tag, discreetly lodged within her bodice, had said five thousand dollars.

"A gift," Charlotte said.

"No, I can't..."

"You make my son happy. That is worth everything to me. And you can wear it at my party," she said. "Next week."

After that, there were other expensive shops and other extravagantly priced outfits. Each time Jaime objected, Charlotte overruled her. "For Reeve," she would say, and as always Charlotte's logic overcame any counter rationalizations Jaime might present.

They dined at the Bistro.

There, too, Jaime drew stares from both male and female patrons.

A waiter approached, and with an air of timid deference, as if forced to speak directly to a royal personage noted for bad temper, he bent close to Jaime's ear and said, "A gentleman, a Mr. Leon Lancaster, has asked that I deliver his card to you." The waiter backed away, his eyes begging forgiveness that someone of her position should have been so annoyed by trivia.

Jaime stared down at the card, wondering at it.

"May I see?" Charlotte relieved her of the mystery. "Leon Lancaster?" Charlotte's eyes scanned the room and came to rest on an elegant man with salt and pepper hair and a deep tan. The man's attention was focused on Jaime. He smiled and nodded. Jaime, who felt disconnected from the scene, merely stared. She saw Charlotte smile for her.

"Well," Charlotte said, her expression one of motherly pride and barely veiled excitement, "you have caught yourself a big fish."

Leon Lancaster was the world's top producer of television shows. He could boast of having four of the nation's top ten shows. Out of those four, two were in worldwide syndication, ranking number one in various countries anxious to imbibe American glamour. He had made media stars of more than one lucky starlet.

"Are you going to call him?" Charlotte asked, placing the card back by Jaime's plate.

Jaime looked at the card, then across the room to the man who was still watching her. She felt herself flushing.

To Charlotte she said, "No. Of course not. Why would I?"

"You could become famous. And rich."

Jaime was quiet. She felt as if she were in a spotlight and the entire room was an audience whose attention was trained upon her. A decision was required to break the suspense. Rich. Famous. The words pulsed in her mind. This was not what she wanted. She wanted Reeve.

"I came here only to make enough money for Jade's operation. And Reeve's the only thing I care about. Nothing else."

Charlotte reached across the table. Her bejeweled fingers covered Jaime's hand. "What a darling girl you are. So true, so real," Charlotte said. "There's no one in this whole town like you. And to think that my son has found you.''

''I love him so much, Charlotte. You can't imagine.'' Tears had come to Jaime's eyes.

''Yes, I know. As I also do.''

''I've been so happy. And Reeve is happy, too. Of course you must have seen it.'' Jaime laughed lightly, imagining the picture they must present to the world, mooning around, touching and smiling, forgetful of packages bought in stores, of time, of the entire world. ''Every day is like a miracle when we're together. Although—'' and Jaime shook her head ''—he worries that I'll leave him. Or that something will happen. Can you imagine! Loving each other as much as we do?''

''It's a great romance,'' Charlotte said. ''Romeo and Juliet.''

''Yes,'' Jaime returned, then with a laugh said, ''no! That had a tragic ending. Juliet died.''

''Ah,'' Charlotte said, ''she did, didn't she?''

Chapter Nine

Jaime had never seen this side of Reeve and could not have imagined it during those years they had been separated. She had thought him invincible, invulnerable to the mortal cares assailing others, particularly her with her chopping and slicing and frowning over gas bills. Although she found his vulnerability made him even more lovable, it made him a stranger to her.

The "Rome thing" had taken its toll on him. It was all very subtle, of course, his concern over his financial future. He tried to hide his worry from her, but in vain. She gradually saw through it.

Two weeks had passed since the night it had been decided she would remain in Los Angeles rather than return home. The time had passed at a frantic pace. Some mornings, she and Reeve worked out on the ice, others at a gym. Sweating and sore, they would fall into each other's arms, laughing and commiserating that they were no longer teenagers. But afternoons were invariably organized by Charlotte, who in the manner of a zealous drill sergeant, instructed Jaime in shopping and dining and led her on daily, serendipitous tours through the city.

Late afternoons, she would return exhausted but exhilarated, to await Reeve's return from business meetings with attorneys, Elliot Cohen, and a team of financial wizards who had lately been summoned to unravel the mess.

At that time she was dimly aware that Reeve was concerned about his financial affairs. But Reeve never had "real" problems like other people. He was immune to life's travails. Soon enough he would skim over the present difficulty, and emerge from the experience unscathed or in even better circumstances. Such was Reeve's luck. So she thought.

Returning from her sprees with Charlotte, she would try to break his pensive mood with her own enthusiasm.

"Look!" She would hold up yet another dress, a purchase paid for by Charlotte, who, if denied the opportunity of satisfying her whim of spoiling Jaime, would settle into a mood of such melancholy that Jaime's objections to the ongoing largesse would seem downright cruel. So Jaime indulged Charlotte, whose pleasure, whose mania, it was to indulge Jaime.

"It's beautiful," Reeve would say, barely paying attention to the garment. "And so are you . . ."

Then, as the pattern went, he would invariably draw her into his arms. Their response to each other was always immediate. Together, they were the world and everything else was superfluous.

One night, however, there was a change.

He had come home before her. Jaime found Reeve standing in the bedroom they now shared. His back was to her as she entered the room amid a rustle of boxes, bags and plastic garment bags—the spoils of that day's hunt.

"Hi!" she said gaily. He was at the door to the large walk-in closet and when he heard her voice, he turned. She ran up with a smile and kissed him. His mouth and eyes were cold. His attention strayed to and settled on the bags still in her arms.

There was no attempt on his part to return the kiss. He raised his eyes again, and now merely continued to study her as if seeing something for the first time.

"Do you want to see?" she asked gamely. She thought she might be misinterpreting his mood, and saw no reason to make an issue out of something that probably didn't exist.

"No," Reeve answered.

Jaime heard the curt "no," but she had already crossed the room, and was surveying the day's purchases spread out on the bed. She reached into a bag and pulled out a red satin jogging outfit.

"It's not real satin," she confided, holding it up to view. "Wouldn't be practical. But it cost as much. More, probably. What do you think?"

Then she saw his face.

"What's wrong?" Jaime asked finally. The red jogging suit was limp in her fingers.

"What is this?" Reeve swept his hand in a way that seemed to encompass the entire universe. "All of this—stuff?"

"Just—" she looked down at her purchases "—stuff, I guess." Jaime gave a bewildered shrug and looked up again. "Nice things."

"They aren't necessary, Jaime."

"Necessary? No. No, I guess they aren't. But they're nice. And—" she felt angry that she had to defend herself "—and, I like them." The last was defiance, not an apology.

"That closet's filled with—"

"Charlotte insisted."

"Charlotte can't force you into buying things, Jaime."

"I'm not. She's buying them. She's doing it for herself, if you want to know the truth. At least that's what she says, and that's what I believe." Jaime sank onto the bed, the jogging suit a vibrant gash of color across her knees. "I'm like a daughter or something to her. She's lonely and this is giving her a sense of purpose. She's showing me the ropes, you know?"

"The ropes, sure. She'll give you enough rope to hang yourself. She's showing you things you don't need to know. It's all irrelevant garbage." He stood near her, his hand lifting a garment bag, throwing it down with disdain, and then dumping out the contents of another sack containing sweaters, scarves and a necklace wrapped in tissue paper that clunked heavily onto the mattress.

Jaime's eyes filled with tears. But she was too furious to cry. "These are my things," she said, gathering up the spilled, the spoiled, presents, and clutching them to her bosom as if she were protecting children from abuse. "They make me happy. I don't see what difference that should make to you, Reeve. What difference?"

He walked away, his back to her as he said, "Suddenly I don't know who you are."

"I'm me, the me I've always been. No, not the way I've been, but the way I never had a chance to be. Who I am—inside. Oh, Reeve . . . I like this. It's like falling into another world. One that's beautiful and easy and fun." Now she was pleading, a little girl again, wanting skates like other children more fortunate than she was. She had looked in so many windows, pressed her nose against so many panes of glass, always on the outside. Now, at last, she was inside. For once she was a part of the "good life."

He had gone to the window. Looking over his shoulder, he said, "It has a price, Jaime. This fun, beautiful world you like so much has a price tag."

"And who have you become?" she returned meanly. She had come home happy, wanting to share, and at the moment she disliked him for having spoiled that mood.

"Me," he answered simply.

"That's interesting. We've both become ourselves, which is to say we've become other people."

"Maybe that's true, more than you know."

He was staring across the room at her. With the garments strewn about her, she felt embarrassed suddenly, as if they were all witnesses against her. It did seem silly, all those "things" cast around her, pieces of cloth that would soon be out of style, or frayed at the edges, or cast off as unwearable. Yet they were "things" she was willing to fight over. She was a hungry person, gorging herself, needing to fill herself up. She couldn't help herself; the hunger robbed her of moral fortitude.

"I don't know who you are, either," Jaime said, not out of spitefulness this time, but because she realized it was true. He had changed from the Reeve she had known. There was a heaviness to his manner, a new maturity.

"I was given a choice today," he said somberly.

Jaime waited for him to continue.

"I could go back to Rome and the slate would be wiped clean. No punitive financial measures would be taken. The daily rushes are supposed to be good. No," he revised with a certain element of sadness, rather than pride, "better than that—great. My break-through role. From movie star to actor, like that." It was sarcasm, but also the truth.

"And what did you say?" Jaime asked. It was clear enough to her than an acceptance of Rome would be a refusal of the skate deal. She didn't know what that would do to her financially now, but she did know that she was looking forward with greater anticipation than she had ever suspected, to her chance to skate on national television. Jaime Quinn, a person in her own right.

"I told them I would rather be a decent human being than a great actor." He strode across the room again. Jaime shrank back as he lifted the clothes out of her arms and tossed them to the floor. "Don't do this, Jaime. It's slow poison. The clothes, the cars, the deal just around the corner. It will kill you eventually."

She was in his arms, responding not to his rebuke, but to his obvious concern for her. "Oh, Reeve..."

They clutched each other; neither spoke, both trembled.

"I'll give everything back to Charlotte tomorrow. She'll understand..."

"No, no," he said, his palm stroking the smooth fall of raven hair. Pulling back from her slightly, he looked into her face. "Keep your pretty things. It's only important that you understand...I didn't think you would. I saw you being sucked into the whirlpool, the same as I was."

Jaime nodded. "I know what's real. And what's not." Tilting her head to the side, she glanced down to that afternoon's scattered treats. "Only I forgot for a moment. Temporary amnesia." She looked back up. "Make me remember," she said. "Make love to me, Reeve." It was a desperate plea to which Reeve responded.

He undressed her slowly, watching her face. He wanted her to be with him completely, as if he were performing an exorcism that required total absorption in the ritual.

His mouth came down on hers, his tongue entering and taking brief possession. Ready for her, he nevertheless continued with his deliberate actions, slipping his hands beneath her arms and raising her to him, his mouth traveling in turn to each breast. He strained against her, hard, a heated brand against her leg. When she reached down for him, he stopped her, and pinning both hands above her head, moved lower to her stomach.

She pressed up, urging him along in his journey. A gentle arching, a short sigh released, her body undulating slowly.

The heat of his mouth enveloped her. She rose to him, knees bent and parted for him. She called out his name wantonly.

He was in her, then she was astride him, their bodies never separating. Her turn to torment, at first with slow deliberation, the tide of passion in her ever-rising but still manageable.

Reeve closed his eyes. His head was thrown back, the pillow a cloud around his face. Teeth clenched, the look of absorption, the famous face in a state of exaltation, a man lost in the sweet torture of a woman's body.

Their motions were a silent dialogue, their mutual ecstasy a pledge of understanding. Always would they exist in the same place for each other, in a realm where fame and fortune were irrelevant. When there was this, when there was love, what else was needed?

Reeve was gentle and controlled. Moving again over her form, he parted her with his fingers. His thrust was deliberate, knowing, an assured male command that was irresistably natural.

Every call of her body resonated with the feel of his. Her heart beat in rhythm to their movements. The air in her lungs danced with delight. He brought her higher and higher, until no longer aware of herself, she became pure feeling, total sensation.

His tongue was in her ear; her hands slipped through the blond halo framing his face.

"Remember, Jaime..." His heat was explosive. The body over hers was slick and trembling, a ripple of steel conquering her flesh. "Remember this is more than all the rest... only this..."

She rose reflexively as he drove harder into her lost in pleasure.

His hands framed her face, and when she opened her eyes briefly, he was watching her. His rhythm grew faster, always unbroken and ever more decisive as he led her further into a state she had never before experienced.

"Now..." he said.

And she obeyed, opening completely to him.

With a shudder, a violent heave of blissful release, his body melted into hers, hers into his.

Afterward, they lay in an invisible nest of warmth and satisfaction. All was as it should be.

"Now I remember," Jaime said.

The following morning, Jaime's new resolve to give up the superficial good life was put to the test.

Charlotte had her own key to Reeve's house. She knocked, then entered on her own. Pressed in her old outfit of faded jeans and a pink sweatshirt, Jaime was on the back terrace repotting an overgrown philodendron.

There was a sudden click of nearby footsteps, and silence.

Jaime raised her head. "Charlotte..."

"One of the gardeners should do that." Charlotte was looking with distaste at the spilled soil as if Jaime were involved with something unnatural.

"I enjoy it," Jaime returned. She brushed an errant piece of peat moss from her cheek, then continued to pat the soil around the roots. She had to finish what she'd started. "I left a message with your housekeeper—"

"I received it." Charlotte's tone was more than cool, it was frigid.

Jaime raised her eyes. She noted Charlotte was dressed for shopping.

"I left it last night."

"I got it last night."

"I see."

Jaime wasn't certain where things were leading, but she already knew it was dangerous territory. Charlotte did not like to be crossed.

Before Jaime's cancellation it was to have been another dizzy day of shopping and lunch, more shopping then late afternoon tea. Charlotte had on one of the new French prints—the incoming season's hot ticket. The dress was decidedly less tailored than her usual uniforms and gave her a softer look. Charlotte's expression more than compensated for any possible hint of feminine fragility. To Jaime, she looked positively fearsome.

Brushing the dirt off her hands, Jaime rose and faced Charlotte.

"Charlotte, I loved all the fun we've had. But thanks to you, I already have enough clothes to last a lifetime."

Charlotte was not dissuaded. "You have a lifetime to make up for. A lifetime that was lost, one that you are only just beginning to find."

Charlotte had struck a nerve. There was too much truth to the statement.

"Maybe," Jaime conceded. She looked away, trying to get her priorities straight again. She had felt so strong, and now, beneath Charlotte's laser-sharp gaze, she was confused, behaving like a moral weakling.

"I was under the impression you enjoyed our times together."

"Oh, I did. I did. But—" Jaime was hoping Charlotte would fill in the blanks.

And Charlotte did.

"But it's all strange. Foreign. You like the security of your jeans, the familiarity of doing things that are beneath your talents and capabilities. I only wanted to help you, Jaime. I know how hard it is for you, coming from where you did. I only wanted to lead you into a better life. One that you deserve."

"I have a better life. With Reeve. Reeve's all I need. The clothes, and all the rest, don't matter."

Charlotte raised an eyebrow in disbelief.

"I liked them, Charlotte. Of course. Show me a woman who wouldn't! But all that stuff takes away from what really counts. It's easy to get lost in just things."

"Jaime," Charlotte said sharply, "I wanted to spare you this. I was hoping to be more subtle. But it doesn't seem that's possible any more, so if you'll permit me. For your own good, let me explain the simple facts of life."

Charlotte turned and reentered the house through the double French doors. Obediently, Jaime followed. She was under the vague impression that having done so, having traipsed after the lofty Charlotte Ferris, she had in some way lost ground.

Charlotte stood by the piano in the living room. A thread of sunlight from the nearby window fell upon an open sheet of Chopin Reeve had been playing the previous night.

"This town is all flash," Charlotte began. "It has the most beautiful and accomplished people in the world, and many of those people are, as it happens, women. It is human nature to be attracted to that which is most alluring, most aesthetically pleasing. It has always been so, and it will continue to be so. From Cleopatra to the First Lady, women who rise to high positions and take their places beside men of position are elegant and assured. Not only inwardly, my dear girl, but outwardly as well. This is a fact. Not mine— history's."

She walked around from the piano. Jaime was standing near the sofa, but did not dare to sit on the fine fabric in her work jeans.

"Take care of yourself, Jaime. Cultivate your talents, improve your appearance with every aid mankind has to offer. Otherwise, you will find yourself a part of Reeve's past."

"That's not so." Jaime even managed a small laugh. "He loves me, Charlotte. Loves me for who I am."

This time Charlotte laughed, but it sounded more bitter than good-natured. "Jaime...once I loved a man for what he was, too. I married him. And then it was over. Why? Because he did not fit into my world."

"But I'm not you."

"But Reeve is a part of me. My son. My flesh. I know him, Jaime. I know what kind of a life he's accustomed to. I know human nature." Charlotte smiled sadly, an additional commentary on that which could not be altered.

"Anyway," Charlotte went on with a slight shrug, "I'll bow to your decision to remain with your plants and your other interests." She reached into her purse and took out a small envelope. "I was going to mail it, but then thought it would be better to hand it to you in person. It will give you more time to prepare," she said.

Jaime took the envelope. On the front was Reeve's name and address, beautifully inscribed, the calligraphy the masterwork of a professional. Opening the envelope, Jaime removed the blue velveteen invitation. A party would be held at Charlotte's house in honor of Jaime Quinn, in celebration of her national debut as Cinderella in the ice extravaganza.

"Oh, Charlotte," Jaime said, looking up in amazement.

Charlotte smiled genuinely for the first time that day. "It's to be your night."

"I don't know what to say..." Jaime ran her fingers through her hair, at a loss. "I mean, all this work and expense, just for me?"

"Don't worry, darling." Charlotte swept her arm around Jaime and squeezed. "It will all be worth it."

"Who'd even want to come?" Jaime asked. "I mean, I'm not really anybody."

"Neither was Cinderella. At first."

Jaime smiled, thinking of Reeve who was in many ways her prince.

"Can I help?" Jaime asked, as Charlotte walked through the foyer. "I could bake something..." Jaime was at a loss to even imagine what such a fete would entail.

"Caterers, darling. One does not squander one's energy on wrapping bacon around shrimp. That is left to the professional drudges. They like to do that sort of thing, and they do it very well. Go play with your plants. Just remember on that night to look wonderful. Exquisite. It will be your night."

Jaime watched from the door as Charlotte got into the Lincoln. She waved, but Charlotte didn't see her. She appeared to be thinking about something and by the look on her face it wasn't a particularly pleasant thought.

Jaime had fallen into a wonderland. All eyes were on her as she moved through the room, sometimes with Reeve at her side, at other times alone, and often with Charlotte making introductions.

There had to be three hundred people there. Charlotte had invited two hundred and fifty, she said, but along the way there had dribbled in the calls from uninvited guests, asking if they might bring along so-and-so, and would promptly give so-and-so's credentials. Charlotte's party was open only to VIPs. They might or might not be associated with the entertainment industry; it was perfectly permissible to be an oil tycoon from Texas, or to have relatives who came over on the *Mayflower*.

Charlotte's home in Bel Air was twice as large as Reeve's and twice as luxurious, yet in perfect taste.

There was nothing crass or ostentatious about the house. It was built in the style of a large New England mansion. The architect's only concession to the more flamboyant Hollywood lifestyle was the indoor-outdoor pool encased beneath an enormous structure resembling a gazebo.

Of course it wasn't any secret that it was Reeve's drawing power that had initially brought people to the gala event; but as the evening wore on it became Jaime's night.

"You seem to be the hit of the evening," Reeve whispered in Jaime's ear as he guided her away from an intense South American filmmaker whose recent entry into the Cannes Film Festival had swept all the awards.

Jaime laughed. "It's the dress."

Charlotte had picked it out. It was floor length, with tiny spaghetti straps, a deep V neckline, and a back that plunged below the small of the back to the curve of the buttocks. The fabric was of heavy gold beading, flowing over Jaime's curves as she moved through the crowded rooms. From her ears dangled yellow topaz earrings cut in a pyramid shape and surrounded by diamonds—a gift from Reeve.

Charlotte intercepted them as they were seeking refuge in the pool area, a spot off the beaten path of the party-goers.

"Darling," Charlotte said, lightly touching Reeve's elbow, "permit me to steal Jaime for a moment."

Jaime and Reeve exchanged looks.

"You'll have a lifetime together," Charlotte coaxed. "I only want five minutes."

A moment later, Jaime found herself in Charlotte's study. It was a large room, paneled in warm wood with floor-to-ceiling bookshelves, a large stone fireplace, and overstuffed furniture.

A man was already in the room when Jaime entered. Charlotte said, "Dak, this is a very special lady."

"I already know that," he returned, his gaze sweeping over Jaime with respectful admiration.

He was tall and tanned with a rather prominent Roman nose and dark compelling eyes that were now boring into Jaime's.

"How do you do, Jaime Quinn?" he said, not moving. "I'm Dak Gallanos."

Jaime turned, seeking support from Charlotte, but found she had been left alone and that the study door was now closed.

Dak Gallanos did not have much time. In little more than an hour he was to board a private jet that was to take him to Spain. In Spain he was to oversee personally the photo session of a new line of clothing. His magazine "Razor's Edge" was internationally famous, a state-of-the-art publication combining the best of fashion and culture. It was literate and avantgarde. Those who appeared within its covers were people of originality and substance. Gallanos's empire extended into book publishing and film. He also owned a chain of private resort clubs throughout the world.

"My offer is this," he began. "I want you to fly to Spain tomorrow. You will be the featured model to launch my new line. There was another girl, but tonight when I saw you, I realized she wasn't right. You are. You're perfect for what I want. Your benefactress, Charlotte Ferris, was correct to have insisted I make time to meet you. And to think I may have missed this opportunity. Charlotte is a very persuasive woman. Yes, you have it . . . the look . . . unique, yet wholesome. Yet there lurks the potential of danger. You represent mystery."

"Me?"

Dak Gallanos laughed. "You aren't the first person who did not know they contained buried treasures. You'll be rich. You'll be famous. And you will not be exploited. What is your answer, Jaime Quinn? I must go."

"I don't know."

"I see." Gallanos nodded. "Call this number tonight," he said. "Eventually, even midway over the Atlantic, you'll be put through to my plane. I will await your decision."

Then he was gone.

Jaime was alone in the study. It was as if the whole thing had not actually occurred. Charlotte entered a moment later. Jaime had sunk into one of the large chairs.

"Jaime?" Charlotte's eyes were bright and expectant.

"He wants me to go to Spain," Jaime said wonderously. "Dak Gallanos wants me to show his new line of clothing."

"And? Are you?"

"He said I'd become rich." Jaime laughed, shaking her head in disbelief. "And famous."

"What did you tell him, Jaime?" Charlotte was coming forward. "You accepted, didn't you?"

"I couldn't decide."

"But you must take this chance, Jaime . . . you simply must!"

"I don't know . . . there's Reeve . . . he—"

"Jaime," Charlotte said, "I can't let you pass up this opportunity. There's something I must tell you.

Reeve is in very deep financial trouble. His career is on the line. Walking out of the film that way—well, it's created a chain reaction of havoc. If you have the opportunity to make money, it would release Reeve from an immense burden. He needs the space himself to deal with these issues. I know I said I wouldn't meddle..."

"Why didn't he tell me?" Jaime asked, stricken.

"Because he loves you. And he's proud. He has always had things his way, and this is...well it's not easy for him."

"Thank you, Charlotte, for being honest."

"It's not that you'd be apart from Reeve forever."

"No, no, of course I wouldn't. It would be only a few days at the most."

Charlotte smiled at Jaime. "Darling girl, you are about to change the direction of your entire life."

Before Jaime could respond, there was a knock on the door.

A guest was distraught. Clumsy bad luck and a drink too many had contributed to the disaster. A fine Chinese vase had been shattered. Charlotte forgot about Jaime, rushing off with the guest to assess the financial damage.

The room was very quiet, with only the faintest sounds of the party seeping into the stillness. Jaime looked down at the card with Gallanos's name and the number she was to call.

She dialed and the phone rang twice. A man answered. She didn't catch what he said the first time. His voice was curt and official sounding, a man who was interrupted in the middle of something more important. "Yes?" he said again. "Hello?"

Jaime said nothing, and the phone went dead on the other end.

Her pulse raced, her arms and legs tingling. She was weak, her muscles having turned to rubber. Short of breath, her whole system was in a state of chaos. Almost desperately, she reached for the chair by the desk and eased herself into it. Then, with a sudden and decisive movement, she dragged the phone in front of her and quickly dialed an Idaho number.

When she heard Pat's voice, her eyes closed in relief.

"Pat," she said, "it's me ... Jaime." The identification was for herself, a reassurance of her own existence.

"Well, girl ... it's good to hear your voice."

He sounded sleepy, and Jaime realized he must have been sleeping.

"I woke you."

"Just dropped off a bit. Not in bed yet. How are you, Jaime?"

Jaime ignored the question, asking instead, "Jade—how's she doing?" If she had called her mother directly, she never would have gotten the truth.

"She's still doing fine, Jaime. Not as well as before, maybe, but the operation's been set. I was going to call you tomorrow, tell you about it. She's going to be just fine after that. Don't you worry."

"Is she still working?"

"Well, yes. And no. Thing is, hasn't been much work to do. Had us a whale of a storm three days ago, then got another three feet dumped on us yesterday, and it was snowing to beat the band all afternoon. Nothing's getting by on the roads. Tomorrow they'll have the snowblowers out. That'll help some. But still, there's the avalanche warning out and we're not supposed to let normal traffic through."

It was an old story to Jaime. She heard Pat's news like a worn-out recording and saw past the words to the reality. The café stove would be cold, pots empty. Jade would stare out the front window into the white landscape, waiting for things to change. Waiting for the snow to stop, for the roads to clear, for customers to come, for the money to accumulate, for the ranch to be built, for Grady to come home to her.

"When's the operation?" Jaime asked.

"Week and a half."

"I'll be there," Jaime said.

There was no hesitation the next time she dialed the number Gallanos had left. "Tell Mr. Gallanos, Jaime Quinn's decided to take him up on his offer."

Chapter Ten

Reeve was standing by the bedroom window, his back to her as she closed the suitcase.

"If it's the money...I told you I'll get it for you."

Jaime sat on the end of the bed. There was only a half hour before Gallanos's limousine would be there to take her to the airport. In ten hours she would be in Spain, her life changed irrevocably. It was paramount that she change, move forward. She would not be Jade, waiting at a window, waiting for a man. Waiting.

She looked across the room to Reeve. "It's not the money," she said, truthfully. Of course, if it had been a financial matter, her response would have been the same. After what Charlotte had told her, the last thing Jaime wanted to do was to burden Reeve with any more responsibility. Wasn't it for her sake he had put himself in this jeopardy?

"Then why?" He looked over his shoulder at her. "I thought we had an understanding."

"Reeve," Jaime said, "it's not the money. It's not. It isn't even the idea of all the fame—"

"No?" At the word, he had spun around and now faced her directly. "Gallanos is a star maker. Fame and fortune are his first and middle names. You're going to tell me this is for charity?"

"Maybe. I'm my own charity. I never had anything of my own, Reeve. If I died this moment, I would have never accomplished a thing besides chopping onions and carrots."

"The skate deal—"

"Is your deal. Not mine. They didn't know who the hell I was, and still don't, for the most part. I'm just an appendage. You think I don't know how people are looking at it? People still think I'm doing the Cinderella role because I'm sleeping with you." She had risen and was walking toward the bathroom. She went in, splashed cold water on her face and returned, almost without a pause.

"When they see you skate they'll know the truth."

"Reeve…" Jaime said, shaking her head, "it *is* the truth! I got that role because—besides the fact that we love each other—I'm sleeping with you. But with Gallanos it's entirely different. He offered me this deal because of *me*."

Lupe knocked on the door; the limousine had arrived.

"It's time to go," Jaime said, standing. Her eyes felt heavy with unspilled tears as she said, "It's only going to be for a few days. I'll be back before you've even missed me."

He picked up her suitcase and started toward the door.

"Reeve..."

He stopped, but didn't turn. Jaime could feel his anger, his refusal to understand the job as a symbol, not as a lifetime commitment to a frivolous career in the public limelight.

"Don't do this...please. I love you. I remember what counts. I do. I'll never forget that. But this is for me, and I haven't had much that's ever been for me. Maybe recently, what you've given me, and Charlotte. But this is something I'm giving myself. And it makes me feel good to know I can do that."

"Sorry. I wasn't thinking in terms of you. I was thinking in terms of us," Reeve said. He continued walking.

Jaime followed. Together they approached the waiting car. The driver opened the trunk and put the suitcase inside. Reeve helped her into the back seat. Before he closed the door, he leaned inside. "I love you, Jaime. I'm not being selfish, really, no matter how it may look. I just see ahead. I've been down that road." He kissed her softly, then shut the door.

She waved from the back window as the car turned in the circular driveway, but Reeve was already gone.

Spain was magical and exciting. They shot the fashion layout in a small village along the coast. It was a medieval town, the plaza still cobbled in gray stone, a fountain in its center sending up spray that caught the light, making rainbows and crystals from ordinary droplets. Gallanos's crew had taken over a large semi-restored castle. Parts of it dated back twelve hundred years. A world-class chef had joined the entourage, and dinners were held in an enormous baronial dining hall, complete with heavy tapestries depicting scenes of courtly love and religious allegory. Standard-bearing flags relating to bygone military campaigns extended twenty feet above their heads as they dined. Off to the side, the hollow forms of knights' armour stood in mute attendance while a guitarist played soulful Iberian songs.

Over each enterprise, Dak Gallanos presided like a modern-day king. Elegance, punctuality and thoroughness were clearly the watchwords by which he lived his life, and he demanded these standards from his associates. But the rewards for the minions of Dak Gallanos were great.

Jaime's room was on the third floor, in a large turret, modernized with an attached bathroom. The heavy, carved furniture was authentic to a period from five hundred years ago. Covering the stone floor was a slightly frayed but obviously valuable Oriental carpet from Turkey, dating back to the Crusades. From her window, Jaime could look out over the plaza and across the square to the cathedral, an imposing structure as large as the castle. She felt like a queen. She was treated royally. She was a star.

The fashions she modeled were romantic and elegant. Given her recent education in fashion by Charlotte, Jaime felt they were sure to be an instant commercial success. She was photographed against the backdrop of the ocean and standing in the spray of the fountain. There was even a picture of her on top of a red tile roof, the sun blazing behind her and a bird flying forward over her shoulder into the camera's lens. A freak shot, but spectacular. Gallanos supervised every angle, and tended to each fold of her gown himself; there was no detail too minute to evade his attention. He advised the makeup artists and redid the work of the hair stylist, even rearranged potted plants seen as no more than a background blur, until all elements agreed with his vision.

He was very pleased with Jaime.

"You have depth," he told her several times. Then, "You have excitement. Immediacy. Mystery."

After dinner one night he took her aside. "I am going to do a film. You would be perfect for the lead role. It would make you into an international star," he said. "Think about it."

She did think about it. She thought all day and all night about what it would be like to continue this life she was now leading.

It took a bit of effort to arrange a call to the United States. She called Pat first, to check on Jade. She heard the reluctance in his voice to admit the truth: Jade's condition was in a decline again. "I'll be there for the operation," she said.

Then she called Reeve. Charlotte answered. "It's Jaime, Charlotte—is Reeve there?" The connection was poor. There was an echo, and now and then silence as some problem interrupted the cable transmission. Charlotte was excited. She wanted to hear about Jaime, about Gallanos, about everything including what she had for dinner. Intermittently Jaime would manage to ask to speak to Reeve. "Yes, darling...of course...he's just at the piano—"

The telephone went dead.

Jaime attempted to replace the call. It took half the night until she accepted the situation as being completely hopeless.

Two days later she was exhausted, but exhilarated with a sense of personal accomplishment as she boarded the private jet belonging to Dak Gallanos. She could barely wait to be with Reeve again. And the stories she had to tell him!

Reeve had drawn a welcome home sign himself and had put it across the front door. The limousine had no sooner pulled up than Reeve threw open the door to the house and ran out.

With the same heedless energy, Jaime jumped from the car and into his arms.

He lifted her, swinging her around as if they were doing a routine on skates. "I love you," she said, crying and laughing at the same time.

"I love you," he said, kissing her deeply. "You were gone a lifetime. But you're here again, here again."

"You aren't angry with me?" she asked, searching his eyes as he lowered her to the pavement.

"You're back, that's all that matters."

"Charlotte told you I called?" Jaime asked, walking to the house with him.

Reeve nodded. "She said she got cut off. I could have dynamited the phone company."

"I tried and tried to get back to you. It was impossible."

Reeve said nothing.

"Reeve?"

"Yes, you tried to get back to me."

"Wait a minute. Don't you believe me?"

"Jaime...it doesn't matter. I told you. You're here, that's all that counts."

"Wait," Jaime said, and stopped. He paused, the suitcase suspended at his side. "I did try to call you. I thought of you constantly. I wanted to share everything with you, everything—"

"Then don't leave me again. That's the one way we'll share everything."

He was on his way again, striding ahead of her, and she followed after, knowing that no matter what he had said, he was hurt or angry or perhaps both.

"I'd go with you if I could," Reeve said. His face was drawn and there was no sign of his usual tan left, the color drained under countless hours, days, weeks of fluorescent-lighted rooms filled with attorneys and accountants.

"It's okay," Jaime said. "It'll just mean sitting in a waiting room. I'm sure it's all going to be all right. The operation will go fine."

"It will," Reeve said, and kissed her fingers.

"And you?" Jaime asked, clasping his hands in hers. "You look exhausted. And you won't tell me anything about the Rome thing." Even she had begun to use Charlotte's euphemism.

"It will all be over soon."

"Over? Bad or good, over?"

"Good," he said, and smiled. Only it was a sad smile, and did nothing to alleviate Jaime's sense of foreboding.

"Why do I have the feeling that that kind of 'good' is the same as my mother's?"

"Good's just good."

"Uh-uh," Jaime objected. "Good to Jade is whatever happens, happens for the best. That could mean a cyclone ripping through your living room is actually a blessing in disguise."

Reeve smiled crookedly. "Maybe she's right."

"Maybe you're both crazy."

"Probably," Reeve said. "Time will tell."

"I hate time," Jaime said. "I don't want to live in the past or the future. I want only now, the present. I don't want my life measured out in dribs and drabs," she finished. It was a vehement little speech, and it surprised even her.

The following day, shortly after two o'clock in the afternoon, Jaime was able to call Reeve and say. "She's okay. The operation went great. My mother's going to be okay."

To which Reeve replied, "I'm sorry, I can't hear—"

In her excitement, the message had come out garbled. She brushed her wrist over a tear-stained face and restated her good news.

Reeve was glad for her, he said. Their conversation was cut short, as she was on the hospital's much-coveted pay phone. It was only after they had said their goodbyes, after her initial flood of relieved hysteria had abated, that Jaime realized Reeve had not sounded happy.

She took herself off to the rink by the lodge, and spent three hours working off tension. When she returned to Los Angeles, she and Reeve would get down to serious practice. She longed for him, for his arms around her, for the taste of his mouth. God, she loved the man!

Pat insisted they celebrate Jade's successful operation with an expensive dinner at the Christiana in Ketchem. It was the only time Jaime could ever recall the café being closed. At dinner she laughed, saying that if Jade wasn't sedated, she'd be out of bed and serving pot roast that very moment.

Maybe it was the wine. Between the two of them, she and Pat had polished off two bottles of a fine cabernet, but Pat broke into sobs over his lobster.

The waiter was concerned. Jaime assured him it wasn't the food; this was how Pat expressed happiness.

Further sated on cheesecake, she and Pat left the restaurant, intermittently laughing and crying, proclaiming resolutions for the future. Large fluffballs of snow were dropping, catching in Jaime's black hair and shining beneath the street lamps like fallen stars. It seemed a magical night, blessed in every way. Jaime began to sing a Christmas song and Pat joined her.

It was Pat who saw it first. He stopped singing midway through "It came upon a Midnight Clear" his voice trailing away.

He stood stock-still, his back to Jaime, and stared down at a newspaper vending machine. Staggering forward a couple of steps, the big man bent down closer to the clear plastic, as if in his inebriated state he had thought his vision mistaken.

"Pat?"

Slowly, Pat Griffen straightened himself. He had worn his only suit, a navy, polyester and wool blend that was no longer in the height of fashion, and over it a dark overcoat that had seen better days. Pat was not a formal man, and earlier Jaime had complimented him, knowing that he had gone to the trouble for Jade's sake. She knew he had meant to make a good impression on the hospital staff, as if in some way, Jade's association with fashionable people might ensure her better care.

It took him forever to turn back to her.

"What is it? What's the matter?" Jaime tried to push past him. A feeling of dread had taken its hold over her. Her thoughts turned immediately to Jade. But Jade's health would never have made the front page of any newspaper.

Pat held her arm, stopping her. "Jaime," he said, the voice only partially slurred now. Reality had shaken him out of his stupor. "Jaime...you don't know if it's the truth. Now, don't go getting crazy on me..."

At that, Jaime freed herself and pushed her way past him to look through the clear plastic.

It wasn't the headline story; that was something in San Salvador. What Pat had responded to was further down the page, the bold-captioned headline shouting out misfortune. Beneath, and off to the side, was a small photo of Reeve's smiling face.

"Movie Star Liable for Ten Million Dollar Film Walkout."

Jaime dove into her purse for change, dropped the three dimes into the coin slot and withdrew the newspaper. Her eyes flew over the print. With heart pounding like an out-of-control jack hammer, she read the account of Reeve's trial.

No one had told her.

Why? Why hadn't Charlotte, who had been so quick to confide in her before, mentioned what was really going on?

All the time she had thought he was just in meetings, but there had been an actual trial. The judge had given his decision that morning. Reeve was liable for damages. The producers of the film had originally sought thirty million dollars—treble damages, awardable in the State of California. Reeve was said to have escaped easily. Easily! Jaime knew he would have very little left.

His attorneys were outraged. Their client would have negotiated; Reeve Ferris wanted time to complete another project, then he would return to the film. There was, his defense claimed, ample additional scenes to shoot in his absence. The prosecution refuted the claim, saying that the director's system was to film in sequence.

In one paragraph, there was a mention of Jaime. She was represented as a beautiful international model, with whom Reeve Ferris had become smitten, a woman who was the subsequent cause of his financial collapse.

The night air was sharp on Jaime's lungs as she took in great gulps to compensate for the experience of light-headedness.

"Oh God...Reeve..."

Pat's arm was around her.

"Girl, you don't know..."

"It's all in there," she said. "It's true. I know it's true. God, he must hate me."

"No, no...no one's gonna ever hate my girl."

Jaime felt her legs losing strength. Wobbling precariously, she leaned into Pat. His arms drew around her just as she felt herself sinking into the pavement.

Chapter Eleven

As Jaime moved onto the ice she felt the stares directed her way. Everyone, from the lowliest gofer to the director of the television production company, was curious to view the femme fatale responsible for the financial downfall of America's most beloved male film idol.

The true picture, that which Jaime carried of herself—a young woman in faded jeans, slinging hash to truckers at a whistle-stop café—was out of sync with the public's fantasy of the dark-haired sex siren. If they only knew, she thought, and skated forward to where some of the others in the skating corps were already gathered. Besides Jaime and Reeve, the cast consisted of forty chorus members and twelve principal skaters.

Reeve was in the center of the rink, conferring with the choreographer, a man renowned for his work on the New York stage and for putting together some of Las Vegas's most spectacular floor shows. Like Jaime, Reeve had not yet changed into his full costume. He wore black practice pants fashioned of a lightweight nylon material, over which flowed the elaborately embroidered tunic top of white and gold, to be worn for the actual filming. It was necessary for him to become comfortable with his movements as restricted by the costume.

The choreographer saw Jaime gliding forward. He gave a bob of his head in greeting. Giving Reeve a pat on the back, he separated himself from their intimate exchange and became accessible to the cast and crew again.

"We're going to take the third act one more time from the top," the choreographer said into a microphone clipped to his collar. "The audience is going to be let in uh . . ." checking his watch " . . . in exactly forty minutes. Let's make this perfect now. Everyone."

Jaime was already in partial makeup and, like Reeve, wore a portion of her costume, a three-quarter length tulle skirt, pink with silver glitter and sequins. She was a girl shot through and through with fairy dust, or so it was to appear to the audience.

"Let's make magic!" called the choreographer. He backed off the ice and became a blur in the shadows.

The camera director, perched high on a camera dolly, communicated with the light and sound booth via a microphone attached to headphones.

The proper lights were on, suspended from the overhead grid. The follow spots were positioned for the first strain of music, ready to capture Jaime's first movement.

From giant speakers, great, sweeping strains of violins and horns and percussion instruments filled the cavernous space of the Los Angeles Sports Arena. A thirty-piece union orchestra would be used for the actual performance before an audience. The members were already assembled in a backstage rehearsal room, their instruments pre-tuned. With the conductor, they were perfecting any rough passages. These musicians would play along with the tape, now sounding over the speakers, which had been prepared earlier in a studio. It was too expensive to leave anything to chance.

Jaime took her position. Huge butterflies batted against the walls of her stomach.

Reeve moved twenty feet away, finding his spot on the ice.

It was hard for Jaime to believe all of it was actually happening. Until that moment, it had all been a living fantasy, a hazy dream from which she would not have been surprised to have awakened. Even after the weeks of practicing every day with Reeve, the payoff for all their effort had continued to seem elusive. But this was real. As Charlotte had said not long before, Jaime's life was being irrevocably altered. *But at the expense of the man she loved.*

It was this certainty that tainted the experience, which otherwise would have been a moment of personal triumph.

There was simply nothing she could do at that point to save the situation that she had brought about. The money for Jade's operation had already been received "up-front," as stipulated in her contract. That money had been spent to cover hospitalization costs, and to satisfy the deficit in the café's ordinary operating expense.

Her life had become a tangled web. To choose between her mother's life and the financial welfare of the man she loved more than her own life, was a proposition dooming her to heartache.

And to think that once she had actually coveted personal power, the chance to be the center of other people's universes.

Reeve waved to her, and she raised her hand and signaled back. They both smiled. Brave, empty little smiles. Great tragedy might bring people closer together, but this sort of whittling away, day after day, at the foundation of people's lives, leached the energy from passion.

The director made his signal. The rehearsal was in progress. In another hour, it would all be for real.

Jaime was perpetual motion. She came out of a scratch spin, immediately gliding to Reeve, who held her waist only briefly until she broke away and did a back crossover—a perfect camel spin, with her body leaning forward, the free leg stretched even before the spin was actually centered.

Reeve responded with a flying camel. The thrust of his body propelled him into the air. His free leg swung wide of his body, the body flat in the air with both the arms and the legs fully stretched. He landed perfectly, outside the spiral he had drawn with his skate, then went into his sit spin.

The music soared. Jaime counted, then leaped. Reeve was there to catch her. She was suspended in air, the tulle skirt floating about her like a pink cloud beneath the colored lights.

There were beads of sweat on Reeve's forehead. She felt his arms trembling slightly, and noted the strain of his jawline.

Suddenly she was no longer airborne, but falling, slipping out of Reeve's grasp and onto the ice.

She broke the fall just in time, her arm reaching out at a safe angle.

A voice in shadows yelled, "Cut! Hold it!"

The overhead lights were "killed," and there was a sudden silence as the music came to an abrupt end; a universal fall from grace into a bleak existence. The temperature cooled immediately.

"You all right?"

Someone was speaking to Jaime. She was looking at Reeve, trying to make out his expression.

"Are you hurt?"

It was the director. Jaime looked his way, but the image of Reeve's face remained strangely superimposed over the other man's questioning expression.

"Fine," Jaime responded distractedly to the concern over her welfare. "I'm okay, really."

The director had reached Jaime, but she had no time for him. Instead, she went after Reeve, hurrying to catch him before he had a chance to shut her out of the dressing room.

Since the trial, he had shared less of himself with her. He told her it was fatigue; there were still meetings with financial consultants as property and other commercial holdings were set up for liquidation to satisfy the court order. Jaime felt the distance between them growing wider.

Even their lovemaking had dwindled to what Jaime felt were mere physical urges on Reeve's part rather than an emotional desire to connect with the woman he loved and who loved him. With all her heart Jaime loved him, and it was driving her mad that she was unable to make things better between them.

When she discussed the matter of their subtle estrangement with Charlotte, Charlotte treated Reeve's behavior as no more than a passing mood, too inconsequential to merit serious discussion.

Charlotte, herself, seemed particularly preoccupied lately; in fact, there seemed to be an element of secretiveness in Charlotte's present behavior.

Reeve was just at his dressing room door when Jaime reached him. Neither of them removed their skates and their progress over the carpeting, laid to protect their blades, had been clumsy and slow, in direct contrast to the high emotional state prompting Reeve's walkout.

"Reeve!" Jaime called.

He stopped. Without looking at her, he waited with an air of weary politeness. A brass plaque bearing his name was affixed to the door. His hand remained poised on the doorknob, ready to turn the handle and disappear into his private place.

"Are you all right?" she asked, padding awkwardly up to him on her skates.

"That should be my question to you, don't you think?" Reeve passed on into his dressing room. Jaime followed, not to be put off by his brusqueness.

"I'm okay, I'm fine," she answered. She closed the door and leaned her back against it, watching him.

Wearily, he sat himself down on the metal folding chair in front of his makeup mirror. The lights surrounding the mirror blazed.

"I'm sorry, Jaime." He looked up, the blue eyes potent as always, magical eyes that could pull at her heart in any situation; only now they were clouded, their brilliance muted by inner turbulence. "This is to be your moment. And I'm spoiling it."

"It's our moment," she said. "Ours," she emphasized again. "Oh, Reeve...this has got to stop." She went to him and sank to her knees, taking his hands, which were limp at his sides, into her own. "We love each other."

She had returned to Los Angeles two days after Jade's operation. Pat had insisted she leave Paradise. In truth, Jaime knew it was more for his own sake, than for hers that she had been banished from Jade's side. He wanted Jade to depend more upon him. This was his chance. And this, Pat had said, was her chance at a life she had missed before. "High time people 'round here started living the lives they were meant to live, full out. Enough of this just plain existing..."

Reeve had greeted her at the airport with a kiss. But Jaime had recognized the change immediately; something had gone out of him. In the space of her brief absence, a light that had been there before had been extinguished. It was as if his inner sun had grown cold and withered during the long legal proceedings.

Fortunately, the furious pace of their rehearsal period following Jaime's return to Los Angeles provided a diversion from the underlying mood of melancholy that might otherwise have been unbearable.

Jaime comforted herself by dredging up some of Jade's old sayings. Such as, "Losing a fortune is the same as losing someone you love very much. It takes the passing of time to heal."

Now, on her knees in the arena's dressing room, Jaime wracked her brain to come up with some appropriate aphorism to make things better for Reeve.

It was unnecessary. Reeve took the initiative from her.

"Come on," he said, standing. He took her hand, and pulled her up to him. He kissed her fingers, just as he would do in their choreographed routine. "The little kitchen girl is about to become the beautiful Cinderella."

"And my Prince...who is he to become?" she asked.

"Himself," Reeve answered. "At long last."

There was a knock at the dressing room door. "Makeup," the voice announced.

"Just a minute," Reeve called back over his shoulder.

"This is your time, Jaime. Go with it, take all the glory."

He didn't add, *Because glory is fleeting,* but Jaime knew it was what he meant.

"Is it money?" she asked, wanting to clear the air immediately before bad moments could build one upon the other. "Losing everything? I know it might matter to you. Of course it would. Anyone would feel that way. But I want you to know it makes no difference to me." She had stopped in the middle of the busy terminal to deliver her speech. She said it earnestly, looking him straight in the eye, disallowing him any chance to doubt her sincerity. "I love you rich or poor. I loved you when things were better. And in a way, I love you even more now that things are worse. I'm no stranger to poverty and I can deal with it. I'll teach you, too. All I want is for us to be with each other."

Reeve smiled slightly. She couldn't quite fathom the meaning of his expression. Ironic, faintly mocking, yet containing tenderness, his glance fell gently upon her as he ran a crooked finger lightly along the side of her face, careful not to disturb her makeup.

"Is that really what you want?" he asked her.

"Yes. Oh, yes..." she responded at once, certain of her answer.

"Then that's what you'll have. At least I can give you that," he said, but there was little resolution behind his words. To Jaime he sounded like a man agreeing to take a trip for which there was no means of transportation.

Jaime threw herself against him, her arms tight around his neck. "I don't know if I want it anymore," she said. "I'm frightened, Reeve. Really frightened."

Reeve laughed, kissing her on the nose, and said, "Jitters. The sign of true talent."

"Thanks," she said, but felt no better. They kissed once again, and then she left Reeve to return to her own dressing room for the finishing touches of makeup and to slip into the rest of her costume.

On the way down the hall, she passed Charlotte. It was only then, as Charlotte smiled and wished her well, that Jaime suspected that the chilling of her soul had nothing to do with stage fright and everything to do with an unknown future.

"No," Jaime said.

"You sound very decided." Charlotte's voice rose in a slight drawl, a tone Jaime had come to recognize as annoyance.

"I am, absolutely."

The two women were on the floor, wrapping presents in the glow of the Christmas tree Jaime and Reeve had decorated the previous night. The heady scent of flower bouquets received after the skating telecast competed with the pine's astringent fragrance for supremacy.

"Why are you so stubborn?" Charlotte asked. She looked up, having finished wrapping another gift, a robe for Lupe. "God only knows why Reeve had to spend that much money on a servant," Charlotte said, shaking her head as she tossed the present aside. "It isn't as if he's exactly rolling in dough these days." She looked at Jaime, her blue eyes a direct challenge. "Why?" she asked again, "Why are you so intent on returning to that terrible place, when you can have the world?"

"It's what we want."

"Really?" Charlotte commented dryly.

Obviously Jaime's choice of the pronoun "we" had done nothing to lift Charlotte's mood; nevertheless, Jaime would not be dissuaded. "Reeve and I want to be together. We want to live our lives, Charlotte. We don't need all of this—"

"Good!" Charlotte snapped.

She stood and, thrusting both her hands deep into the pockets of her tailored slacks, looked down at Jaime.

"That's good to hear, dear. I can't tell you…a great relief. Because there isn't going to be *all of this* much longer. Not unless Reeve decides to come to his senses. And you, too." Charlotte turned and walked away. She stopped in a shadow, and a cold disembodied voice spoke words that Jaime could not discount as being untrue.

"Be reasonable, Jaime. My son is bewitched by this foolish idea that he can give up everything that he is and become someone else entirely. He'll merely drop out, and pitch camp in that bump-on-a-road town, which someone with an absurd sense of black humor chose to name Paradise. It is not paradise. It's purgatory."

"Some people like it," Jaime defended.

"Do you?" Charlotte asked bluntly.

Jaime was still.

"Didn't you enjoy Spain? Didn't you enjoy it here in L.A.? The shops on Rodeo Drive? Ma Maison? Dinner at the Bistro? Jaime?"

"Yes," Jaime whispered truthfully. She stared down at the gilt paper she had just cut to wrap another gift for Reeve.

"You have offers for a career in the entertainment business coming out of your ears. Commercials. That series—they want you for a series, Jaime. Do you know how much money that means?"

Yes, Jaime was aware of the money, and of more. Elliot Cohen had explained everything to her. Several times.

The Cinderella and the Prince ice extravanganza had been aired as a pre-Christmas family telecast. It was the perfect show for the perfect season, and was lauded by critics and public alike for championing quality family entertainment. Given Reeve's recent financial problems, it also made him appear as a generous, wholesome man, devoting himself to the improvement of general humanity at his own expense. After all, he might have gone back to the film deal. As for Jaime, she was no longer viewed as the wicked seductress. Rather, she was now perceived as the incarnation of Cinderella herself—a poor, sweet girl who, after much personal travail, had claimed happiness in the arms of America's foremost romantic figure.

Both she and Reeve had become the current darlings of the news media. There were offers for both of them to expand their careers.

"Yes!" Jaime said, reacting at last to Charlotte's badgering. Still in her seated position, she had twisted around to face Charlotte. "Yes, yes, yes! I know, and Reeve knows, that we can do movies and television and all the rest of it. We know that eating out in fancy restaurants is very nice. And I like to wear pretty clothes. I love all of those things, Charlotte! So you're absolutely correct about that.''

Jaime jumped up, borne by some invisible force that she knew might never again visit her if she failed to make rightful use of it now.

Charlotte remained veiled in shadow, a slim, pale outline in her slacks and sweater outfit of cream-colored wool.

Jaime moved closer to her, inexplicably feeling unsafe, as if in not being able to see Charlotte's expression, she was leaving herself open to some danger. At that moment, Charlotte had undergone a mythic transformation. She was, in Jaime's current emotional state, the ghost of every past desire Jaime had ever entertained, come to taunt her, come to lure her.

Jaime drew in a breath. "All of those things are fine, but you can't turn them off. They have a funny way of taking on lives of their own and they steal away the person you are.''

"I don't know what you're talking about," Charlotte said from the shadows.

"I know you don't. Anyway, it's the way Reeve and I feel. We both want to go back. Back to the bump-in-the-road town.''

As Jaime spoke, Charlotte had faded farther back into the dusky recess of the room, her powers perhaps temporarily vanquished beneath the weight of Jaime's rebuttal.

Glittering like an eye, Charlotte's immense ring flashed at Jaime from the dark.

"Nicely said. But, oh, how wrong you are, my dear. I know human nature. It is romantic and commendable, your little dream of starting over with a sweet grass-roots life. But that's all it is—just a dream. You'll never make it, Jaime."

"Well, in my family we happen to believe in dreams," Jaime returned defiantly, and with a degree of surprise. It was as if someone else, some passionately assured person had spoken from within her own body. Behind her, Jaime could imagine the presence of Jade and all of Jade's ancestors, those believers of the improbable and impossible.

"Yes," Charlotte said, "your family would. Why not? They had nothing else to do but hold on to their little fantasies of better times. Fantasies don't cost anything. But you, Jaime, you can have everything . . . the real thing. Don't throw it away."

Having said her piece, Charlotte excused herself, leaving Jaime to wrap the remaining gifts alone. She was sitting by the fireplace, her knees pulled up beneath her chin, when Reeve returned.

"Hi!" he said, his voice carrying from the foyer. "I'm home. Anybody around?"

"In here," Jaime called over her shoulder.

He entered, a smile on his handsome face. In his arms, he carried a stack of boxes, the smallest ones teetering precariously on top as he crossed the room to where she was sitting.

Lowering himself to one knee, he set his burden on the carpet by the tree. "If I'm going out, I'm at least going out in style," he said. He looked up, merriment dancing in his eyes. "As of today, I'm paid up."

"The ten million?"

Reeve nodded, then shrugged. "Easy come, easy go. What can I tell you?"

Jaime sighed, looked away from him, into the fire. "You could get it back," she said resolutely.

"What? The money?" Reeve walked over to her. Kneeling behind her, he rubbed her neck, then bent to kiss her right ear. Nibbling lightly, he said, "What's money when I have this?"

"They aren't the same," Jaime returned. "Having one doesn't necessarily mean you can't have the other."

He leaned far over to the side and gently urged her to lie on the floor with him. His hand went to the soft mound of her breast and he stroked. Almost instantly her nipple stiffened to a hard point.

"I have you. And I have myself," Reeve said, rolling her over on top of him.

"You do," Jaime concurred. "That you certainly do."

Her mouth parted and his tongue found hers. Jaime closed her eyes, but even so the firelight danced against her lids. The dancing light punctuated the delight rising from her loins, expanding into her belly, and making her gasp.

Already she was forgetting Charlotte's upsetting caveat.

Reeve's hand roamed restlessly over her jeans. She felt him harden beneath her, and teasing him, she moved her pelvis against his in a slow, provocative grind.

In response to the deliberate teasing, he began to work the bottom of her sweater upward, until, with some help from her, it was peeled off entirely.

Her breasts were ready for him, full and heavy in the thin lace bra and his tongue danced upon the point of each nipple.

Jaime let out a small cry, not out of passion, but from a delight that transcended even the physical pleasure she experienced at his touch. She was so happy with him, happy in a way she had never dreamed would be possible in this world. It was the kind of joy people fantasized about and prayed for on their knees, but never truly expected to have. Fulfillment was hers now, with Reeve; and as she lay with him in the glow of the Christmas tree, she could not imagine a hereafter to surpass this immediate sense of wholeness.

Reeve had slipped easily out of his clothes, which he tossed to the side. From where she lay on her back, she looked up at him. The firelight flickered against his skin. In the glow, the contours of his body appeared luminous, and she reached out to run her fingers down the smooth, flat incline of his stomach. The stomach muscles rippled slightly, and beneath there was a sudden urge of response to her touch. He had the body of a man born to be an athlete: strong limbs, straight and long, shoulders proportionate to his height.

Reeve moved against her again, guiding her hand to his body. He kissed her, his tongue moving in the same suggestive way as her hand. Neither of them could last much longer that way, and Reeve drew slightly away, working his tongue between the valley of her breasts.

Jaime arched against him, and he moved lower, with every inch becoming more completely her master.

His fingers moved to her waist. There was the slight popping sound of a snap being released, then the sinuous whirring of her zipper being lowered. The material was pushed aside.

His mouth was hot against her stomach; inwardly, she burned even more intensely and whimpered as he slipped his hand beneath the nylon binding. With the flat of his hand he pressed hard against her femininity, increasing the pressure building within her.

It only took a second to slide off her jeans, yet in her aroused state it seemed an eternity until she was free of all constricting material.

Reeve pulled her astride him. "You're beautiful," he said, in wonderment.

It was, she felt, even at that moment, a time that could never come again. With the tree over them, and the surrounding scent of flowers pervading the atmosphere, they were in a secret, magical glade. It was very still.

"I love you," she said.

The fire crackled, sending sparks against the wire mesh.

He lifted her up, then lowered her to fit over him.

Jaime closed her eyes as he began to move.

The lights from the tree blinked off and on, creating a kaleidoscope of soft, colored pools of light on their skin. Encircling her waist with his hands, Reeve moved her with him. Amid the changing shadows cast by the fire, with the mysterious reflection of the firelight in Reeve's hair, they were secure in the circle of their love.

"Everything else may change, but for us, it will always be like this," Reeve whispered.

Jaime leaned to kiss him. A shadow formed, where her body blocked out the light, and for a second Jaime started.

"What's wrong?" Reeve asked, alarm for her welfare causing him to tighten his hold on her. "Jaime—you're shivering."

He averted her kiss and looked into her face for the answer she did not volunteer.

"I was frightened for a moment. It was nothing." Her eyes drifted to where Charlotte had stood earlier, to a place where the light could not reach.

Reeve followed her gaze. "What?" he asked. "Did you hear something? See something?"

"No. No, there's nothing there. It was just my imagination," she said.

"Santa Claus?" Reeve wore a half smile. He was at a loss to understand what she herself could not.

"Santa, yes . . ." Jaime said.

"Wait until the morning," Reeve said. "Wait until you see what I've bought for you. It's the most beautiful—"

Jaime's hand flew to his lips and she pressed her fingers to silence him. It was as if for a moment, she had heard Charlotte again, her warning that without wealth and material possessions they could never be happy.

"This is all I want, all I need," Jaime said.

They made love with a fury, the early tenderness vanished. Three times he brought her to that place where only sensation existed. The final time, he joined her, trembling from the power of their union.

"Jaime?" he whispered afterward.

She lay against his chest, her face turned toward the fire where only embers remained. His heart was still racing. With her ear pressed against him, she could hear all the sounds of his body.

"Are they gone now, Jaime? Are the demons gone now?"

She shifted her face to the other direction, and through her partially drawn lashes, looked at the gathering darkness waiting to claim even more of the waning light.

"Yes," she said. "The demons have fled."

She closed her eyes then, shutting off a tear. It was the only time she had ever lied to Reeve.

Chapter Twelve

January First. The date not only marked a new year, it also heralded a new life for Jaime and Reeve. They were to begin it in the presence of Charlotte, who had prepared a celebratory meal at her house in keeping with the calendar date.

Jaime, Reeve and Charlotte sat at the polished oval table in Charlotte's formal dining room. It would not have surprised Jaime if a liveried footman in a white powdered wig had stepped into the room.

Jaime's seat faced the bank of windows that were elaborately draped in light blue velveteen, the draperies drawn to the side and held in position by golden braid with tassels at the ends. It was a brisk day, almost wintery by Southern California's generally mild standards, and Charlotte had lit a fire in the dining-room hearth. Beyond the window panes Jaime could see trees bending to the wind. The sky was a clear, honest blue against which groupings of tall white clouds moved in stately clusters. Jaime felt safe and warm, happier at that moment than perhaps she had ever been.

Charlotte's maid had just finished clearing away their dessert dishes. Reeve excused himself and rose to fetch a bottle of champagne he had bought especially for the occasion at hand.

"Reeve," Charlotte said, eyeing the French label and identifying it not so much by quality as by cost, "you shouldn't have."

It had seemed to Jaime, of late, that Charlotte never missed an opportunity to remind Reeve of his fall from financial solvency.

"Which is precisely why I did," Reeve replied lightly and without irritation.

With an expert twist he removed the cork, catching a bit of escaping froth in his own glass, and filled the other two goblets in turn. "I would like to propose a toast," he announced.

Jaime discerned a flicker of apprehension from Charlotte, who was not fond of surprises that she herself did not plan.

Each glass was raised, held in abeyance, while Reeve came around to where Jaime was sitting. With his hand on her shoulder, he said, "With this toast, we officially announce our engagement to be married."

Jaime caught his hand on her shoulder and squeezed his fingers. With silent meaning, he returned the pressure. Their intimate gesture was not lost on Charlotte whose gaze was riveted to their clasp of hands. Her lips were turned down, and when Jaime smiled expectantly, Charlotte quickly came to and made an effort to return the smile with a quick quirk of her lips.

The expression Charlotte arranged on her face only remotely mirrored pleasure.

Still, she said nothing.

Reeve had shifted his position by Jaime's side. "Okay," he said, "are we going to do this?"

Jaime giggled. "If you spill it on me..."

"Hush, you're ruining it. This is a romantic moment."

Somewhat awkwardly, but with the right feeling, they managed to entwine their arms and sip from each other's glasses. They kissed tenderly, lost in their private moment.

Straightening, Reeve poured more champagne for both himself and Jaime.

He walked around to Charlotte, then stopped, the bottle poised in midair. "You haven't had a sip, Charlotte."

Reeve's mother's face was ashen, and she stared straight ahead. "No." She set the glass down.

"And, you haven't said anything."

"You might have warned me." With hollow eyes, Charlotte stared into space.

"Warned you? You had to have known. We're going back to Paradise. Of course we're going to be married."

"But under the circumstances—"

"The circumstances? We're in love with each other," Reeve said.

"But everything's so unsettled. If you were to wait—"

"For what?"

"You can rebuild, Reeve." Charlotte's eyes were brilliant again. "Elliot says if anything you may have grown in stature as far as the public's concerned. Like

Liz Taylor. All her personal traumas only made her more accessible to the public.''

''I don't want to be accessible to the public. All I want is to be accessible to the woman I love. And to myself.''

Jaime had been observing the interchange between mother and son like a spectator at a tennis match, her eyes following the play, back and forth. She was amazed. Always in the past, Reeve had either placated Charlotte's emotional whims, or merely avoided a confrontation. This was partially out of love for her, love mixed with a dollop of pity, knowing she was alone in the world but for him. It had always been better to give in, and one way or the other, Charlotte had always managed to have her way.

Now Charlotte appeared as a petulant child, stunned at being denied her desires. In contrast, Jaime could not help but compare this to her own mother's forthright selflessness.

''When will you be married?'' Charlotte said in a pinched voice.

''Jaime's going home to tell her mother in person. I've an offer on the house, and can't go with her until the papers are all signed and the legal stuff's cleared away. As soon as the house business is finished, I'll fly up, too. We want to be married up there, in a small and private ceremony. The wedding will be for us and for the people we love.''

''I thought you might like to stay at the lodge,'' Jaime said quickly, making it understood that Charlotte was definitely included in the plans.

''The people you love,'' Charlotte muttered softly to herself, but loud enough for the phrase's mournful tone to have its effect. ''If it were true, that you loved me, Reeve...Jaime...you might have discussed your plans with me before this. I feel," she said, and rose from her seat, "that I've been excluded. A cast-off in your lives." Placing her napkin at the side of her plate, she moved from the table, going swiftly from the room.

Jaime started to rise to go after her, but with a gentle touch, Reeve motioned for her to stay.

"She's hurt," Jaime whispered.

"She hurts herself," Reeve said sadly.

The airport bus from Boise let her off in Sun Valley. Pat was there waiting for her, just as she knew he'd be. She waved happily, calling out to him. He responded with a listless nod. He moved forward, having to pick his way through the turmoil of passengers, ski equipment and luggage, to reach her.

Before he had crossed even half the distance to her, Jaime knew something was wrong. It was something bad, very bad.

"It's Jade," Jaime said as soon as he stood before her.

Pat grabbed her two suitcases. "Come on," he said. "Blazer's over there." Jaime followed him over to the new car Pat had bought recently.

"Tell me," Jaime said, her hands thrust deep into her pockets. The temperature had to be close to zero.

"Get on in there," Pat said gruffly, still avoiding her question. "You'll freeze out here and then I'll have a ton of paperwork to do on your dead body."

Jaime climbed into the passenger's seat. Pat threw her suitcases in the back. A moment later he joined her. They drove in silence for a minute.

"She's dying, Jaime."

Jaime looked at him, denial in her eyes. A tear was winding its way down Pat's stubbled face. He made no move to wipe it away. Jaime realized his inner grief was so deep he had lost all consideration for his outward appearance.

Jaime couldn't have spoken had she known what to say. She felt as if she had been hit in the gut.

Pat was going on, anyway, his large, ungloved hands gripping the steering wheel. "Found out for sure this morning," he said.

"Does she know?" Jaime asked finally. She stared straight ahead, dry-eyed, her soul as withered as the frozen landscape outside.

"I think she's always known, Jaime...I think the woman's known even before she went to the doctor and he did those first tests."

"How long's she got—?"

"Six months on the outside. Less, most likely."

"Pain?"

"Pills help a lot. So far."

They drove in silence after that. A few flurries began to drift down. They dissolved on the heated windshield. Pat activated the wipers. Jaime stared at the blades moving back and forth monotonously, their actions ultimately futile against the unlimited resources of nature.

Pat took the turnoff to Paradise. Jaime touched him on the arm. "Pull over for a minute," she said. The Blazer slid hesitantly to the road's edge.

Jaime spoke over the gurgle of the engine. "Her whole life, Pat, she hardly had anything. All she ever really wanted was to see that ranch built."

"Not just her dream," Pat reminded. "It was Grady's." He sounded bitter.

Jaime nodded. She knew it hurt Pat that Jade had never given up on a man who wasn't a tenth the person he was.

"I can't get Grady back for her, but I can see she gets her ranch. At least that'll be something."

Pat looked at her wildly. "Damn..." he said, "to see her face! To see the happiness in that pretty face of hers. What I wouldn't give." His eyes grew misty, and he turned away. With a catch to his voice he said, "I've thought about it. Yeah, I used to think it could be me who gives her the ranch and me who lives there with her. I used to think about it at night. Her and me, sitting out on a porch summer nights. Hear the sheep, the horses—we'd have a few off to the side where we'd have a little corral. Hire some of the Basques, a cou- ple'd come riding in at sunset to tell us something or other—we'd have dinner, talkin' and laughin'." He broke off.

Jaime covered his hand, his knuckles white as he gripped the steering wheel.

"Well, hell..." he said. "Well, hell..."

"You can do it," Jaime said. "You can have that. Maybe not for always, but for a little while," she said. "Maybe just for once, but at least once. For Jade," she said.

Pat turned his head. He was crying openly. "How? You tell me how the hell we can make all that happen, girl. I'll cut out my heart to pay for nails if I thought there'd be enough left over to cover the wood and livestock. There's nothin' I wouldn't do for that woman."

So Jaime told him how it could all come true.

"Damn," Pat said when she had finished. "It could happen. It really could."

"Will," Jaime corrected. "It will happen."

"You sound like your mother, Jaime."

"Yeah? Well, maybe, after all, that's not such a bad thing."

Jaime did not tell Pat or Jade about her plans to marry Reeve. For the time being, it wouldn't have made any difference. She had to focus on Jade's happiness now, not her own.

Jaime called Dak Gallanos from Pat's house. She didn't want Jade to know anything about her plans, for fear they might not turn out.

Her fear that Gallanos might not be as predisposed to furthering her career as he once was turned out to be groundless.

"I'm delighted that you called me," he said. "And I'm aware that you could have called many other people. You were a great hit on that television special. For my clothing line . . . well, I needn't tell you again the sensation you've made in the photo layout. There is something," Gallanos told her, "very important, very big for you. A film. It is being shot in Paris and in Rome. It's my own company, but I try to keep a low profile in its operation."

The following day, he called her back. "The part is yours," Gallanos said. "I had to speak to the director first. He agreed after seeing your pictures you have the right quality. He is very excited. And so am I. Yes, and the money you wanted? It's quite a lot."

"I'm not doing this for the stardom," she said. "I must have the money."

"Yes," Gallanos said. "It's yours."

Jaime was shaking when she put down the receiver. Pat stood several feet away. His face was white, his eyes fearful.

"Two hundred and fifty thousand dollars," she said.

Pat's face relaxed into folds of flesh made weary by the constant worry of the past several months.

"I have to leave tomorrow. For Paris. As soon as I get the money, I'll send it to you and you can begin."

Pat nodded. "What about?" Pat hitched his head slightly. Jaime knew Pat still refused to trust Reeve with her heart. He rarely brought himself even to speak Reeve's name outright, preferring to clear his throat or let sentences trail off instead. The reference was merely implied.

"I've got to fly out of L.A. I'll tell Reeve myself then."

Reeve spread the plans for the house on the floor in his living room. He had spent the entire morning with the architect, a friend of his for many years, who had volunteered his services, *gratis*. That the living room was practically bare of furnishings disturbed Reeve in no way. Almost all of the house's furniture and artwork had been sold, some of it to satisfy the ten million dollar court order, and the rest of it was happily deposited in the bank. It was to be used to begin his new life with Jaime in Paradise.

The plans for the house were to be a surprise for Jaime. He was going to bring them with him when he joined her there. If she didn't like something, it'd be changed to her satisfaction.

In a way, he knew it was selfish of him to have begun the project without her. But he needed to involve himself in something concrete that would make the reality of their union tangible to him.

He had waited so long—forever it seemed—to live his own life. Yes, he knew what he wanted. Yes, he knew his own mind. But there were the constant reminders of what he had given up for those years under the domination of Charlotte. He had lived everyone else's vision but his own.

There were constant temptations to fall back into the easy life he had lived. The offers came in every day. Elliot would ring up, frantic that the deal of a lifetime was slipping away. Charlotte would appear in person, carefully broaching the subject of opportunities she foresaw for the future of his career.

"You can't mean to become a—a farmer," she scoffed.

"There's nothing wrong with being a farmer," Reeve said.

Charlotte would laugh with an alarming hilarity that Reeve recognized as a reaction to stress.

"Anyway," Reeve had answered during one of these dialogues with Charlotte, "who knows what might happen when a person lives in Paradise?" It was a deliberate pun. Charlotte did not catch it.

"Nothing," she retorted, "has ever happened in that town. And nothing ever will."

"You have no faith," Reeve said.

"I'm not Jaime," Charlotte spat, feeling herself the object of fun. "I'm not that foolish."

"Perhaps you should be then," Reeve said, and Charlotte had picked up her purse and left the Spartan remains of his living room to return to the real world filled with people of sensible viewpoints coinciding with her own.

On his knees, Reeve carefully unrolled another set of architectural drafts, and carefully went over the details of the film studio his friend and he had been working on. In the top right corner, the identifying name of the drawings was Paradise Films.

A tiny electrical charge coursed through Reeve as he envisioned the studio complete and operational, situated against the backdrop of the Sawtooths. In all ways, his life with Jaime would be paradise. It was in-

trinsic to this vision that nothing would originate from
Paradise Films that would not in some way uplift humanity.

He didn't mind that he came to Jaime practically
empty-handed. In a way that was the best part of it,
being able to start out together, the two of them, with
nothing but each other. Had they married when they
were young, it would have been that way. Yet, he
would see that Jaime was given her chance in life, as
well. She might not mind chopping onions at the café,
but if she wanted more, he wanted to help her have her
chance. After all, she was giving up everything for
him. He knew she could have had a future every bit as
brilliant as his own. She turned away from that to be
with him. It was one thing for him to have given up the
life of a movie star, for he had become satiated with its
richness; but Jaime's cravings were still there. He had
sensed it, seen it in her eyes, when the proposals came
in for her from Elliot Cohen. Jaime could have had it
all; instead, she had settled for him. He would make
it up to her.

Reeve rolled up the plans for the studio. He had an
appointment tomorrow to see about obtaining fund-
ing for his enterprise. He would put it all together before raising Jaime's hopes needlessly.

He dialed Charlotte's number. She answered it,
sounding sad.

"Hi," he said, "Could you do me a favor?"

Charlotte agreed to be at the house the following
day. There was to be a walk-through with the real estate agent and the new owner before the sale of the
house could be completed.

"Where are you going to be?" Charlotte asked.

"I'm going to visit a friend. He's drawing up some
plans for a house I'm building for Jaime in Para-

dise." It wasn't entirely a lie that way, merely a twisting of the truth. The studio was sacred, and still in its fantasy stages.

Even over the wire, Reeve felt his mother's rush of fury and wave of despair at the mention of the house, Jaime, and Paradise all in one sentence.

"Why not?" Charlotte said listlessly to Reeve. "What else have I got to do now?"

Reeve almost suggested she might try living her own life for a change, which was the crux of the issue. Instead, he bit his tongue and said, "Thanks. I appreciate it."

Charlotte had just shown the realtor and his client around the house. The client was Randy Ring the King of Chrome, a corpulent man from Detroit who had made his fortune in used cars and was now into the Hollywood scene. The man had stared more at Charlotte than at the condition of the home he was to purchase for over a million dollars. Clearly, he was smitten with show business, and through her association with Reeve, he apparently found Charlotte a goddess. "Bet you made him what he was," Randy Ring said when they were in the master bathroom. "That kid of yours."

Charlotte noted the use of the past tense. "I had a great deal to do with his success," she said coldly, but was also secretly pleased that her contribution and worth were being acknowledged, if not by someone who counted, at least by someone. If it were not for Jaime... Charlotte sighed, and continued with the tour.

The cause of Charlotte's downfall appeared in the flesh soon after the realtor and the Chrome King departed, satisfied with the house's condition. Charlotte was already feeling sad, and now, as she stared at Jaime's smiling face in the kitchen, her mood became mean. If it were not for Jaime...

"Where's Reeve?" Jaime was asking. Charlotte poured a diet drink into a glass and took a sip.

"He had to go somewhere," she said. It would turn her stomach to say the truth, all about the sweet little house for Reeve's sweet little wife and their sweet little future—exclusive of her. Instead, she said, "I don't know where exactly." Not a total lie. "Did you tell them about the wedding?"

"No, no I didn't." Jaime told Charlotte about Jade's condition. She told Charlotte that she had accepted the job in Paris as a way of earning enough money to pay for the ranch.

"That's admirable of you, Jaime. I'm so impressed." Charlotte could hardly contain her elation. Charlotte felt as if the gods above had only been trifling with her—a little joke, and now she was being let in on it. Jaime was going to be snared by the entertainment bug again. She'd be out of the country, out of Reeve's life. All of her efforts to launch Jaime into a career that would separate her from Reeve were not in vain, after all. Charlotte took her first happy breath in months.

"Would you tell Reeve?" Jaime said. "Explain that I'll call him from Paris. I've got to go right now, today. They're beginning filming in three days."

Charlotte was all too pleased to help Jaime pack. Together they took the outfits Charlotte felt Jaime might need while overseas. "I'd wanted to pack up all this stuff myself and send it back to Paradise," Jaime said with concern.

"Let me," Charlotte said. "I'd be more than happy to lend a hand."

Charlotte insisted on taking Jaime to the airport. They were already in the car, when Jaime said she had forgotten something and ran back into the house. Snatching a piece of message paper by the bedroom's telephone, Jaime jotted down a quick note telling Reeve she loved him and hated having to be away, but that she had to get the money for Jade's ranch. She'd call. And again and again she scrawled, "I love you!" She signed the note: "Your Wife-to-be."

At the airport, Jaime thanked Charlotte many times over for her help. She hugged Charlotte, her eyes brimming over. "You're going to be my only mother pretty soon."

Charlotte patted Jaime's back and broke from the embrace. "Don't miss your plane, dear..."

Charlotte fairly floated home in the white Continental, the music on the radio playing some light classical piece that matched her buoyant mood. She stopped at a grocer's and scavenged for as many old cartons as she could get into the car, then returned to Reeve's home.

Feeling exhilarated and energetic, she piled Jaime's belongings into the boxes and transported each box into the garage for future disposal. She was finished with her task and was leaving the bedroom with the last carton in her arms, still feeling happy and strong, when she caught sight of the slip of white paper on Reeve's pillow.

She snatched it up and read it. Her face blanched when she realized how close she had come to disaster. Quickly, she put the note in her purse, just as she heard the front door open.

The piece of paper stuffed in her purse was like a smoking gun as she stood before Reeve a moment later, explaining the situation.

He didn't believe her.

"But it's the truth! Look for yourself." Charlotte opened the dresser drawers, forced him to see how the closets were bare of Jaime's clothes.

"She came back and took the things she would need in Europe. She said it didn't matter what I did with the other things. She may have suggested charity. I don't remember," Charlotte said, shaking her head wanly. "I was in such a state," she said. "I just wanted to get everything out of here, every final trace of that terrible woman out of our lives before you came back." She looked down at the box she had not yet taken into the garage.

"I don't believe it," Reeve repeated.

"I know. I was shocked, too. But call Gallanos yourself. It's his film."

Reeve shook his head, partly in denial that such events could be happening at all, and to refuse the telephone Charlotte held out to him.

"Why?" he asked himself, and slumped down to sit on the edge of the bed. He stared at the place where Jaime's body had lain close to his only three days before. They had made love, had held each other, had spoken of the future. Their children. "Why?" he repeated.

"Oh, Reeve, darling…" Charlotte went to him and sat beside him. Her arm circled him and even though he gave no notice of her, she continued in her soothing manner. "It was destined from the beginning. I tried to warn you. I saw it right from the start. She was just a young woman like any other. You shouldn't really blame her. She had never had anything in her life that remotely smacked of glamour, and then— *voila*—the world was suddenly hers on a golden platter." Charlotte lowered her voice a bit and took a different tone, matter-of-fact and conspiratorial. "She said she went back to Paradise, and one look at the place...well, she just couldn't bear the thought of living there. She said she finally knew who she was and where she belonged. Reeve," Charlotte said, with a sigh, "she is a young bird who wants to try her wings. I suppose we shouldn't hate her."

Reeve had grown very quiet. He felt totally alone, a man on a small raft becalmed in a vast sea. "Our marriage?"

"It's over, darling. She's gone. Out of our lives."

"I don't have a life anymore," he said, and walked away from Charlotte.

"You have me..." Charlotte went after him.

He stopped her with a fierce glance. "No. No, Charlotte, I do not have you. You do not have me, either. All I have, all I want is my own self. With or without Jaime, at least I have that left. Now leave me alone."

Chapter Thirteen

Paris, the City of Lights, held only darkness for Jaime. It had been a week since she had left Los Angeles, and although she returned each afternoon from a day's filming with the hope there would be a message from Reeve waiting, each day delivered nothing more than fresh disappointment. She did not understand what the trouble might be, and was beside herself with worry. For three days, no one answered the phone at the house, and the next time she phoned, the recording said the number had been disconnected. There was no new listing.

Yesterday she had phoned Charlotte. She was told Reeve had sold the house and had left for parts unknown to start a new life. There was no message for Jaime, Charlotte said.

"I don't understand," Jaime whispered, as bewildered by the situation as she was troubled. "You told him why I had to take the film job, didn't you?"

"Jaime," Charlotte said, "I told him. Look, you can't really blame him, can you? He gave up everything for you, and now you run off to Paris—"

"But it isn't for me," Jaime said miserably. "I explained that. And it's only temporarily."

"He felt abandoned. Betrayed."

Jaime knew the feeling well. "Did he . . . did Reeve say anything about our marriage?" Jaime asked. She shut her eyes, silently praying.

"Jaime," Charlotte said kindly, "I believe you can consider the future with Reeve permanently terminated. I'm terribly sorry, but of course there's nothing I can do."

In her room at the Crillon Hotel, Jaime looked down at the *Place de la Concorde*. She was staying in a hotel whose clientele consisted of royalty and diplomats, some of the richest and most beautiful people in the world. Her room was furnished in old Louis XVI furniture and her bathroom was entirely of marble. In spite of her surroundings, she felt impoverished. Jaime stepped back from the window and let the heavy silk fabric of the drapes fall in graceful folds, covering the glittering splendor of the world's most romantic city.

She cried until dawn, each minute of the night an interminable waking nightmare flooded with memories of her past with Reeve. There were times during her fevered ruminations when she became so lost in the beauty of what they had shared, that the pain of the present was temporarily obliterated. Her heart soared again as she reexperienced the feel of his silken skin. She saw again in her mind, as if it were happening at that moment, the light spark behind his eyes as their joining brought her to peaks of physical and emotional ecstasy.

All that could not be gone, her heart screamed in protest.

But, yes, it was finished, said her mind, ended like the last frame of a beautiful romantic film. Reeve had not called her; he had made no provision for her to be able to reach him. Even if Charlotte had not delivered her message, he would have found her note on his pillow. From that, at least, she could have been certain of a sympathetic response.

Jaime's wake-up call from the hotel's office came at the first break of dawn. Her lids were puffy and her face splotched and swollen. No amount of cold water could compensate for the night's ravages.

In an hour, the limousine was at the hotel's entrance to drive her to the filming site on the banks of the Seine. The director took one look at her and threw up his hands. He could not shoot a single frame of her in her present condition. Makeup would do nothing to help.

She was sorry, she told him. It would not happen again, she vowed in all earnestness.

The truth was, it had frightened her badly that day when the day's shooting was postponed on her behalf. The night's crying jag had inconvenienced at least a hundred people, from extras to technicians. There was little doubt in her mind that if such a thing were to occur a second time, she would be replaced. Temperament might be acceptable, even glamorous in a star, but in a virtually unknown actress who desperately needed the money, this behavior was untenable.

After that, Jaime complied with the director's every wish. No one could have wished for a more accessible

and agreeable artist. When the day's shooting schedule was complete, Jaime made herself available for
publicity stills. She attended strategic interviews with
the international press corps. There were even public-
ity-oriented "dates" arranged for her with a French
rock star, a member of the English peerage who was
famous for racing Formula One automobiles, and
several actors of varying degrees of fame.

In the daily rushes, she was frequently lauded for
her work. Her best performance, however, had anyone known her inner state, was in appearing cheerful
off camera. In her scenes of tragic consequence, the
tears were genuine. Her loss of Reeve still ran like a
wide, empty valley through the center of her soul. It
was the smile she wore, fake through and through,
that was truly deserving of accolades.

On two or three occasions, trapped by the loneli-
ness of the night, she lost her resolve to keep her heart
hardened against any hope the past might be revived,
and called Reeve's old number. It was her only contact with him, that mere physical exercise of dialing.
The sound of the recording was like a knife in her
heart. It jangled her nerves, tore at her. She forced
herself to listen, punishment for having been weak,
hating herself for loving, hating the world for still existing when she had died.

In the daylight hours, full of resolve to make Jade's
dream come true, she would speak to Pat about the
plans for the ranch. They had borrowed against her
contract, and the bank was releasing funds as the
building progressed.

Jaime spoke to Jade almost every day. Jade never
mentioned that she was dying, nor did Jaime. But it
made the phone calls all the more precious.

Reeve's high rubber boots sank ankle deep into the valley's rich soil. Wild flowers had begun to sprout from the thawed earth, tiny blue and yellow and orange dots appearing over the vast landscape in greater profusion with each day's passing. Sometimes the smell of the air, the feel of a breeze, particularly and unseasonably warm on the side of his face, filled his senses with all the erotic seductiveness of a beautiful woman's perfume. A sudden wrenching feeling would overpower him, and he would stand stripped of all defenses, succumbed to the bittersweet sensation of his remembered love.

There were days when he was particularly vulnerable to these fleeting glimpses into the past. Caught in the emerald green of a blade of grass, a dewdrop, trapped like an unspilled tear in its crease became the memory of two bright and laughing eyes. *Jaime!* his heart would sing. And then reality would hit and the dull ache would again resume its cruel and relentless throb.

On such days, he would hurl hammer against nail with the fury of a demon, and if he were lucky he would fall asleep quickly, exhausted. But sometimes he was not so lucky. When he had misjudged his energy and found an excess at day's finish, he would walk over the land that was his, purchased with the sale of his house and what little was left over from his estate. In the moonlight the land seemed to go on forever, melting into the Sawtooths, which loomed darker against the purple night sky. He thought sometimes that he was walking into a vast ocean, going ever deeper, and that he might, if lucky, eventually drown his sorrow. If it were particularly bright outside, there would be patches of silver detectable on the peaks, and he would think of white coverlets lying over the mountains. A coyote might howl, another answering, and an owl would pass silently on a nocturnal hunt.

Several times, he had stayed out until the sun rose over the horizon, and would find himself at the edge of the little village that was Paradise. Smoke from the few cabins snaked upward out of chimneys. A light shone from the odd porch or window. Nestled among the brown and gray clapboard structures was the one building sacred among the others—the café where she had lived her life, and where once she had loved him and had waited for him to return. In the morning haze, in that in-between time when creatures of the night were settling in to sleep and those of the day were not yet risen, he would stare at that single building and remember.

A dog's bark would bring him back, and as the sun's rays burst from behind a mountain, he would turn and trudge back to his temporary home.

Home was a tent, large enough for his clothes, bedroll, cooking supplies and tools. He kept a couple of shotguns loaded just in case. Bears were curious and unpredictable, like women. Nearby were high mounds of lumber covered by plastic tarps kept in place by spikes. Three months after he had left Los Angeles, the house that was to have been his and Jaime's was three quarters finished. He had done the work himself, needing the silence and the physical labor as therapy for his pain. Rarely would he venture into town, and when he did it was only to confer with someone experienced in construction or to purchase more supplies. The Porsche had been exchanged for a pickup truck with an extra-long bed.

He did not miss the company of other people. He called Charlotte occasionally to see that she was all right. But this was a duty he disliked, as there was always in the back of his mind the faintest hope that Jaime might have contacted his mother and wished to reconcile. Jaime had not called, had never called. She had never once looked back from the moment she had packed her bags and walked out of his house. Out of his life. Jaime, Charlotte insisted, had gone on with her life and Charlotte prayed that Reeve would likewise come to his senses and do the same. There were other women... *For other men,* Reeve would complete silently.

It was also as if he required this freedom from other people to adjust to himself, to become acquainted with the man he was, but had never known before. With each succeeding day of his solitary existence, he felt more certain that the man he was, was a man worth knowing.

His labor on the house took on the erratic rhythm of his inner moods. At the start of construction he had slammed nail and wood with an alternating anger and despair. Later the despair had abated and his work became characterized by fury at Jaime for having ruined their future. She had cheated him and herself of a life of such happiness, that to even think of it was unendurable.

Now, of late, his emotions had taken another turn, and in the middle of leveling a window sash, he would pause and see the view from the spot as Jaime might see it, as she had been *meant* to see it. Soft and beautiful Jaime. Jaime, whose eyes had flashed at him with green anger when he had come speeding into her life that morning at the café. Jaime, whose body had given him such exquisite pleasure. Slender and firm, her legs had encircled him and he had been satisfied to burn in that ring of fire for all time. Her breasts, full and high, yielding to his slightest touch...the sweet curve of her hip, a hollow of desire...the bent grace of her elegant swanlike neck. He had known all of that once, and it suddenly came to him that he would rather protect those memories than shatter them. The Jaime who was then, still remained in his heart; it was for this Jaime that he continued to labor on the house.

The other Jaime, that woman who had chosen the false glitter was an unknown woman, and therefore not to be thought of again.

It was more or less a milestone. Glass windows were in place, the walls plastered, and the hardwood floor laid throughout the house. Reeve was feeling proud as he drove the beige pickup into Ketchem. His hands on the steering wheel were rough. They were the hands of a stranger, speckled with white paint and scored by cuts in varying stages of healing.

He was at the lumber yard, pricing varnish for the floor when the familiar face rounded the corner. Pat Griffen did not recognize him at first. When he did, he did a double take worthy of any first-class comedian.

"How's it going?" Reeve said with offhand cautiousness. After the initial surprise, the big man was eyeing him warily, the way one viewed a dangerous animal previously thought dead.

"Gettin' by," Pat said, and brushed past him to another section.

Reeve took what he needed from the shelf and went to the counter to pay for his goods. When he left the store, he crossed the street diagonally, and from the side he saw the big man watching him.

Two days later, as Reeve adjusted a wind deflector to the top of his chimney, he looked down to see Pat trundling down his potholed excuse for a driveway in a Blazer. Like Reeve, he was wearing the uniform of a construction worker, paint-splattered coveralls and pockets bulging with the telltale evidence of nails.

"What do you think?" Reeve asked making his way down the slant of the roof.

"Good job," Pat replied, looking at the house, then squinting up at Reeve. "You do it all?"

"Every last nail." Reeve held up his welted hands.

Pat almost smiled. He was silent, looking around.

"Take a look inside, if you want."

Pat nodded and went in through the front door. He emerged a few minutes later, said nothing, but tipped his hand in a salute as he got into the Blazer. In another minute he was only a dust cloud, and Reeve stood on the edge of the roof feeling slightly sick inside. The man had been a reminder of Jaime.

Two days later as Reeve was working to sand the bedroom floor, Pat came stomping in through the front door.

"What is this?" Pat asked. "What the hell is all of this for?" he demanded to know.

So Reeve told him the way it had started out, the plans for the house, and the way it had come to be, the defection of Jaime from those plans. Pat said nothing, showed nothing on his broad face but perhaps the outline of worry, which Reeve took as displeasure that his "type" was moving into the area to stay. Reeve guessed he was considered to be ecologically unsound, a human nuclear generating plant with a high-risk contamination factor.

The big man nodded now and then, seemed to want to say something, but didn't. Again Reeve watched him drive off, more slowly this time, as if Griffen were lost in thought.

Reeve was still asleep when the pounding sounded on the front door. He had moved into the house, sleeping in the living room in his sleeping bag. It was light outside, and he realized he had already overslept. A glance at his watch said it was eight. The pounding continued in the absolute silence.

"Yeah, yeah! It's unlocked."

The door swung open. Pat Griffen stood in the doorway. He brought with him the scent of paint and turpentine. "We got something to talk about, you and me."

The two men walked beside each other in the chill morning air. That way neither of them had to see the other's face. It was like a long distance phone call, Reeve thought, where you could look about and think your own thoughts without the necessity of having to respond with polite facial ticks to the other person.

"She won't talk about you," Pat said. "That was my first clue something bad had happened. Not that I was ever much for the two of you getting together. Didn't even know you were going to be married, till you said it yesterday."

"Maybe she never mentioned it because she never meant it," Reeve said.

Then Pat turned. His weathered face was screwed into a tight ball of pain, and his mouth was twisted into something that looked at first like a crazy grin, but altered midway into the first trembling fits of a man who was trying hard not to wail.

"Her mother's dyin'," Pat said. "Jaime took that job because she was being paid a lot of money. She and me, we're fixing up the ranch Jade was saving for all this time. We plan to have it ready before Jade's time comes."

Reeve felt the ground sway beneath him. A wave of something akin to relief and sorrow, and a wild sense of having in some way failed as a man, overcame him.

His condition must have showed, for Pat was propping him up.

"Why didn't she tell me?" Reeve asked, the words coming out in a fitful gasp of agonized bewilderment. "Why the hell?"

"Don't know," Pat said. "Maybe there was a letter? May have gotten lost in the mail." He shook his head. "She sounded so damned sad all the time. 'Course she tried to hide it, but she can't hide things from me much, and when Jade or I'd ask her about you, she'd clam up."

Pat and Reeve made their way back to the Blazer. "Thanks," Reeve said. He put out his hand. Pat took a while, stared down at the outstretched arm for a long while, then slowly reached forward and the two scarred hands clasped and held.

"Just a neighborly thing to do," Pat said. "Looks like we're going to be seeing more of each other..." He cast his glance toward the house.

"I want her," Reeve said, and he kept his eyes firm on Pat's.

"Aw, maybe you aren't such a bad dude, after all," Pat said. He averted his eyes and followed the loop of a hawk overhead. "I love Jade," Pat said. "And I love that girl of Jade's just the same as if she was my own daughter. I wouldn't mind giving her away at a wedding to the right guy."

He slipped off to the side, his big frame slightly slower in its movements than it had been months before when he had threatened Reeve's life. Pat opened the door of the Blazer and stepped up into the driver's seat. He started the engine. Reeve stood off to the side as Pat wheeled the car into position to head back up the bumpy driveway to the main road. The Blazer stopped a few feet ahead and Pat leaned his head out the window. He looked back at Reeve.

"You just might be that guy," he said. He looked long and hard at Reeve. "Just might be him, after all."

Chapter Fourteen

With his own house finally completed, Reeve worked like a man possessed on Jade's ranch. He was possessed with love for a woman who was to be coming home to him forever, although at the moment Jaime did not know it. Reeve laughed, dropping the nails he had been holding between his teeth as he forgot himself with happiness.

Pat Griffen cast him a harsh look from across the roof where he was laying another shingle in place. Reeve laughed again.

God, he thought, throwing back his head and drinking in the sunlight with his entire being, *what a world it was!*

It could already be considered the beginning of the summer season. Backpackers and rock scramblers had replaced the winter tourists who came to the valley. These last days of May were warm and the light was lasting longer, making it possible to work farther into the day. By midsummer, Reeve remembered, the sun would not disappear until as late as ten o'clock.

His skin was a deep tan and his eyes a vibrant blue, shining with satisfaction and a secure joy he had never before known so completely. He was certain, at last, of himself. He knew absolutely that things were going to work out exactly as he had planned them.

But in the presence of Pat he would often feel guilty over his good fortune and whenever possible attempted to subdue his excitement. This morning, after his sudden outburst, he and Pat continued their work with a respectful solemnity for the project's underlying purpose.

The two men broke for lunch promptly at noon, the way they always did, as if a loud industrial bell had sounded their release from labor. Pat had brought some oversized sandwiches from town for both of them. He kept a cooler on hand stocked with beer and soft drinks. They sat on the house's porch with their lunches. Both men were silent, as usual, while they ate and sipped and stared out into the valley.

"No need for you to keep up that act," Pat said, spitting out the stem of a green jalapeño pepper.

"What act's that?" Reeve asked, glancing sideways at Pat.

"That long face of yours. What else's it for—life— if you can't enjoy it?"

Reeve nodded. He stared straight ahead again. "I'm really sorry about Jade."

"Can't change that." Pat watched the sky. Reeve did the same. Towering white cloud castles floated overhead. "Almost makes you believe in heaven, seeing something up there like that." Pat was thoughtfully silent for a while more. "We gotta pick up the action around her. Jade, she's getting worse every day."

They broke from lunch earlier.

When they had climbed back onto the top of the roof, Pat asked Reeve to hand over the bag of nails. He slipped a handful into his pockets and turning back the bag, said to Reeve, "Jaime called last night. She's coming home."

Reeve stood stock-still. His legs were spread-eagle at the peak of the roof. A gust of wind hit him full force in the face. It smelled of mountain flowers and melting snow. "When?" Reeve asked. His throat had constricted and his heart was pumping rapidly in his chest, which seemed oddly hollow. He felt weak with a sense of longing, and at the same time exhilarated, charged with a sense of purpose to life.

"Two days," Pat answered. "She's expecting me to pick her up when the bus lets her off."

"I'll go to meet her," Reeve said quickly, knowing he wouldn't be able to stand another second's wait until he could see her again.

"That's what I was about to suggest."

Jaime stood at the side of the bus, surrounded by her suitcases and several heavy cartons filled to bursting with gifts she had brought back from Europe for Jade and Pat. She wanted whatever time she had left with her mother to be special; each day would be a celebration of life. There would be lovely presents and good dinners with flowers on the table, with laughter and hugs between them. Birthdays would not be treated as a once-a-year occasion; instead, days would be honored as they existed, one after the other, each one special. Until there were no more, Jaime thought with a sadness that had become a part of her.

The crowd was beginning to thin, and Jaime thought perhaps Pat might have misunderstood her time of arrival. Then she thought, with a sudden sense of panic, that something terrible might have happened to Jade since she had last spoken to them. Although Jade could no longer hide her weakness, not even over the telephone, she still wouldn't admit to her condition. Pat, however, gave Jaime the news straight. Jade didn't have long.

At least the ranch was almost done, Jaime thought. The fences were going up in a few more days and the livestock would be delivered as soon as that happened. The money she had earned from the film turned out to be just barely enough, even with Pat taking a leave of absence from his regular job, and doing as much of the physical labor on the ranch as he could.

During the nights, when she was able to put Reeve out of her mind, her thoughts would turn to visions of the completed ranch, and of Jade seeing it for the first time. Now that she was home, she wondered what it would be like in reality.

She looked around again in search of Pat. She was looking for a large middle-aged man, when suddenly her whole being froze.

He was standing a few feet off, staring at her, as if at a ghost. It was impossible, but it was Reeve.

A thrill passed through her at the sight of him. Darkly tanned, his hair had lightened to a pale blond that emphasized the startling blueness of his eyes.

Totally transfixed, hopelessly unable to move, she watched as he shouldered his way through the remaining bus passengers.

"Don't say a word," he said, looking into her eyes.

Jaime started to speak, and he cut her off.

"Not a word." He looked down at the disarray of suitcases and boxes surrounding her. "Don't tell me these are all..." When he looked up, she was staring at him with those remarkable, wide green eyes, eyes more brilliant than Venus, eyes, which as he walked through the valley at night unable to sleep for his yearning and heartache, had burned in his imagination. For a terrible instant, he thought that her presence might be only a dream.

Suddenly, unable to keep up the pretense of being in control of his emotions, he swept her up into his arms. "Jaime," he whispered in a graveled voice, rent with desire, "I love you more than life itself. How could you have ever doubted that?"

She was clutched against his chest, which was warm and smelled of the air and the sun, of trees and of the rich earth. It was a scent far surpassing the most elegant of French colognes, and in his arms she felt safe and, yes, that she had come home where she belonged.

He released her, and his smile was sheepish, like a teenage boy's when he was with a girl he was crazy over.

"These are mine," she said, averting her eyes from his and pointing out the various bags and boxes belonging to her. Her body burned from his touch. She could feel his gaze on her, but could not bring herself to respond to his words. Whatever she felt within herself was now locked so tightly, so deeply, that she had forgotten how to bring it forth into the sunlight. It would take time.

On the way to Paradise she learned of Charlotte's duplicity.

"I had a feeling..." Jaime began. The pickup's motor purred softly. She looked across at Reeve. "I left a note for you. Just in case."

Reeve shook his head. "She must have taken it." He reached over and stroked the side of her face, as if needing to convince himself she was truly there. "Do you mind?" he asked when she had still given his affection no sign of acceptance or of refusal.

She shook her head, keeping her eyes on the scenery.

"You may or may not be pleased to know this. Charlotte's found a new lease on life. The man who bought my house." Reeve laughed, thinking about it. "Randy Ring, the Chrome King."

"What?" Now it was Jaime's turn to laugh.

"Yeah," Reeve said. "She always wanted to hook up with royalty. They're very happy. He's loaded with dough and wants to take over Hollywood. Charlotte's right there behind him, meddling in his affairs."

"That I can believe."

"He's already producing a movie. I understand it has no socially redeeming values. It's being touted as a certain blockbuster. Something about cheerleaders going wild on a trip to Hawaii. They have a sequel in the works even before release."

Rather than take the turnoff that led straight into Paradise, Reeve turned down a narrow dirt road some distance past the exit. Jaime gave him a questioning look, which he answered with a wink. After bumping along for some distance, Reeve slowed.

Straight ahead was a timber fence, interrupted by a large square arch, beneath which a wood sign swung in the wind. It bore the inscription, "Paradise." Farther down the road, she saw a medium-sized house with its roof peaked to withstand the winter snow. Its exterior was of stained natural wood, and even in the distance, she could make out pots of bright geraniums on the front porch.

"Welcome home, Jaime," Reeve said, watching her reaction with strained pensiveness.

"Home," Jaime whispered, not moving her eyes from the sight before her. Her eyes glistened and she bit her lip. Trembling, she took in several short breaths, but in the end broke down in sobs.

"Jaime!" Reeve cried, beside himself with apprehension. He grabbed her and, clutching her shoulders, spoke directly to her, his words desperate, tumbling out one after the other. "If you don't like it . . . Well, maybe it should have been a white fence. I thought about it, but it seemed better, the raw wood…" He hit his fist on the dash. "We'd talked and I thought this was the way you'd want it. Everything, Jaime, everything here was done just for you, to please you. But, if it's not right," he took in a deep breath, "I'll tear it down, start over. Oh, Jaime!"

She had been crying, and now, inexplicably, she had begun to laugh. "Oh, darling Reeve…" And when she raised her head, the green eyes glistened with undisguised love for him. "It's the most beautiful home in the world."

She went to him, then. Reeve shuddered, his body wracked with desire and relief.

"It's your home, Jaime. Ours," he amended. He waited, but she said nothing to either confirm or deny what he had just proposed.

They left the pickup truck, and together they walked through the rooms. Jaime admired everything, noticed each small and loving detail he had put into the home.

"It doesn't look like Charlotte had a hand in it," Jaime said, smiling. The whole home was solid and honest. There was a wholeness about it from the foundation up. A home built to last forever, Jaime thought.

The master bedroom was large and spacious. It had white walls that sparkled in the sunlight let in by the sheer drapes, which, fluttered in the breeze from the open window. Jaime's eyes fell on the bed. It was large, its frame of white metal formed in a pattern of graceful scrolls, trimmed in gleaming brass and with a bedstead raised very high off the ground. There was a thick down comforter on it, also white, and matching pillows trimmed in eyelet lace, balanced against the headboard.

"I've never slept in it," Reeve said, staring across the room to the bed. "I used my bedroll," he added, and Jaime saw the two-toned blue sack rolled neatly in a corner. "Sometimes at night, I'd lie awake and—"

Jaime, who stood beside him, tilted her head up questioningly.

"I'd remember how it used to be between us."

Jaime nodded, and without a word, turned and walked silently from the house.

Reeve helped her into the pickup, trying to discern from her expression what might be going on in her mind. As for his own internal condition, he was beside himself with need for her. When they had stood in the bedroom, so close to the bed, he felt a surge of desire so strong he could barely stand. The curve of her body, the sheer accessibility of her flesh so close to his, was unnerving. He had come close to being undone.

There was no way for him to know if she still truly wanted him. So far her response was admiration, appreciation. Damn! He wanted more. Paris and Rome—the experiences of those months may have changed her whole perspective on life. He reminded himself that she had come back to Paradise not for him, but for Jade.

He would be patient. He had to be.

The dinner Jaime prepared was held in the café dining room because Jade was too weak to make the drive into Ketchem or Sun Valley.

Since she had returned, Jaime helped run the café's daily operation along with Pat's sister. They maintained the charade of allowing Jade to help them, insisting that all they wanted was for her to write down her recipes. Even this was becoming too much of an ordeal. Each day Jade slept longer, partially because she wasn't able to rest at night. Every so often, Jaime would awake and see her mother standing at the window, peering at the moonlit road.

Jaime had closed the café early that night. The dinner was for the four of them. Pat's sister had to return home to her family.

It was a lovely meal with all of them together. The front door was open to the night, which was unseasonably warm. Some of the cowboys had come in from the hills and music could be heard floating from the neighboring saloons. There was the neighing of horses communicating with each other as they stood hitched to posts. A dog peeked in, yawning.

"Present time!" Jaime said when dessert had been eaten and coffee served. She returned a moment later from the kitchen, her arms laden with colorfully wrapped gifts.

Jade flushed crimson as Jaime placed them before her. "It's not my birthday," she said softly.

"It's your un-birthday!"

"It's not necessary," Jade said, still looking down.

"I wanted to, Mother. I made heaps of money in Paris, and I had a ball going shopping." Jaime exchanged quick glances with Reeve and Pat.

Without enthusiasm, Jade undid the ribbon and loosened the wrapping paper. She pulled out the silk robe, a stylized version of a kimono. "It is very beautiful," she said. She traced thin fingers over the embroidered pattern of roses and birds.

"It'll look beautiful on you," Pat said.

Jade nodded, and listlessly continued to unwrap the other gifts. When she was through, she thanked everyone for her un-birthday and asked to be excused.

The three of them sat around the table, staring at the paper and ribbon, the cast-off gifts, which, of course, were superfluous to a woman whose life was ebbing from her.

"If she would just admit it," Jaime said. "She seems so alone."

"She has her dignity," Pat said.

Jaime saw the two men exchange glances. "Jaime," Pat began, "we wanted to ask you first. I'd like to have your permission to track down Grady. The ranch is almost finished. Jade doesn't have long. This way, if I can find him, she can have her dream. At least for a little while."

Jaime stared down at her fingers. She thought for a long while, then lifting her face to Pat, said, "Can you do that? Find him?"

"I can try. Reeve, here, he's got some extra dough to help with a private investigator. And I can pull some favors and use the police computers." Pat paused. "I never wanted to see that man's face around here again. But when you love someone...well, you put some things aside."

"Try then," Jaime said quietly, "try to find the rat."

It was extraordinary.

Jaime had finished with the early afternoon's preparations for dinner, and she went back to check on Jade in the cabin behind the café. She expected the curtains to be drawn against the harsh July sunlight, but instead found daylight filling the room.

Jade was not on the bed asleep. She had somehow lifted an old suitcase onto her bed and was rummaging through a pile of clothing. There was a faint musty odor to the air.

She turned to Jaime and smiled. A hint of color was in her cheeks, and to Jaime her mother looked suddenly youthful again, almost like a young girl flushed with some secret romantic thought.

Jade responded to Jaime's questioning glance by holding up a dress. It was silk with an overlay of lace, very white, and Jaime recognized it at once as being a wedding dress.

She stepped forward, and Jade put it into her arms.

"It was yours?" Jaime asked.

"The dress I wore to marry your father."

"It's beautiful," Jaime said.

"It was the most beautiful dress." Jade's eyes glistened.

"It still is." Jaime handed the dress back.

"No," Jade said, and refused it by stepping away. Smiling she said, "It will fit you."

Now it was Jaime's turn to flush. "It's a dress to be married in."

Jade's face softened, "Jaime, I am a dying woman."

Jaime closed her eyes. Now at last, when it was out in the open, she didn't know how to deal with the fact.

"Do not make so much trouble over a little thing like death," Jade said. "It happens to everyone sooner or later. With me, a little sooner. But while we are alive we should make the most of life."

Tears were streaming down Jaime's face. Instead of being strong for Jade, she was falling apart. She tried to wipe away the wet trail with the back of her arm. Jade stopped the action by taking her by both hands. "Look, my daughter, you must not weep for me. This death is only a brief sleep. Then I shall awaken and continue on."

"You really believe that?" Jaime asked.

Jade nodded. "You love this man, Reeve. He is a very good person, and he loves you a great, great deal. Take the dress, Jaime. Use it. You will be very happy together."

Jaime sighed, knowing what Jade was thinking. No doubt her heart was still telling her that Grady would come walking down the road for her. But Jaime knew better. Nothing had turned up about her father, although a detective agency had been working full-time on the case, and Pat had all but blackmailed every person he had ever dealt with in the police agencies into making concerted efforts to find Grady. The last news was that a Grady Quinn had died in New York three years before. He was an indigent.

Jaime had not been to Reeve's house since the day she had first come back to town.

Now, she walked through the rooms again, alone this time. It was as if the walls had feelings. Somehow they had absorbed the man's passion and radiated it back to her. When she entered the master bedroom, she saw the bedroll lying open in the corner.

Her eyes moved to the large bed.

So, he had still not slept in it. Like Jade, the man never lost hope.

It was already late in the day and he would be home soon. She had to be quick. Without further daydreaming, she took care of her errand and left.

Reeve parked the pickup in front of the house. He was covered in dust but happy as he stomped up the stairs of the front porch. He had been out on the projected site of his studio. Pat had gone with him, and agreed that if he kept to his word and produced only films of a high moral caliber, he wouldn't have the locals on his back. That had made Reeve feel good. It was further confirmation that he belonged in Paradise. With each passing day, that fact became more deeply embedded in his consciousness. This was his home.

If only he could share the home he had built with Jaime. After that first day, when he had brought her to see the house—their house—he hadn't pushed her about their marriage, afraid if he did she might reject him totally. He clung to the hope that one day Jaime would come to him.

He noticed the geraniums on the porch were drooping and took time to water each pot before removing his shoes and entering the house.

The moment he entered he sensed it. He was accustomed to the house's stillness, but today there was something different in the atmosphere. Like an animal attuned to intrusion in its environment, Reeve paused, listening to what the silence could tell him. In the months he had lived in the country, he had become more trusting of his senses.

Warily, he made his way through the house, checking each empty room.

At the door to the master bedroom, he paused, and seeing the bed, was overcome with a rush of adrenaline. Almost dizzy with disbelief, he strode to the bed.

Tentatively, he reached down and lifted the delicate material from the bed where it had been spread out. The silken texture felt like cool skin between his fingers. Jaime's bare, unclothed body flashed before him, and he felt another rushing sensation, this time through his loins. The dress smelled faintly of perfume. Or was he imagining that he wondered. He was lightheaded with joy.

It was still light out when the beige pickup truck stopped in front of the Paradise café.

Reeve had showered and changed into a clean pair of jeans. He wore a leather vest, a plaid shirt, and boots of polished brown leather. The only thing he lacked was a Colt in a holster and a pair of spurs on his heels when he walked into the café dining room.

The room was filled, even at nine o'clock at night, with herders who had ridden in for food and other nocturnal pleasures available during Paradise's peak summer season.

He stood in the doorway, just stood there still and quiet and serious, staring across the room.

There was a sudden hush. All eyes moved to Jaime. Her face went pale.

"Come here, woman," Reeve said in a deadly quiet voice. He didn't move a muscle, but for the silent accompanying order of hitching his head back.

Slowly, Jaime put down the plate she had been carrying. She wiped both hands down on her apron, and began a timid approach in his direction.

The stillness was acute, all eyes straining.

When she reached him, they looked squarely into each other's eyes, then, as fast as a snake, Reeve's arm shot out and pulled her to him. He kissed her hard and full on the mouth, lifting her off her feet.

When he was through, he put her down on the ground. She backed away, and with her eyes flaring, said, "I'm not the kind of woman who just gives her kisses away."

"What kind of a woman are you then?" Reeve asked, his eyes glimmering with a slow, dangerous fire.

"The kind you marry," Jaime snapped back, and spun away on her heels, only to be hauled back into place by Reeve.

"You drive a hard bargain, woman."

"I'm a mighty hard woman."

"When, Jaime?" Reeve asked.

"When the moon's full," she answered back.

Every head in the room swiveled in the direction of the windows. A collective sigh sounded. Rising in the heavens was a pale, perfectly round and full globe.

"You got it, babe."

This time when Reeve kissed her, there was a round of applause and some raucous whistling in the background.

"Hey! You guys ought to make movies."

Jaime and Reeve turned and took small bows. Laughing, they looked into each other's eyes. "I'd rather make love," Reeve whispered to her.

"Me, too," Jaime whispered back. "Hey! You guys, how fast can you be out of here and breaking chairs over each other's heads next door?"

Chapter Fifteen

It was decided at the last minute that Jaime would drive Jade to the ranch alone. Pat and Reeve would come later, but the first sight of that ranch had to be shared only between mother and daughter.

Jade sat beside Jaime in the Blazer, which was more comfortable than Reeve's pickup and had therefore been chosen as the best means of transport. The doctor insisted Jade's recently improved condition was merely a state of remission; she would weaken again soon enough, probably for the last time.

"But," he had told Jaime, "she's a remarkable woman the way she hangs on. There must be a good reason," he said.

Jaime smiled sadly and shook her head. "She's stubborn. She refuses to believe she can't get her way. She's had this dream, you see..."

"Don't we all," the doctor said, and showed Jaime from his office.

Jaime nodded. "Yeah, but Jade doesn't give up on hers."

Jaime's wedding band gleamed brightly, turning rose in the brilliant sunset staining the early September sky. Soon it would be winter again, Jaime thought. She glanced at Jade, wondering if her mother would see the first snowfall. A rapturous expression graced her mother's face. Her green eyes were wide, as if she meant to capture within their green depths the beauty of everything they touched and take the world's splendor with her.

Jaime stopped the truck at the entrance to the ranch.

Jade looked up at the sign, lit by directional floods at the side of the road.

DREAM RANCH, the letters said.

"You were right, Mother," Jaime said, placing her hand on Jade's. "Everything's possible. Right there's the proof."

Jade nodded and with a slight smile, she said, "Of course. Did you ever doubt it?"

Jaime laughed. She threw back her head and laughed until there was a stitch in her side. She laughed so hard the tears stung her eyes.

"A little," she said when she had collected herself.

Jade walked through the ranch house with the dignity of a Chinese empress inspecting a palace that might or might not be worthy of her.

"It is very good," she finally said. "How did you pay for all of this?"

"Well, funny thing, Mother...but see, your daughter had this dream, too. And I got it, just the way you did. I wanted to be famous for a while. The money was from my Paris gig.''

Jade nodded.

That evening the sky was bursting with color. It was an enormous watercolor canvas spread over the valley. Jade sat on the porch alone. She rocked back and forth in the swing chair, the joints making tiny squeaks. Crickets had come to serenade and now and then a frog would croak.

Jaime was in the house, preparing the refreshments for when Reeve and Pat would join them. Now and then she would look out of a screen window, or move silently to the doorway to check on her mother.

She was on one of these inspections when her heart suddenly constricted. Jade was no longer in her chair. Jaime threw the dish towel down and hurtled out the front door.

The dusk was gathering fast. The sunset had turned crimson streaked with darkest purple. Panic clutched at Jaime, and then she stopped, relief filling her. In the distance, she saw her mother's form silhouetted against the painted sky.

Jade had walked out past the driveway. She was moving down the road, moving toward another dark figure that was approaching.

Jaime strained her eyes to see, but the figure, which was male, was not Pat and for a moment, Jaime's heart quickened with the sense of danger.

She was about to call out to Jade, when Jade's voice sounded. Sweet and clear as a bell, it rang out with a single word "Grady!"

The figure answered in a long whistle, the single note a familiar prelude leading into an old Irish song Jaime had sung with her father when she was only a child. The song took up again, floating through the twilight air.

So they did it, Jaime thought, *Pat and Reeve pulled if off after all.*

She watched for a moment, long enough to satisfy herself that Jade was truly all right, then retreated from Jade's private dream and went back into the house.

Grady Quinn stood with his head bowed. Jaime and Reeve had bought him a new suit to wear at the funeral. He wore it now, eight months later. To anyone seeing him in his present condition, standing in the living room of the *Dream Ranch*, he might look like any other proper member of society. But there were slight, telltale clues that the man did not quite fit the image. His face was more lined than that of the average citizen his age, and his hands were rough. There was a suggestion that he had lived a life often at the mercy of the worst of the elements. But the eyes often danced—and all the rough edges were lost behind the sparkle of his free-spirited laugh.

At the moment, Jaime's father was as sober as she had ever seen him.

"I am what I am," Grady said. "I'm not saying I'm proud of what I am, but I can't pretend otherwise. I tried that once," he added looking sadly at Jaime. "And I made a right mess of it, didn't I?" He shifted his weight, and scuffed one of his shoes on the floor while thinking of what he wanted to say. Finally, he looked up, and said, "You know I can't run this place. I gave it a try, but it's not in my nature. All this responsibility, and I'm making a mess of it, too. Same's I made things bad with my family. I'm just a roamer and a drifter, Jaime." He shook his head. "I'm sorry, daughter. It's what I've always been."

Reeve shook his hand. "A man's got a right to be true to his own nature," he said. "It takes more wisdom than most people have, and a rare talent to do that."

Grady's eyes were moist. He nodded, then hugged Jaime. "Take care of my girl," Grady said. He picked up his new suitcase, then placed it down again. "Naw," he said. "Too much responsibility. Give the stuff to someone who can use it."

He was whistling his Irish tune as he disappeared from their view, moving off the beaten path and cutting across the pasture to the main road.

Only three years later, Paradise was no longer a one-bump town in the middle of a single-lane road. Paradise Studios, the amazingly successful venture of Reeve Ferris, who had stunned the film industry by doing things his way, had seen to that. Every week there was another story in a national magazine about the place seen as the entertainment industry's version of Camelot. Guinevere was Jaime Ferris. She had set up a scholarship fund in her mother's name to ensure that young people with great dreams, without the financial resources to realize them, would have a crack at the golden ring. She taught skating at the rink, but also worked together with Reeve at the studio. In three years, they had never once been separated for more than a day.

On an early spring morning, when the sun was barely breaking over the Sawtooths' craggy white peaks, and the tenderest shoots of grass had just broken through the softening earth, a patrol car with its sirens howling into the vast, empty countryside whipped down the interstate blacktop doing one hundred miles an hour.

Pat Griffen's hands were tight vises on the steering wheel and beads of sweat dotted his receding hairline as he glanced into the rearview mirror.

In the back seat of the car, Jaime Ferris was taking a deep, happy breath as the labor pain ebbed. Reeve's eyes were misty with sympathy and joy and a touch of apprehension.

"Hey!" he called up front to Pat. "Someone's gonna' haul your tail in for speeding!"

"Let 'em try to catch me," Pat shouted back with an accompanying hoot. "I've got me a godchild to get born this morning!"

The exit sign marking Paradise listed the town's official population at sixty-five. Pat Griffen made a mental note to talk to someone that very day about changing that number to include one more.

The Silhouette Cameo Tote Bag Now available for just $6.99

Handsomely designed in blue and bright pink, its stylish good looks make the Cameo Tote Bag an attractive accessory. The Cameo Tote Bag is big and roomy (13″ square), with reinforced handles and a snap-shut top. You can buy the Cameo Tote Bag for $6.99, plus $1.50 for postage and handling.

Send your name and address with check or money order for $6.99 (plus $1.50 postage and handling), a total of $8.49 to:

**Silhouette Books
120 Brighton Road
P.O. Box 5084
Clifton, NJ 07015-5084
ATTN: Tote Bag**

SIL-T-1

The Silhouette Cameo Tote Bag can be purchased pre-paid only. No charges will be accepted. Please allow 4 to 6 weeks for delivery.

Arizona and N.Y. State Residents Please Add Sales Tax

Offer not available in Canada.

AMERICAN TRIBUTE

Where a man's dreams count for more than his parentage...

Look for these upcoming titles under the Special Edition American Tribute banner.

LOVE'S HAUNTING REFRAIN
Ada Steward #289—February 1986
For thirty years a deep dark secret kept them apart—King Stockton made his millions while his wife, Amelia, held everything together. Now could they tell their secret, could they admit their love?

THIS LONG WINTER PAST
Jeanne Stephens #295—March 1986
Detective Cody Wakefield checked out Assistant District Attorney Liann McDowell, but only in his leisure time. For it was the danger of Cody's job that caused Liann to shy away.

AM-TRIB-1

Silhouette Special Edition

AMERICAN TRIBUTE

RIGHT BEHIND THE RAIN
Elaine Camp #301—April 1986
The difficulty of coping with her brother's
death brought reporter Raleigh Torrence
to the office of Evan Younger, a police
psychologist. He helped her to deal with
her feelings and emotions, including love.

CHEROKEE FIRE
Gena Dalton #307—May 1986
It was Sabrina Dante's silver spoon that
Cherokee cowboy Jarod Redfeather couldn't
trust. The two lovers came from opposite
worlds, but Jarod's Indian heritage taught
them to overcome their differences.

NOBODY'S FOOL
Renee Roszel #313—June 1986
Everyone bet that Martin Dante and Cara
Torrence would get together. But Martin
wasn't putting any money down, and Cara
was out to prove that she was nobody's fool.

MISTY MORNINGS, MAGIC NIGHTS
Ada Steward #319—July 1986
The last thing Carole Stockton wanted was to
fall in love with another politician, especially
Donnelly Wakefield. But under a blanket of
secrecy, far from the campaign spotlights,
their love became a powerful force.

Silhouette Special Edition

COMING NEXT MONTH

LOVE'S HAUNTING REFRAIN—Ada Steward
Amelia had left the East Coast to join King on his Oklahoma ranch.
Theirs was a marriage of love and passion, yet it was threatened by
the secret that King dared not reveal.

MY HEART'S UNDOING—Phyllis Halldorson
Colleen's love for Erik had grown from a schoolgirl crush into the
passions of a woman. Erik had loved before.... Could he forget the
woman who'd broken his heart, or would she haunt their future?

SURPRISE OFFENSE—Carole Halston
Football superstar Rocky Players had a reputation as a womanizer,
so why was he treating Dana like one of the boys? Dana was
definitely a woman, as Rocky was soon to find out.

BIRD IN FLIGHT—Sondra Stanford
When Andie and Bill met by chance in London, they were each
flooded with memories. Had a three-year separation taught them
enough to overcome their differences and rediscover their love?

TRANSFER OF LOYALTIES—Roslyn MacDonald
Adrienne was a dedicated employee who thought of little but her
career, until Jared Hawks came along and showed her the truth in the
old adage "all work and no play..."

AS TIME GOES BY—Brooke Hastings
Sarah needed the funds that Jonathan Hailey controlled in order to
continue her underwater exploration, but slowly her need for funds
was overridden by her need for Jonathan.

AVAILABLE NOW:

RETURN TO PARADISE
Jennifer West

REFLECTIONS OF YESTERDAY
Debbie Macomber

VEIN OF GOLD
Elaine Camp

SUMMER WINE
Freda Vasilos

DREAM GIRL
Tracy Sinclair

SECOND NATURE
Nora Roberts